THE GOLDEN ROSE OF SCOTLAND

THE LADIES OF LORE II

MARISA DILLON

CROWN & CASTLE
PUBLISHING

DEDICATION

To my husband, Jim.

All other heroes pale in comparison.

THE GOLDEN ROSE OF SCOTLAND

Published in the United States of America by Crown & Castle Publishing

1143 Belvoir Ave.

Dayton, OH 45409

eBook ISBN: 979-8-9917402-5-8

Print ISBN: 979-8-9917402-6-5

www.marisadillon.com

The publisher does not have any control over and does not assume any responsibility for author or third-party websites or their content.

ACKNOWLEDGMENTS

The author thanks:

The professionals: editor Debby Gilbert; author and mentor Terri Valentine; and authors Violetta Rand and Karin Shah, who lit the path to publication.

My family: sons Jamie and Zach, who are my best creations and who support me in so many ways; my parents Alf and Celia Hansen, who took me all over the world as a young girl, influencing my storytelling today; my brother Eric, writer and author; my supportive sister Carina; my Aunt Linda, the ultimate beta reader; and my husband, the best surrogate critique partner ever.

My friends and neighbors: so many to thank who helped me through a very difficult time while this book was written, but particularly Robin Michaels, who provides the best emotional and promotional support; Melissa Johnson, whose counsel is invaluable; Cairo Mama, who is the best dance sister ever; and my advisor Jeff Bruce, whose guidance is essential.

Without their support, this book would not exist.

CHAPTER 1

erwick-upon-Tweed, England 1486

"Damn the English!" Lady Rosalyn burst out. Swearing caused her trouble, but she refused to curb her tongue if the situation demanded and now was one of those times.

Wrestling against her bound wrists in the stifling dungeon, Rosalyn blinked through the prickling sweat that stung her eyes and seeped through her thin chemise.

"The English? They be damned already," croaked her unwelcome companion. His cocky reply echoed through the chamber that reeked of stale stench.

Ignoring the prisoner they called Lachlan, she focused on her escape. Raising her wrists, Rosalyn dug her teeth into the knot again. Moistening the heavy twine made it pliable.

"We're both damned," he added with aristocratic finality.

Was it his condemning reply or the rope between her teeth that made her choke as she spit out stray bits of twine? Either way, being tied back to back with this criminal, even with a hitching post between them, was causing her proper manners to unravel.

"

"I will nae have a part of any Englishman's sentencing. You be damned on your own," she huffed, twisting her hands back and forth between the ropes. "The chancellor will hear my plea," Rosalyn shouted, determined to reclaim what had been stolen from her family, no matter the sacrifice.

"A Scot given a fair trial on English soil?" Lachlan scoffed. "An Irishman's luck you'll be needing to avoid a hanging."

Hanging? Nay, she'd find a way. English judge or not, her da had raised a fighting Macpherson, clan loyal, and Fyvie Castle was like family.

Yesterday, with her royal-stamped parchments in hand, she had expected the court proceedings to be uneventful. Even as she'd sailed into the port of this border town between two kingdoms on high spirits and plucky optimism, she'd never expected to be held prisoner. Her treatment proved abhorrent. No solid meals or soft bed had left her wanting to poison someone. *And she knew who and how.*

"Damn," she cursed again, seeing no need to apologize to her coarse companion. The light shining in from the tiny loophole window, like a bright gem set in the middle of an ashen stone wall, signaled the time to defend herself was only moments away.

With her confidence deflating and her fear rising, Rosalyn slumped against the post. A desire for escape, no matter how childish, had given her hope until now.

Accepting the harsh realization, she struggled to find a comfortable position on the floor of the godforsaken dungeon. Yesterday's memories swirled like a fog except for one: when they lashed the English prisoner to the post between them.

A torch light had woken her when the guard led him into the cell. Dressed in a cloak, a hood covering his head and face, he'd almost stumbled onto her lap in his drunken state. When he caught his balance, he'd said something odd to her.

"My brother killed her, not me." After that, they tied him to the post behind her. She'd caught his name when the guards were leaving, but he'd said nothing more the rest of the night.

As his thrashing started again, Rosalyn's anger intensified, reminding her this English criminal was strapped to her back.

What was his crime? Stealing? Murder? The unpleasant musing made her queasy. She dare not ask, for he'd probably tell her the sordid details just to torture her.

"What have the English done to earn your tongue-lashing?" the prisoner asked, breaking the silence once more. He'd been out cold most of night and had done little but moan until her damning outburst moments ago.

"How can I stop your English tongue from wagging?"

Lachlan chuckled, a deep, throaty sound. "If only I wasn't bound, my lady," he began, but his retort was interrupted by a scraping sound just outside the cell. A guard appeared at the barred door. Letting himself in, he plodded toward them dragging a gimp leg.

Rosalyn shuddered when he stood over her, his one eye covered by a black patch, but she didn't divert her gaze even when he withdrew a dagger. Instead, she fought against her fear and the urge to scream. If she'd just inhaled her last breath, it wouldn't be as a coward.

With a few quick swipes of his weapon, the guard cut through the ropes that bound them together to the post, then hauled the Englishman to his feet. "Your time, Lord Lachlan," the guard grunted.

As the released prisoner stood, his hands still bound, he ignored the soldier and gazed down at her instead.

Rosalyn smothered her surprise. Lachlan was not the scruffy ruffian she'd expected, but a distinguished nobleman dressed in a chestnut silk cloak and sporting a meticulous goatee. His snobbish confidence complemented his sleek, black hair and wicked widow's peak.

"I had a dream about a beautiful lass with long, auburn locks and eyes like warm honey. You do not disappoint."

Ignoring the guard's disapproving glare, the prisoner knelt beside her.

"What are you doing?" she gasped as he leaned forward.

"Answering your first question," Lachlan said crisply, then he reached his bound hands over her head and secured them behind her neck. The prisoner tossed her a sly grin before his lips made their assault and he crushed her to his chest. Using equal parts speed and agility, his tongue tunneled its way in to claim her mouth as if he'd been appointed its new ruler. Even if she wanted to fight him off, she couldn't.

"Your time," the slow-witted guard shouted again, hauling Lachlan off her.

Once he got his footing, Lachlan held her gaze and crinkled one eye into a mischievous wink. "Enjoyed your English tongue-lashing, did you now?"

Rosalyn pursed her lips. They tingled, slightly swollen from the stranger's rough kisses. Not sure whether to lash out with a diatribe of why that was wrong, or to thank him, she gawked up at him instead, her mind as numb as her mouth.

Just when she thought she'd be left behind, the guard's blade ripped through the ropes around her chest that bound her to the post.

"Your time, woman," he grunted and dragged to her feet.

As she stretched her arms forward for the other ropes to be cut, the guard's dulled gaze lingered on her bosom.

Beast.

Rosalyn clenched her bound hands to her chest.

The guard grunted again, then pointed to the hallway outside the cell.

She gave the officer a warning stare as she passed him and fell in step with Lachlan. The soldier's bad leg made a scraping sound behind her as he prodded the two of them down the dim hallway with his dagger drawn, eventually driving them out of the prisoner's tower and into the blindingly bright courtyard.

Squinting into the sunlight, Rosalyn was grateful to be free of the dungeon. Sucking in gulps of fresh air, she followed the limping guardsman as he now led them on the short jaunt across the lower bailey and into the great hall of Berwick Castle.

Filled with dread and fighting a rising panic, Rosalyn walked behind the gimping guard, slowly making her way toward the Chancery Court bench in the grand and well appointment hall filled with quarrelsome, noisy English.

The damning evidence had caught up with her again. With her father gone, and the clan riotous, the Lord Chancellor would need to understand her motives were for self-preservation.

As she passed the front row of commoners, who'd come to watch for nothing but sport, an unsavory peasant to her right grabbed her arm, dragging her off her path.

"Follow my advice and I'll save you," he promised in a harsh whisper.

Startled, Rosalyn spun around, her hand reaching for the dagger at her boot. But the trusted knife wasn't there waiting for her. Stripped of her dirk and her dignity at the arrest, Rosalyn realized she'd have to use words as a weapon instead.

"After my money or my bed? I need the likes of you like a noose about my neck." She spat on the offender and yanked her arm free. Following back in step behind Lachlan and the guard, she came to stop in front of the bench.

"Hear ye, hear ye, the court now calls Rosalyn

Macpherson and Lord Lachlan de Leverton," the bailiff announced. "Stand before the court."

Rosalyn felt her knees go weak and she grasped Lachlan's arm. He was an unlikely savior, but perhaps her only chance of avoiding a devastating verdict. She flashed him a weak grin when he put his arm around her waist and hoisted her fully upright.

Brushing stray strands of hair away from her eyes, she reached up on tipped toes to whisper in his ear, *"Docha gum bi thu mo dhochas-mhain." You may be my only hope.*

Now that they were front and center, the chancellor began. "Yesterday in this court during separate hearings, Lord Lachlan de Leverton and Rosalyn Macpherson both laid claim to Fyvie Castle in Aberdeen, with papers signed by James III, the King of Scots."

Rosalyn gasped. *This* was why she was back in court? *This Englishman* had challenged her claim?

Furious, Rosalyn turned and grabbed Lachlan's cloak. The prospect of losing Fyvie sickened her. Tossing reason aside, she shouted, "The land of my clan will nae be taken again!" Crumpling his silk fabric into her clenched fists, she tried to shake him. "Only when my body is cold and the last shovel of Scottish earth strikes my coffin, will I release Fyvie."

"Order. Order. Order." The pounding noise coming from the chancellor's gavel finally broke through her rant and she released Lachlan.

Lord de Leverton smoothed the crumpled edges of his garment, then leaned in, his lips brushing her ear. "Let me speak to the judge for you."

She nodded weakly in agreement and glanced at the floor while she struggled to regain her composure. Hysterics wouldn't save her as she'd learned from past digressions. Damn her emotions. They were her enemy, not Lachlan.

"Your Honor," Lachlan began, but he paused as if searching for the right words.

Waiting for the silence to be filled, Rosalyn glanced up, only to meet the scrutiny of the bespectacled justice, who peered down at her with a smirk, making her wonder if he'd toss her back into the dungeon.

"This woman *is* guilty of forgery," Lachlan announced.

"Guilty!" Rosalyn shouted and almost fell to her knees at Lachlan's lie. If she could throttle him now she would.

"Yes, your Honor." Lachlan turned toward her and winked. "You heard the plea of guilty from her lips just now," he said, giving her a reassuring look before he turned his attention back the judge. "However, I must ask that you be lenient with her. An orphan from birth, abandoned by her husband, the woman has taken to stealing from the rich, even though she knew, in God's eyes, it was wrong."

"My husband abandoned me?" Rosalyn whispered in disbelief. Her head was spinning. What diatribe of lies was this? What was his plan?

"Your Honor, she's without a moral compass," Lachlan continued. "She has no man in her life to tell her right from wrong."

The judge eyed her up and down. "I see, and what do you propose?"

"I pay her forgery fine and become her guardian."

Sounds of shocked reactions bounced off the tapestry-covered walls, while whispers tossed between jurors faster than fresh gossip among old maids. The Lord Chancellor gave a reprimanding glance to the jury as he hammered his gavel, his desk serving as barrier from the people, like a castle's iron portcullis gate guards its king.

When the chancellor's actions didn't quiet the crowd, the court bailiff slammed the bottom of his lance hard against the wooden floors.

Finally, the twittering and shocked, loud voices faded to hush whispers as the judge commanded the room once more.

"Granting guardianship to you would be condemning the lass to a fate worse than debtor's prison," the justice replied, his voice booming through the hall.

Rosalyn was mortified. Neither verdict, prison nor guardianship, was acceptable. Her mind whirled, desperately seeking another plea. Could she blame someone else for the forgery?

After a long pause, the judge addressed her. "Lady Macpherson." He leaned forward, sobering. "The evidence here today demands a higher court and a jury of *your* peers." At those words, the great hall went silent. "A claim of Scottish land disputed between a clanswoman and an Englishman cannot be decided in an English court. King James would have my head if word reached him that I'd levied a judgement under such circumstances, or determined which papers were forgeries."

The judge drew in a deep breath and leaned back into a massive chair as if satisfied with his decision and continued with his hands steepled. "You and Lachlan will be awarded guardianship under my sheriff and will join a party leaving soon for Edinburgh. There, you will both learn your fate." He slammed the gavel head against the desk. "Dismissed."

Rosalyn's knees almost buckled again as the great hall erupted in a flurry of reactions over the verdict, but Lachlan grabbed her elbow tightly and guided her over to the bailiff, who led them away from the curious onlookers to the back of the great hall where he finally cut the remaining bonds.

"Good man," Lachlan said as he rubbed his wrists, "were the ropes really necessary? We're gentry, not common criminals."

"If ye'd be treated as criminals, ye'd be in chains and an executioner would be leading you to the gallows, instead of a sheriff assigning you to your guest chambers at Berwick Castle." The court bailiff laughed at Lachlan's aghast expression.

"I'm accustomed to having dinner with dignitaries, not being held prisoner in a dungeon," Lachlan responded with disgust. "I was serving King Henry's court here at Berwick until just yesterday when this misunderstanding took place."

Stone-faced, the bailiff stared at him. "Your misunderstanding included a drunken tirade after you found out someone else had laid claim to Fyvie Castle."

Lachlan responded first by stroking his perfectly plucked goatee. "Well, then, that explains my confinement, to sleep off my over-indulgences and my lack of good manners, but what of the woman? Why was she bound like a prisoner?"

"She's not English," the bailiff stated as plainly as if he'd called her a bastard.

Rosalyn bit her tongue. Another glaring example of why she hated everything English.

Lachlan raised a fist, but reconsidered when the bailiff reached for his sword. "I would fight for any lady, English or Highlander," he declared gallantly, then put a protective arm around her shoulders. "She's not guilty of a crime yet, so she shouldn't be treated as such."

Rosalyn appreciated Lachlan sentiments, but she was still suspicious of his motives and was anxious to be out from under the scrutiny of the crowd of onlookers. He'd lied to the judge about her background and that didn't set well with her.

"I must get some air," she declared and spun out from his unsettling embrace.

The bailiff nodded, but that didn't stop Lachlan from chasing after her. In moments, he nabbed her elbow and ushered her out of the great hall with grace and superiority. He didn't say a word, but nodded at each passerby with that conceited grin of his.

As he led Rosalyn out of the keep and into the gardens, she worried about her mother and sister, now that her plans had been delayed. A trip to Edinburgh before returning to Aberdeen would take at least a fortnight.

Lachlan settled on a bench behind a row of rose bushes. Taking her hand, he ushered her to the seat beside him. He finally leaned forward ready to speak and it broke her trail of worry.

"I'm sorry for all that," he said, gazing at her over their joined hands.

All that? If ever she was speechless, it was now. Whatever did he mean? The kiss? The lies? The discrimination of the Scots? But her heart thundered against her ribs like a wild beast thrashing against the bars of its cage.

"You needn't worry, Rose." He kissed her hand. "As your guardian, I'll save you from harm."

She straightened her spine and yanked her hand from his too-familiar grasp. "My name is Rosalyn," she hissed, "and I'm nae in need of saving." No one called her Rose, except her da, and he was gone.

"Is it the fiery red hair that makes you obnoxious?" he asked, giving her a curt nod after she shot him an icy glare, but he continued to serve her that smug smile. "Call me Lockie," he suggested, keeping her gaze and taking her hand in his palm again. "You are quite worth saving, Rose—" He paused as if taunting her, then finished with "—alyn."

"I'm quite sure your promises are as sincere as your kisses, and as untrue as your testimony against me in court." She didn't realize until she finished speaking how sarcastic she sounded.

"Quite the contrary, my lady," he said, inching closer. "You have no guardian. I'm at your service."

His charm was disarming, but she had to fight the urge to be taken prisoner by his charisma. The fact that her escort to

Berwick-upon-Tweed had fallen ill shortly after they arrived by ship did not concern him. "I think not," she said, shaking her head to dissuade him and clear her thoughts. "You're a liar, Lachlan."

"You're safe with me, Rose," he promised again. Still holding her hand, he closed the gap between them, gazing down at her with pitch-black eyes that hinted at mischief.

She wanted to tell him that he couldn't call her by that name again, but his mouth smothered her objection, just like he'd done in the prison cell. Lachlan stole her breath away with his gentle assault. And when she wanted to, she couldn't breathe.

Finally after breaking his hold, she grabbed his arm to steady herself. "What's happening? I—"

CHAPTER 2

*L*achlan caught Rosalyn before she fell face first into a bed of wild red roses. The irony of it should have caused him some amusement, but right now, he was disturbed by the potential consequences this lady's death could have on his reputation.

Killed with a kiss? As the once-feisty Scot hung limp in his arms, he imagined the rumors swirling and the gossips describing his lips as deadly. His normally cool composure was interrupted by a disgusting trickle of sweat dripping down his brow. As much as he hated soiling his silk coat, Lachlan adjusted his shoulders until he could dip his head and wipe off the offense with his sleeve.

Standing straight again, he glanced about the courtyard garden to confirm they were still alone.

"Damn the Scots," he said half to her and half to the heavens, swearing about his father's likely displeasure over his inability to secure Aberdeen castle. Even though he'd been distracted by the beautiful Highland lass, how had a simple land hearing gone wrong? Now he'd been ordered to appear before a Scottish high court. The highest.

When Rosalyn moaned, Lachlan turned his attention to her and a spark of recognition flared.

Is she Dengas Macpherson's daughter?

When she moaned again, Lachlan decided he should seek out a healer and quickly wash his hands of her malady. The gossips from the court would be milling around the bailey soon.

Tucking his arm under her legs, he hoisted Rosalyn up into his arms, shifting her weight against his chest. The lass was so light it made it easy for him now as he took great strides back the way he'd come. It didn't take long before he reached the keep and rushed to the nearest chamber, kicking the half-closed door open.

Expecting an empty room, Lachlan was halfway to the bed when his ears were assaulted by a woman's scream. Turning toward the noise, he discovered a maid and her paramour in the middle of a romantic embrace wearing nothing but their embarrassment.

The servants dove for their clothes, heads knocking in a comedic scramble to get covered. Eyes downcast, they bowed incessantly. He found himself relieved when they finally reached the door.

"Bring a healer to me," Lachlan demanded, impatience resonating in his clipped order as he reached the bed and the embarrassed couple rushed out.

With the utmost care, Lachlan lay Rosalyn on the bed's fur coverlet. Giving her a quick assessment, he was pleased to find her ample bosom rising and falling. As distracting to him as it was, he relaxed a little. At least she was alive. Fainting spells were rarely fatal.

Without breaking his gaze on the lass, as if she'd stop breathing without his watchful eye, Lachlan took up a sturdy stool by the bedside and studied the woman who'd challenged his family's land holdings. Pale-faced, she was still stunningly beautiful in her sleep like state, and he was determined not to let this Highland lass keep him from his claim. Even though his time spent at Fyvie had been short, he knew of the Macphersons and her father, Dengas. But the clan leader had died four years ago. What claim could his daughter have on Fyvie now?

The sound of approaching voices through the half-opened door had Lachlan scrambling to his feet. He raked his fingers through his hair and straightened his cloak.

"She's in here, Ursula." The voice from the hall echoed into the chamber where he waited. Finally, the castle's healer swept into the room with a mini army of servants in her wake. They carried buckets of boiling water, fresh linens, and trays of herbal concoctions.

Tossing him an icy glance, Ursula rushed to the other side of the bed. The healer lifted Rosalyn's limp wrist and pushed her fingers against it, gently seeking a pulse. Seemingly satisfied, Ursula peeled back Rosalyn's eyelids and inspected the girl's empty stare. Once the healer had enough probing and poking of her charge, she snapped her fingers and one of the servants brought forth a tray of herbs and potion bottles.

Lachlan had been smitten by the sultry woman when he first arrived at Berwick Castle. She'd escaped his advances thus far, but every time he was around her, he was aroused. Bedding the lass had occupied his thoughts until he'd been able to find satisfaction elsewhere.

Mesmerized by her delicate moves as she carefully selected a miniature-sized, purple glass bottle from the tray, he still couldn't fathom why she kept her distance.

Holding the delicate bottle at arm's length from her nose, Ursula carefully opened the top. A *pop* sounded when the cork was removed. Even from where he stood, his nostrils were assaulted by a strong, pungent smell. All the servants took a measured step backward.

With the grace of a dancer, Ursula waved the purple glass container under Rosalyn's nose three times, then quickly recorked the top. Right away, Rosalyn's lashes fluttered, then her almond-shaped eyes opened wide.

"Oh, oh, my," the lass sputtered, blinking hard and taking Ursula in with a dazed gaze. "Wh-Where am I?" Rosalyn asked in a shaky whisper, color flushing back in her cheeks.

When Rosalyn leaned forward, propping herself on one elbow, the healer held up her hand.

"Under my orders, you are not to move from this bed. Understand?"

"I speak the same English as you," Rosalyn responded, her speech now more rebellious than timid.

Ursula cut a dominating figure, even without her potions about her. Waist-length, obsidian-colored hair framed her deep, brooding eyes. Her skin was a stark contrast, as if she'd avoided the outdoors and spent her days under the covers. When Ursula clapped her hands together, Lachlan snapped out of his seductive thoughts.

"The lady's feeling much more herself. Out you go, now," she instructed, rising to her feet and shooing the servants toward the open door, like herding wayward sheep.

But Lachlan lingered, caught web-like between the two, blood pulsing through his groin. Thoughts of all three of them together in the chamber bed made him hard against his breeches.

He caught Ursula's eyes first and she cooled his intention with her obstinate glare, her hands on her hips. Reticent and unyielding to his pleading grin, she pointed to the door.

Admitting temporary defeat, he shrugged his shoulders and left.

Once out of the room, Lachlan turned toward the main hallway, ready to retire to his chamber with a tanker of strong ale when his boot kicked something that blended in with the gray stone floor. Studying the mound more closely, he found the creature to be covered in fur.

A mouse? He'd saved one the other night from being beaten to death by a maid with an empty chamber pot. He smiled at the memory of the terrified servant, happy the mouse was spared and he'd rescued the maid from the harmless critter.

Picking up the fuzzy wad, he held the bundle in the throbbing light of a wall sconce to discover it wasn't a rodent after all, but a drawstring bag made of rabbit's fur tied together snugly at the top by a leather thong. Curiosity outweighed courtesy as he loosened the leather knot and eased open the pouch.

Peering inside the opening did nothing to reveal its contents, so Lachlan poked his fingers inside, his hand too big for the job. Soon he found an object that felt familiar and drew it out. Even in the semidarkness, the impressive, unset red stone gleamed and sparkled. This was clearly no chambermaid's pouch.

Whack! Lachlan felt his heart jump. He'd nearly lost the jewel when the sound of Ursula slamming the door shut behind him made him bobble it, but he managed to jam the stone and the pouch into the empty tankard hanging from his belt before he spun around to face her.

She appeared rattled at finding him outside Rosalyn's door.

He cleared his throat. "At the ready," he offered, then swept into a low bow, his gaze holding hers.

Ursula eyeballed him suspiciously as he rose. "Your guest has lost something personal," she informed him. "I was going to call for a maid to see if she could help in the search."

"Don't trouble yourself," Lachlan insisted. "You stay with our *guest*. She's a ward of the courts. Someone should keep an eye on her."

"The woman's a victim, not a prisoner," Ursula said, her dark eyes narrowing, full of distrust.

Lachlan chuckled nervously while he slowly backed away. "What tis the missing item?"

"A fur pouch."

"Yes, right. I shall see to it," he promised and turned, heading toward the great hall. After ascending the stairs to the guest chambers, he paused on the landing to listen. Once he was sure Ursula hadn't followed him, although he would enjoyed the minx's company, he hurried in alone and bolted the door behind him.

Curiosity still overrode his sense of duty as he dumped the contents of the pouch on his desk. He combed through the tokens. A scrap of plaid, frayed around the edges, caught his attention first. He turned the fabric around in his hands, the fine wool soft against his skin. He set the plaid next to a lump of yellow wax. But it was the stamping seal, tipped on its side, that he sought next to examine more closely.

After loosening a burning tapered candle from the wall sconce above the desk, Lachlan softened the bee's wax over the flame until it became pliable. When his fingertips started to burn, he dropped the gumming wad onto one of his parchment papers. Scooping up the stamp, he pressed it firmly into the naked wax anxious to find what markings it would reveal. He counted quickly to ten, then with care, peeled off the stamp to reveal its fresh imprint.

Lachlan stumbled back a step when he read the words on the hot wax. "*Tha Séala Mor na h-Alba*", he uttered in disbelief. How could it be? He'd seen the symbol of the monarch on horseback before. It was unmistakable. The King of Scots' seal.

Lachlan shook his head. Was it a fake? Part of Rosalyn's forgery tools? How had she managed to keep this from the court? This very device could have proven her guilt.

And guilt was what he'd have on his conscience if he turned her over to the court with this evidence. How he wished he could be honest with her and the court as well, but he couldn't. Not yet. Not until they appeared before the King of Scots, then Lachlan would need to prove his legacy amounted to more than just a surname.

When a sharp rap sounded on the chamber door, he quickly began shoving Rosalyn's belongings back into the fur pouch. "What do you want?" he asked, hoping if only a servant, they'd leave him be.

"Sheriff, here." The door rattled against its hinges. "Open up."

With no time to consider an iron-forged key, Lachlan tossed it into the pouch and drew the drawstring taut. Later, he'd find a suitable hiding place. For now, he'd stash it in his crotch.

Lachlan chuckled after securing the soft fur. It tickled him as he walked to let the sheriff in.

The soldier stumbled into the room as if he'd been braced against the door. With a huff, the officer addressed him, "What are you hiding in here, Lachlan?"

CHAPTER 3

Grateful her accommodations had improved and feeling more herself, Rosalyn cautiously surveyed the chamber with half-closed eyes, admiring the rich, tapestried walls and masterfully carved furnishings, a stark contrast to the dank dungeon. But she couldn't deny the truth, no matter how glamorous the surroundings. She was still a prisoner with a sheriff as an escort. And that's why no matter what the chancellor had said, Rosalyn was certain her king, the King of Scots, would award her Fyvie if she could make her plea first.

But she needed an ally.

As Rosalyn's determination to control her fate bubbled, her gaze finished sweeping the room and settled on Ursula working meticulously over a cauldron hanging in the hearth. Rosalyn squinted through her lashes, secretly studying the woman, grateful she was the only guest left in her chamber after the healer had ushered out the rest, including Lachlan.

The English bastard had thwarted her plans for Fyvie and taken liberties. He'd kissed her. Twice. With the first, she'd been defenseless. The second, she should have given him a black eye for his trouble. Instead, she'd swooned from the lack of air. Because he was English, she should have been abhorred by the idea of kissing him, but he'd been so kiss-able. And handsome.

She sighed.

"Watching me, are you?" Ursula accused without turning around.

Rosalyn coughed.

"You know my intentions?"

"No. Well, yes," Rosalyn finally admitted. Of course, how could she be so idiotic? Most healers were also seers. Better concede now, or she'd stand to lose the woman's trust.

"Rowan berries?" Curious, Rosalyn sat up, still under the covers, propping her elbows on her knees. "And you've heated them?"

"Red berries from the Faerie tree. 'Tis what I know," the healer said, turning toward her. "This will settle your stom-ach," she promised as she made her way to the bed with her pestle and mortar.

Rosalyn's nostrils flared as the unmistakable aroma filled her sinuses first, then her lungs, soothing away the nausea that accompanies a fainting spell. Uncooked, she was certain the berries were poisonous. At least she might relax a little knowing Ursula wasn't trying to put an end to her. Rosalyn hadn't been able to trust anyone since arriving in Berwickshire.

"*Caorunn!*" Rosalyn said with conviction, finally recalling the Gaelic name. She'd been taught much of the healing arts from her mother. "Good for many uses including witchcraft protection."

Ursula confirmed her appraisal with a nod and a reluc-tant smile, the first to grace her striking features.

Rosalyn grinned and narrowed her gaze on Ursula. "You arenae English?"

The healer sobered and studied Rosalyn for a moment, like a Scottish wildcat would before a retreat or attack. A smile flickered, then turned into a grin of acceptance when Ursula hiked her skirt to her knees and flipped up the hem to reveal a swatch of red, purple, and gray tartan sewn into the underside edge.

"Highlander?" Rosalyn squealed, struggling to hide her enthusiasm.

Ursula nodded.

"Macpherson, sept and clan," Rosalyn said proudly, wanting to show her plaid, but quickly remembering she couldn't with her pouch missing.

"Mackintosh sept, clan Fraser," Ursula said, bursting with pride.

"We're near-cousins. Is your da Big Douglas? Is the laird still alive?"

Ursula's grim expression answered for her. "I donna know who my da is. Whether he's alive or dead." Ursula swiped a tumbling tear from her cheek, then sat on the bed next to Rosalyn. Scooping up some of the paste she'd made, the healer offered Rosalyn the concoction.

Rosalyn swallowed the bitter herbs, then waited patiently, hoping the healer would offer more of her story. As if reading her thoughts again, Ursula scanned the chamber, then walked to the door and put her ear to the wood. Once she was satisfied no one would eavesdrop, she worked her way back to Rosalyn's bedside and took up the stool.

"As I was saying," the healer started again, "I donna know who my da is, or was. I came to Berwick-upon-Tweed when I was six and ten. But living on this land, fought over by decades of rival kings, I've witnessed the English shedding Scots blood and murdering our legacy. I'd rather see the French, even the pillaging Vikings have Berwickshire than let English rule what's rightfully ours."

Feeling an immediate kinship, Rosalyn's heart went out to the Highland lass beside her. They'd both suffered from the loss of land and family.

She is the perfect ally.

While she mulled over how to approach Ursula on the subject, the woman placed a warm hand over her own. "You didnae need to convince me, I'll help you escape." Then she squeezed it and released a deep, back-of-the-throat chuckle. "And nay, I didnae share Lachlan's bed."

Rosalyn couldn't help but gasp. She didn't recall thinking about the two of them together. Or had she? Of course, she was curious about the man who'd been strapped to her back. Not a criminal, but a lord. A man who was accustomed to serving at court, accustomed to getting what he wanted.

"Nay, he donna always get what he's after. And his thoughts are muddled. I cannae read them all the time," she admitted with that cautious smile.

"If don't read his thoughts, then what has he told you about himself?"

"Not much at all, really. He's brooding and I catch him staring at me most days. Not that I'm a beauty or anything, but he just does. It's unsettling. He's handsome, but conceited."

"Conceited?" Rosalyn giggled.

"He likes his own appearance." Ursula leaned in closer to share more whispered gossip. "At the end of a meal in the great hall I've caught him grinning in his goblet's reflection."

That conceited smile. She'd been a witness.

"And he takes liberties with unmarried noble women," Ursula said, staring off into the hearth.

"Aye! That I've seen firsthand," Rosalyn confessed. "Just moments after I met him, he ravaged me with kisses. My hands were tied, and I couldn't fight him off. 'Tis not a noble way to treat a woman. Is he a bastard?"

"You could call him a skirt-chaser, stealing kisses and embraces like a thief, but the gossips say he doesnae bed his dalliances." She leaned in closer as if happy to have a confidante. "No one knows much about his family, the de Lavertons. A few of the ladies of the court started looking into his heraldry, but couldn't find much. Probably trying to decide if he's a noble worth having or a bastard who should be passed up. But many enjoy his flirtatious attention."

Rosalyn considered all Ursula had said and cocked her head. "Does he nae have one redeeming quality?"

Ursula's gaze traveled to the ceiling and her face scrunched up as if her mind was occupied by a complex problem. After a few moments of contemplation, Ursula finally released a little "ah."

"Aye, he does," the healer admitted as she focused on Rosalyn again. "He can be kind."

"Kind?"

"Not like you and I would be kind." Ursula stole a look at the ceiling again. "Mayhap *considerate* is the better word?" Then she nodded as if satisfied.

"Aye, now that you mention it," Rosalyn said, "he did question the bailiff about my abhorrent treatment in the dungeon." As much as Rosalyn wanted to dislike Lachlan for all the reasons she should—he was English; he was conceited; his nobility was in question; he took liberties— there was something about him that drew her to him.

"Damn good kisser," Rosalyn responded in a dreamy tone, but then she gasped, covering her mouth when she realized what she'd said aloud.

"Ursula gave her a disgusted glare and a *tsk* before she continued. "From afar I've watched him work his hands through his hair until it gleams in an unnatural manner. But that doesn't deter most of the available ladies of the court who swoon at his glances. He could have any one of them, but says he's waiting for me." She drew her gaze from the fire and gave Rosalyn a he'll-be-damned reaction. "Well, he can wait until his cock falls off, because it's nae going to be. My heart is promised to another."

"Scot or English?"

"Eww! My distaste of the English is as strong as yours." Ursula nodded knowingly. "His da is a MacDonald."

"Enemies! No, Ursula. The fates are cruel to you."

"Aye, they are, lass. That's why we are apart for now. He travels from near Edinburgh through Berwickshire once a fortnight bringing the raw wool to be sold at market."

"So you see each other in secret."

"Aye, we slip away to the woods by the sea. There's an abandoned farm by Marshall Meadows. For now, that 'tis what we have."

A sharp rap on the door shattered their cocoon of intimacy and startled Rosalyn so much she shook as if a cold draft had entered the chamber.

Ursula's head jerked toward the door.

"Open up. It's the sheriff."

Rosalyn sucked in a sharp breath, unprepared for more questioning. She was hoping to avoid a conversation with another English official altogether. But before she had a chance to figure out a stall, Ursula was at the door opening it a crack only a mouse could navigate.

"Making my rounds." The sheriff's gruff voice filtered in through the narrow slit.

"Your charge is in my good hands, resting," Ursula said.

"Let me enter," the sheriff persisted, pushing against the door and making his way into the room past a ruffled healer.

Rosalyn swallowed a snicker.

"The Bishop of Imola," he began, addressing them, "we're honored to have him as a guest at Berwick Castle. He's traveled from Italy, sent by the pope for King James." He paused.

"The bishop has requested a Scot be present at the feast tonight." He shuffled his feet. "You are the only Scot in residence," he said, looking directly at Rosalyn.

Rosalyn resisted the urge to glance at Ursula, who until they'd been alone had hidden her Gaelic lilt.

"Will she have to attend in ball and chain?" Ursula asked provokingly as the sheriff's gaze shifted. "As her healer, I cannot promise she has recovered enough to attend." Her accomplice crossed her arms over her chest and waited.

The sheriff cleared his throat. "What would assure her good health for tonight's festivities?" he asked in a low, toneless voice, his gaze moving to the glowing hearth.

"Her dirk returned and no guard to watch over her chamber. I'll be her guardian from now on," Ursula said, as simply as if she'd asked for sweet cream.

"Then it will be quite the blessing in the great hall to see you both for the ceremony," he replied with sarcasm, watching Ursula on his way out the door. As it closed with a hard slam, the healer's eyes gleamed with victory.

CHAPTER 4

$\mathcal{P}$rimping, pinching, and pampering. Rosalyn was not accustomed to the pompous fussing she'd received in the past few hours preparing for dinner with the Italian bishop. Rarely did she receive this kind of attention. Of course, her mother had once had staff, but even then, Rosalyn and her sister Rowen shared a maid with her and most days dressed themselves.

It went against her nature to accept the assistance. But when the handmaiden explained she might be beaten if she didn't perform her duties, Rosalyn gave in.

First, she was dressed in a silk lavender chemise that was topped with a deep purple velvet overdress.

Next, her wild, red locks had to be tamed. As nervous as she was, Rosalyn couldn't help but fidget while her hair was plaited into one long braid down the middle of her back. The maid wove in stings of amethysts before it was twisted into a crown shape atop Rosalyn's head.

Finally, when all the fussing was complete, the maid walked with her to the mirror's view. Smoothing out the folds of her gown the young girl gushed, "You look like royalty, my lady."

When she took it all in, Rosalyn stepped back, surprised by the result of all the primping. "I do feel quite grand," she admitted. At least more worthy of her clan's station than she had in the past four years. She sighed deeply, reflecting on how much had changed. The dress she wore now reminded her of the finery her laird father would bring back from his wool trade travels to France. Before that he'd imported the raw wool to be spun in Aberdeen from the wild land of Norway. Then, he'd brought her beautiful jewelry made of silver. That was long ago.

She was grateful to Ursula for the dress and blinked away a tiny tear, covering a sniffle with a cough. "Yes, quite grand. Surely, I'm ready to meet the bishop."

After a few more moments of fussing, the handmaiden finally led her to the grand hall entrance, instructing her to sit at the dais. Then with the confidence of a Macpherson, she walked into the great hall. Crossing the room crowded with the curious and the courtly, she joined Lachlan, the only familiar face in the place. Once she was at his side, he gave her a puzzled look.

"Do I know you?" he asked, almost snarling.

Ruffled at his obstinacy, she shot back a query of her own. "What kind of greeting is that coming from a nobleman who kissed me and vowed to protect me?"

"God's blood. If I'd kissed you, I'd remember it," the man said, grinning wickedly.

Rosalyn reassessed the man smiling at her. The cocksureness was there, but the charm and confidence were lacking even though the face looked the same. She huffed, "What have you done with Lockie?"

A clean scowl replaced the dirty grin. "Lockie?" he growled.

"Right here, Brother." The response came from behind her.

Rosalyn whirled around to find the charming smile she'd been seeking. "Lockie?"

He caught her up in his arms, leaning close to her as if he'd kiss her. "You've been looking for me?"

With a gasp, Rosalyn stumbled backward only to be caught in the arms of the Lachlan impostor behind her.

"She's my ward." A hand reached out to tug Rosalyn free of both men. She caught a glimpse of the black, glossy hair and recognized the gentle but firm grip even before she could breathe a sigh of relief.

"Identical twins?" Rosalyn whispered to herself, the resemblance remarkable. Ursula held her elbow protectively as she tried not to gawk at them. She glanced at her friend looking for an explanation, but the healer shrugged.

Awkward silence prevailed until Lachlan put his arm around his brother's shoulder and offered an explanation. "You must have mistaken me for my brother, Ethan. He just arrived today from Aberdeen."

Rosalyn's eyes narrowed. Aberdeen? What was an Englishman doing in the Scottish Highlands?

"Just arrived, aye. Sent by our father to investigate," Ethan said, shoving his brother's arm from his shoulder in an odd show of animosity. "In his words, 'Find the bastard judge keeping Lachlan from settling our claim and take care of it.'"

"Your claim?" Rosalyn's cheeks flamed. Ursula's grip tightened, but Rosalyn shrugged her off as she strode forward to stand toe-to-toe with Ethan. Glaring up at him, she didn't let his dominating figure or returned scowl dissuade her from what she was ready to say. "Tis nae your—"

She was interrupted by a hand clapping over her mouth. Lachlan had come behind her and stopped her from telling his brother all about the court and her claim. She wanted to bite his hand so she could get on with it, her blood boiling, but he held a firm grip. Tantrum-like, she stomped on his boot, but he didn't even flinch. Instead, his other arm wound around her waist as he drew her close.

"Unhand her!" The command came from an authoritative voice to her right. Lachlan's hands went limp and Rosalyn let out low whistle, a puff of air leaving her lips. She was relieved a referee had stopped the tiff and gave her a moment to let her anger subside.

She turned to find the sheriff staring at the group of them, but he addressed Lachlan. "You are still under my guardianship, so mind your actions lest I have to bind your wrists again," the court's servant warned.

"Bind your wrists?" Ethan asked, his expression giving away his disgust. "You told me you were dealing with a trivial delay."

"I'm the trivial delay," Rosalyn said, speaking up, but calmer now that the sheriff had intervened. Even though the guard was English, he'd more likely protect her interests than Lachlan or his brother. But any further words on the matter would have to wait. A hush fell over the room.

Covered in gilded regalia and followed by six priests, the Italian bishop entered the great hall. Ivory robes flowing, as if gliding on angels' wings, the pope's emissary cut a path through the great hall while courtiers gawked. Most had at least the courtesy of bowing with respect when he passed. As the holy man came closer, Ursula pointed to a chair for Rosalyn to take on her right at the end of the head table.

While she took up her place, Rosalyn's gaze followed Lachlan as he steered his brother to a long trestle table nearby filled with ladies of the court who giggled as both men took their seats.

When Ursula nudged her ribs, Rosalyn turned toward the

healer, ready for a query or comment, but felt a hand on her leg instead. Resisting the urge to swear, Rosalyn locked her gaze with Ursula while her Scottish ally handed her something cold and heavy beneath the table.

Her missing dirk?

When the reigning Lord of Berwick Castle met the bishop at the dais and bowed deeply with hands in prayer, Ursula whispered in her ear, "That's First Lord Hailes."

"Thank you," she said more for her dagger than the information, then she turned her head to follow the proceedings as she slyly tucked the covered weapon into her boot.

"Rise, my son," the bishop said softly, stepping up to the dais and taking a place beside the castle's lord. The six Catholic priests, also richly robed, joined them.

Lord Hailes signaled for all to rise and everyone in the great hall stood. Sweeping an arm toward his guest and beaming with pride, he announced, "Courtiers, welcome Giacomo Passarelli, the Bishop of Imola, sent by Pope Innocent VIII of Italy."

The bishop extended his left hand and Lord Hailes kissed the holy man's golden ring. Then with gentle grace, Bishop Passarelli reached his hands out in supplication to the reverent courtly guests. Blinking heavy-lidded dark eyes, he exuded peace and calm as he glanced about the room. His linen headdress crowned a head of graying, shoulder length curls.

Rosalyn had never seen a bishop before and found herself intrigued by his presence.

While the lord continued his address, Rosalyn worried over the reasons why the bishop wanted her at the high table. Surely, human sacrifice was not a catholic practice, but she'd heard stories of Vikings taking virgins for their God Odin at ceremonious occasions. *Are the Italians as primitive?* She couldn't help but wonder why a Scot needed to be on the dais. Even with Ursula at her side as her guardian, there was little the healer could do if an agent of the pope made a formal request.

When hushed exclamations of surprise and admiration began rippling through the great hall in reaction to a new group entering, Rosalyn returned to the present as Lord Hailes waved the new procession forward.

Dressed in full battle armor, three guards approached the dais, the one in the center cautiously carried a gleaming object while the castle's host gushed with pride. "He's gracing us with his presence during a brief stop after arriving today at port. From here, the bishop will travel by guarded caravan to deliver the Golden Rose to James III, the King of Scots."

"The Golden Rose?" Rosalyn whispered in Ursula's ear, but the healer gave her a gentle elbow and a tiny, "Shh!"

The castle's lord turned to the bishop, "Your Excellency, please present the Rose."

"*Grazie*," the bishop thanked him, his serene face glowing. "I will speak in English," he promised with only a hint of an accent, although there were many in the room who would have understood Latin.

"What makes this Golden Rose special is not only its pure and precious metal, but the mystical significance and honor it carries. The Rose represents love after hate, joy after sorrow, fullness after hunger," the holy man explained, his voice full of reverence. "Blessed at the solemn Mass in the papal chapel," the bishop said, picking up the gift and raising it in exaltation, "the Golden Rose is given once a year to a worthy king as a token of admiration for the leader's Christian virtues." The bishop paused, then bowed his head. "Let us pray."

As the holy man began a poetical prayer appropriate for the occasion, Rosalyn bowed her head slightly, but kept her eyes open. She was close enough to study the object that measured about eight inches tall. Ten golden roses were nested in a golden urn, with the largest rose centered in the middle and smaller ones clustered around it. Rubies and other gems decorated the petals. Nature captured in a metal form. She'd never seen anything more stunning.

When she heard the word, "Amen," she mumbled it under her breath and was startled when she looked up to find everyone else seated but herself. With a shrug, she slid silently into her regal chair at the end of the row. Her eyes involuntarily darted to Lachlan, whose gaze she caught unexpectedly. He'd been watching her and flashed her a charming grin. She returned a sheepish smile before she realized she'd done it.

Where was her ire when she needed it? Being angry at Lachlan made it easy not to like him. And right now she should be plotting her escape from him, not swooning under his attention.

The bishop brought her focus back to the high table when she found him by her side.

"*Scusami*," he said with a slight Italian lilt.

Rosalyn's lips froze and her mouth went dry. She wanted to speak, but not even a squeak would come forth. Ursula elbowed her in the ribs again, and Rosalyn started breathing, thankful for the poke.

"Your Excellency," Rosalyn said in a wispy voice she did not recognize as her own.

"No formalities, my dear. Are you the Scottish lass I seek?"

CHAPTER 5

*S*itting on the dais speaking to the bishop, Rosalyn was a vision of desire. But a dalliance with a Scottish lass would not allow Lachlan to earn back his father's respect. Besides, Rosalyn was proving to be a worthy adversary. She wanted what he wanted: *Fyvie Castle.*

What had started as an exercise in forgery to claim the Scottish prize at his father's request, had turned into another opportunity for his twin brother to best him.

Now that the proceedings had concluded, he couldn't avoid a conversation with his brother any longer. Lachlan braced himself for the worst as Ethan turned.

"Explain how Fyvie's land title eludes you," his brother asked as though he didn't know already, his gaze intense as always.

"You met my trifle inconvenience," Lachlan said, nodding toward Rosalyn at the dais, holding back his anger, wanting to remain neutral. "Any self-respecting English judge would have tossed the twit out on her pretty arse after making a land claim." Then Lachlan leaned in and said, "But the local chancellor treated her like Scottish royalty. He must be in King James's pocket."

"No doubt you have a plan?" Ethan asked.

Nothing sparked his ire more than his competitive brother's scrutiny. "It's not a matter of *if*, but *when* I deploy it. I suspect I'll join you in a fortnight or sooner." Lachlan bristled. He'd answered enough questions. "Where's Father?"

"Dunster Castle in Somersetshire." Ethan took a long swig of mead from his goblet as if to provoke Lachlan further with the delay. After wiping his mouth with the back of his hand, Ethan continued. "He has a score to settle with a Garter knight, but promised to return to Aberdeen before Easter."

Lachlan was repulsed by how much Ethan was like their father in manner, mind, and where money was concerned. "Father always has a score to settle." Lachlan rubbed his beard and reflected on how his father pitted the two brothers against each other as young lads. Whoever was the boldest and pleased Father the most slept in feather-bed comfort while the other slept on woven rushes on the floor. Even then, Lachlan knew Ethan was Father's favorite.

"And so do I. Off to King Henry's coronation on the morrow, then to Dunster to give Father my report. He may have to get involved after all," his brother threatened, a sneer curling his lips.

Wanting nothing more than to punch Ethan's face, Lachlan gritted his teeth instead before replying, "Your report? Now, what might that be about?"

"Your actions," he said, then ticked them off with his fingers. "At Berwick court for months. Leaving Fyvie without an overlord. Avoiding the mutinous clansmen."

Lachlan forced a hard smile. "You tell him Fyvie's ours. I have the means. I'm pondering the method." Lachlan wanted to be as vague as possible about the whole affair. No longer willing to defend his actions, he turned his back on Ethan and focused his attention to the dais, hoping his disinterest would end the discourse.

"Your inconvenience is beautiful," Ethan said dryly, "but not worth your inheritance."

"No need to worry, Brother. I fancy the black-haired beauty Ursula over the angry redhead."

"I fancy Ursula as well."

Of course he did. Ethan fancied anything Lachlan did out of spite. Ethan was beyond jealous. Some called him mad. He'd stop at nothing to take from Lachlan: women, land, titles, if he could. But Lachlan was ready for battle and turned back to face him. "Are you up for a wager, Brother?"

"Perhaps." His brother stroked his goatee like a lover. "What are the stakes?"

"You bed Ursula and my future title is yours." That was one thing Lachlan had over his brother. He was first out of the womb.

Ethan chuckled loudly, drawing the attention of the flirtatious noble women. His brother ignored the curious and slapped him on the back. "Earl? Yes, that's acceptable. What's the rest of the wager?"

"You lose, you do my bidding for a year. What I require. Whatever I want you to tell our father. Agreed?" Lachlan shot out his hand.

"Done," his brother said, accepting the wager with a handshake.

Now it was Lachlan's turn to smirk as he turned his attention to the dais. Even if his brother was as notorious as his father, he'd learned from an early age that Ethan couldn't resist a good wager. Never had Lachlan put so much on the line, but never had there been so much to gain.

Knowing Ursula as he did, though, it was a gamble worth

taking and perhaps the only way to accomplish his goal. Right now, he had make sure Father stayed out of Scotland.

Just then, Ursula shifted her gaze from the bishop to the table where they sat. She glowed with an earthy confidence as she stood. His gaze followed the redhead and the bishop off the dais. He turned to find Ethan's gaze tracking her movements, his brother's breathing heavy as if hunting prey. "Take me to her room. Now," he demanded.

* * *

Knees knocking, but determined to stay strong, Rosalyn carried the Golden Rose following Ursula and the bishop as Lord Hailes led them from the great hall down a winding, narrow corridor to the courtiers' small chapel. The bishop had made it clear at dinner that it was God's calling she needed to answer. He told her the Lord had put her in the bishop's path for a reason.

Oh, praise Mary!

Rosalyn considered the invitation both a blessing and a curse. Surely, arriving in Edinburgh with a reverent entourage and the Pope's emissary to deliver the Golden Rose would give her much-needed esteem and a stronger position from where to argue her cause. On the other hand, she'd need to figure out a way to make sure Lachlan, her curse, was sidetracked so she could plead her case first.

Trailing behind the grand robes of the bishop as she entered the small chapel with Ursula, Lord Hailes, and the six priests, Rosalyn found herself greeted by a beautiful statue of the Virgin Mary gazing at her from behind the altar. Awe and reverence stirred inside her.

While they walked in a slow procession, the bishop began a beautiful chant, his Latin words bouncing off the high beamed ceilings.

Although it wasn't heavy, the Golden Rose felt like a burden, as if she carried all the hopes and dreams of her countrymen in her hands.

When they reached the font of the chapel, Bishop Passarelli directed her to place the precious gift on the altar. Then after gesturing for all to kneel, he began a prayer.

"Oh, Lord, most powerful and forgiving, we have set foot on English soil this day, the first part of our journey, to deliver the Golden Rose to the one most deserving. Please bless our steps as we travel to Scotland with the chosen one. Provide your protection and your divine love. Amen."

As the bishop began chanting again in Latin, Rosalyn held her spot among the kneeling congregation curious as to who was the chosen one. King James, no doubt, was the most deserving. She tried her best to put her mind at ease until more was revealed, but couldn't stop her feelings of frustration now that the path to win back Fyvie was no longer her own.

When the chanting stopped, she opened her eyes just as the bishop gestured to her.

"Lady Rosalyn, come before me."

With knees knocking again, Rosalyn did her best to navigate the narrow path between the priests and the altar until she was in front of the bishop. She knelt with her head bent and her heart pounding.

He put his hand on her head and said softly, "My child, do not be afraid. The reasons you are the chosen one are many-fold. Some of that I will reveal to you now, the rest when you are ready."

I'm the chosen one? As much as she wanted to feel honored, she couldn't help but want to disappear into the heather-filled woods of her homeland with her land title tucked into her boot, gone from the worries of court, free of a kissing Englishman, and of any obligations to the Catholic Pope.

"Rosalyn."

When the bishop spoke her name again, she snapped out of her pondering.

"The Golden Rose is one of the greatest treasures of the world and each year when it's en route to its final destination, a ward of that country is chosen as its champion," he explained.

Rosalyn gulped, wondering how she could escape when she was going to champion a public treasure as the holy man kept his hand on her head.

"How appropriate too," he continued, with a slight Italian accent, "that your name means *rose* in Latin." Then he chuckled and his mirth traveled through his hand to her. "Of course, it is no accident, it's God will."

God's will be done on earth as it is in heaven.

"*Si,* Rose, God's will be done," the bishop answered, as if hearing her thoughts. He'd called her Rose, but she would forgive him as he reached for her hand and helped her up.

Filing in behind Bishop Passarelli, Rosalyn let out a little sigh, happy she would not become a sacrificial casualty. Of course, it had been ridiculous of her to think that possible, but her fears often overrode her sensibility. Sadly, it was when she was angry that she had the best clarity. But she could not be angry with the bishop for his request. In a strange way, it gave her purpose for the journey to visit her king beyond the court proceeding she was dreading.

The bishop led them back to the entrance of the great hall. After the group said their goodbyes and offered wishes for a good night's sleep, Ursula and Rosalyn walked the short distance to the healer's chamber door.

Rosalyn was a step behind her friend when Ursula opened the door and screamed. Covering her ears, Rosalyn wasn't sure whether to follow Ursula inside or run for help.

"Lachlan!" Ursula's voice boomed across the room and

brought Rosalyn inside to look. Barely covered, he lay in her bed. The healer shook with anger, her fists at her side, her chest heaving. "Not now, not ever. You are a verra selfish man to risk my reputation. Certainly, you do not care about your own," Ursula ground out, no doubt unaware her brogue had entered the room with her.

The awkwardness of Ursula's refusal hung in the air for a few moments until Lachlan sat up.

"Your escort can leave now," was his response.

"You can leave now, or I'll scream down this hallway until the chamber is full of gossips. Is that what you want?"

Ursula appeared angry enough to follow through on her threat, jamming fisted hands against her hips, eyes blazing.

Rosalyn shifted her stance, ready to reach for her dirk if Lachlan made a threatening move.

Anticipation stretched to anxiety for Rosalyn as time passed in silence. Finally, Lachlan let out a grunt and threw off what little silk covered his naked form. Taking his time to leave the bed, his manhood rose before he did.

Heat rushed to Rosalyn's cheeks. Aye, she was still a virgin and this was her first contact with a naked man. His full arousal was intimidating, but even though his body mesmerized her as he moved, she was taken aback by his primordial nature.

Ursula didn't flinch and even walked over to stand protectively in front of Rosalyn while Lachlan dressed and finally left the chamber without another word.

Once he was gone, Ursula slammed the chamber door shut and drew the heavy bolt into place. Then they ran toward each other before collapsing into a huddle.

"It's time to leave this place," Ursula finally said. "I won't be safe here any longer. If he tried this once, he'll be back." She gazed into Rosalyn's eyes, fear swimming in her black pools. "The only thing that kept him from taking me was you."

Rosalyn hugged Ursula tightly and guided her to the bed's edge, easing them both down. "We must honor the commitment we made to Bishop Passarelli, but we need a device that will keep Lachlan here. At first I hoped to escape with your help and travel to King James to make my plea without Lachlan, now I must make my way with the protection of the bishop."

Ursula stared at her blankly. But after a few silent moments passed, the healer arched one perfect brow. "*Och*, I could retaliate by poisoning his food!" She cackled wickedly. "Wouldnae have to kill him, just make him sick enough to keep him in bed a few days."

"Enough days to hold him at Berwick until Fyvie is mine," Rosalyn agreed, and she laughed wickedly, too.

Yet Ursula did not seem satisfied. With her brows knitted together, lips forming a firm, straight line, she gazed into the hearth.

Rosalyn considered the delay as it went usually long. Ursula wasn't angry enough to change her mind and kill him, was she?

But after a few more moments of contemplation, Ursula finally rose with a glazed-over stare, then walked to a tall, ornate cabinet covered with plant carvings and Rosalyn followed.

The healer slowly opened the cabinet doors as if a vicious beast were caged inside. But instead of something awful, Ursula revealed rows of vials and potion bottles.

As Rosalyn peered inside, a waft of odor assaulted her senses even though all the containers were sealed. She gagged from the overwhelming smells.

But Ursula appeared unfazed. She spun and danced in front of the cabinet as if in a trance.

When the healer finally stopped what was either a cele-bration or ritual, Ursula got to work taking what she needed from the shelves.

"Nightshade, eye of a frog." The healer turned around to face Rosalyn, her hands full of bottles that tottered precari-ously between her fingers. Ursula gestured with a beckoning head nod. "Help, please?" she asked, pointing her elbow toward a twisted vine basket by the door.

Rosalyn hurried to retrieve it. Then after she helped Ursula unload her precious cargo, she took her time to scan the chamber. The shock of seeing Lachlan naked had kept her from doing so until now.

The room—a virtual lab within a bed chamber—would make any healer envious. And because Rosalyn was a healer, too, she appreciated the collection. Not only did the cupboard contain curious concoctions, but the wall rack by the window also held treasures of many plants. Some were freshly picked, others dried on the rack. Under the window, an impressive marble-topped table stood covered in mortars of many sizes.

Rosalyn slowed to a stop at the table, admiring the resources until Ursula loudly cleared her throat and tapped her foot.

"Oh, of course," she mumbled, finding Ursula with another handful. The two quickly filled the basket to the brim with great care and efficiency.

Humming, the healer almost skipped to the marble table and began unpacking her arsenal of Mother Nature's ammunition.

What type of poison is she making?

Immersed in her work, Ursula pointed toward the drying rack. "Fetch me the dried hemlock. You should know it," she ordered as if Rosalyn was a loyal lap dog.

"*Arf, arf*," Rosalyn barked, then panted.

That made Ursula laugh, but the healer didn't lift her eyes from the ingredients before her. Instead, she reached out her open hand and waited for the requested dried herb.

After providing the required assistance, Rosalyn grabbed a short stool by the bed, then took up a seat by the working table to observe in silence.

Humming a pretty ballad, Ursula combined the herbs and potions with skilled hands as Rosalyn watched in awe.

Finally, after a long spell of concocting, Ursula let out a satisfied sigh. "The deed is done," she said, turning to Rosalyn and offering her the mortar with a sly grin.

"Outside of what I know, what else have you added?" Rosalyn asked, taking the mortar from Ursula and peering over the top of it, finding a dark-red liquid, almost like wine.

"Most of what you might expect. The forest mushrooms, toad blood, meal worms. Typical healer resources." The dark-haired beauty rubbed her hands together in glee. "But also dragonfly wings, snake eyes, and mercury."

"Mercury? Isn't that deadly?" Hadn't Ursula said she didn't want to kill Lachlan?

"Not when it's shaved into bits so fine you can't detect it with your tongue when it's in liquid. The elements virtually dissolve. This needs to be placed in Lachlan's chalice on the morrow."

"How will you manage?"

"I shall manage just fine, because I will nae be the one to deliver it, you will."

"Me?" The response came out of Rosalyn's mouth like a mouse's shrill squeal.

"Aye. I'm certain Lachlan will want to break his fast with you in the morn. He's interested in the final travel plans with the bishop. He'll seek you out. Me, on the other hand, he'll avoid for sheer self-preservation." She chuckled at what Rosalyn assumed was her expression of dread.

CHAPTER 6

The next morning, Lachlan rushed into the great hall anxious to hear from his brother. Taking the seat next to Ethan, Lachlan snatched up a hunk of cheese from the trencher and grinned. If his twin claimed he'd won the wager, Lachlan would insist he hear it from Ursula himself.

"Before you begin," his brother said, staring straight ahead, looking half-drunk already, "I want you to know it's clear that you sent me to fail."

Lachlan gloated inwardly as he took a satisfying bite of the imported Jarlsburg. Savoring his victory and the cheese, a servant interrupted him, curtsied apologetically and asked meekly, "Wine, my lord?" When Lachlan nodded, she filled his goblet to the brim.

After taking a few sips, he turned to his brother. "How could you fail? You're a handsome-looking fellow," Lachlan bragged, nudging him in the ribs.

"I was too quick to gamble." His brother's glaring stare and stubborn set jaw said more than his words. "However, I will honor my wager and do your bidding with one condi-tion." He waved a heavily ringed hand like a king, paused dramatically, then said, "Only when it suits me."

Lachlan sighed. He should have known. Controlling his brother was near impossible. He sighed deeply. "I shall concede to you, but with one condition—that you not share our surname while you are here, or in Scotland."

"We're Luttrells after all. Notorious as our family is, you venture to hide your heritage, even now that father has been vindicated and he calls the King of England cousin? Are you ashamed?"

"I have my reasons, Lachlan said. "Until you embark on your journey to Windsor, you will be known as Ethan de Leverton. Agreed?"

"So be it!"

Skeptical of his brother's quick agreement, his promise most likely a lie, Lachlan frowned. Like when he lied to his father about his mother's death. "Have you poisoned anyone lately?"

"Perhaps, why do you ask?"

"I was deciding if I could count on your promise, or if it was yet another lie."

Ethan ignored his brother's doubt. "Do you need the Scottish lass poisoned? Surely, I could volunteer."

"That's what I'm afraid of," Lachlan said. "Just because you want someone out of the way doesn't mean poisoning them is the answer."

"Poisoning is an everyday occurrence, especially in our family," Ethan said, as if boasting. "Which reminds me," he said, stroking his beard and studying Lachlan with a critical eye, "did you hire a new food taster? I believe you lost the last one."

Now it was Lachlan's turn to ignore his brother. "I must

ready for the journey to Edinburgh." He was ready to be rid of Ethan. "As far as Father is concerned, I have Fyvie in my possession. That will be your report."

They both rose.

"For now I leave you," Lachlan said.

Ethan grasped his shoulders, then wrapped one arm around his back in an awkward embrace, more ceremonial than sincere.

As they parted ways, Ethan toward the bailey, Lachlan took the stairs to the solar anxious to embark and plead his case before King James.

Once inside the chamber, his first task was to retrieve the drawstring fur pouch that belonged to Rosalyn. Even though he'd sworn to himself that deception no longer served him as he planned for a new life with the de Leverton name, Lachlan was smart enough to understand old habits die hard. His family's obsession for land was one of them.

After taking the pouch from behind the tapestry, he spread the contents on his desk and shifted the items around. Wanting to restudy the seal, Lachlan rolled the heavy stamp around in his hands. He'd seen forgeries before, even made some of his own. The weight of it felt substantial enough to be legitimate. Rotating the head to examine it more closely, he squinted his eyes and lifted it closer to the wall sconce. This one was real. He was sure of it now.

How had the lass managed it? Paid for it handsomely, he supposed. He chuckled thinking about the false imprint he'd used on his papers, but not the king's seal. No, the penalty for forging or misuse of a royal seal was a beheading. Lachlan shuddered. Fyvie meant everything to him, but his integrity meant more and he promised himself he could make the claim without the king's seal as evidence against her.

To avoid temptation, he returned to his hiding space and shoved the stamp and the wax into the dark recess. Greed was an ugly companion and in some ways, he wasn't sure he could trust himself once he was ready for the king's final judgment.

When he righted the tapestry, a streak of sunshine cut a swath across the desk, reminding him that it was time to saddle his destrier. As he picked up the pouch, the sunlight struck a piece of Rosalyn's odd red stone, making the edge gleam from underneath the frayed tartan. The heavy iron key rested on top, creating an awkward mound of her treasures.

After packing the key and the tartan away, he studied the last, the red stone, wondering if it was precious or merely a fancy piece of glass. But as much as he wanted to act honorably at the Scottish hearing, Lachlan was grateful to have this pouch as leverage against the Scottish lass. Even if he left the most damning evidence behind, any one of Rosalyn's personal belongings might prove useful at Edinburgh.

Filled with confidence and a clear plan, Lachlan stashed Rosalyn's possessions in the bottom of his travel satchel. Knowing the servants would gather the rest of his belongings, he left the chamber with a cocky stride to find the Scottish lass.

* * *

Waking with a satisfied stretch worthy of a lazy cat, Rosalyn rolled over and squinted from the sun pouring in between the cracks of the plum velvet drapes. Foggy-minded and warm, she whispered the words on her lips. "Again, Lachlan, again."

Bolting straight up in bed, she shook the fuzzy images of the dream from her mind. Aghast at her flushed cheeks and moistness between her thighs, Rosalyn tried to destroy the image of a naked Lachlan seducing her. "Father, forgive me," she said beneath her breath, "for I have sinned."

Tossing back the warm fur covering, she quickly planted her feet on the threshed matting, fishing for her soft slippers. Heart thundering, the image of a naked Lachlan entwined with her in bed came back. How could she face him after yester eve? Meet his eyes after meeting his cock? Would he gloat about it? Tease her? What then?

Damn Ursula. Rosalyn had agreed to slip Ursula's wicked wine into Lachlan's goblet. She'd have to see him at least once before she left for Edinburgh. Her cheeks burned after another vision of Lachlan popped into her head. She swore again.

As she reached for her linen chemise and began to dress, she shifted her attention to her task. Could she pay a servant to do the deed? But then the thought of it all going wrong squelched that idea. Even if she bribed a servant with gold, how could she be certain an English wench would honor a Scotswoman's bidding? No, Ursula would never forgive her if the deed was not done right. The deceptive task would have to be her responsibility alone.

But she'd need a distraction.

Hoping she wasn't too late, Rosalyn checked the flask tied to her belt and made sure it was secured as she left the chamber and headed for the great hall, anxious to find Lachlan.

Once inside the great hall's main entrance, Rosalyn slid into the shadows by the trestle table, still laden with meats, pies, and tarts. She scanned room for Lachlan, her charming adversary.

Finally, her eyes settled on the back of his head. Finding him sitting alone, she walked quickly through the retreating courtiers, nodding politely as they passed. Then she rushed to the table.

"Oh, I'm so glad I found you," she said breathlessly as she took a seat beside him. "The bishop was looking for you," she lied.

With his eyes upon her, she froze. Then she panicked and looked away. She counted to ten and prayed for courage. When it did not come, she decided being silent was worse and turned to face him.

"Lachlan," she finally said in a big gasp, "Bishop Passarelli wants to speak with you about Berwick-Upon-Tweed and why it's a prosperous seaport. About the history of how it's been fought over centuries between our nations." She took a hard swallow and pressed on. "I told him as an English lord in residence, you'd have much to say about the matter."

"Well, you were wrong," he replied dryly, his condemning gaze not wavering.

"*Scusami*," mumbled a soft voice from behind.

Startled, Rosalyn almost knocked over Lachlan's goblet with her hand as she turned. But it was the bishop who put a kind and steady hand on her shoulder.

"God forgive me for alarming you, lass." The bishop chuckled softly.

Even Lachlan laughed for a moment, his harsh gaze softening.

Rosalyn hopped up and curtsied deeply with her head bowed and Lachlan stood.

The pope's apostle put his hands in prayer at his heart. "I was looking for you, lass," the bishop said, turning to her.

"Well, of course, because you must have known I'd be with the Englishman," she said, taking her seat with her heart beating frantically. To Rosalyn's relief, Lachlan settled back on the bench next to her and the bishop took a seat across from them.

As the Lachlan and the bishop began to talk, she seized the distraction and whisked Lachlan's empty goblet off the table and into her lap. Keeping her gaze on the two and pretending to be engaged in their conversation, she fumbled with the flask top anxious to get the wicked wine in front of Lachlan.

Finally, victory was hers as she finished filling the cup and slid the goblet back in place without notice.

Now, the most difficult part. Rosalyn took a deep breath and waited. And waited. And waited.

As much as she wished for Lachlan to grab the goblet and guzzle the poisoned wine, after about ten minutes of conversation with the bishop, his hand had not raised it.

She wanted to appear at ease, but it was difficult not to fidget as the conversation appeared to be ending.

The bishop stood. "*Si*, a prosperous seaport will be the envy of any nation," the bishop said, then turned toward her. "We will go now," he instructed.

She stood slowly, stalling, as her mind scrambled for a reason not to leave Lachlan's side until she was sure he drained his goblet. Then an idea struck her.

"Your Holiness, would do the honor of blessing Lachlan's wine?" she asked, handing him the filled goblet. "Pray for good health and good fortune in the days ahead?"

The bishop's eyes softened like a father's would when honoring a daughter's request, and he accepted the cup.

Lachlan stood and bowed his head as the holy man placed his hand over the wine and softly said a prayer in Latin.

To her relief, Lachlan took the goblet from the bishop and after a raised salute, drained the cup of its contents. He glanced at Rosalyn. "Looking out for my wellbeing, how selfless of you."

"How selfless, indeed," she responded, choking on an embarrassing giggle and bowing low. "Now, I shall excuse myself to ready for the journey." She straightened, waiting on the bishop.

"When the trumpets sound, we will embark," the bishop said.

Rosalyn snickered to herself as she almost skipped out of the great hall.

CHAPTER 7

$\mathcal{A}$fter packing the suitable travel clothes her lady in waiting had provided, Rosalyn rode her palfrey to meet the group gathered at the front gates, giddy as she thought about how she'd deceived Lachlan. But then she remembered what her father used to say when she was a little girl and she'd done something wrong, "Blessed are the pure in heart, for they will see God." She sighed. No doubt, she was headed for hell.

Tightening the reins in her gloved hands, Rosalyn tried to feel remorseful about drugging Lachlan. With the exception of his defense of the Scots and his chiding the bailiff over her poor treatment, he'd been a selfish oaf.

Well, except when he had rescued her from the swoon, but he'd caused it. No, she couldn't feel remorse now that it was only Lachlan that stood between her and reclaiming Fyvie.

Damn the English.

She was just getting used to the cold leather saddle under her skirts when another rider approached her. Mounted on a black-as-night destrier that matched his own dark coloring, her mouth gaped as Lachlan rode up beside her. Flipping his cape back over his shoulders to reveal a heavily decorated armored chest plate, he bridled his horse.

"Good, I caught you," he said rather breathlessly. "The Garter knights have yet to arrive, so I have suited up along with a few other former knights. We've been asked by Lord Hailes to assist in protecting the bishop's group and ensure the success of the Golden Rose's delivery. I did not want you to worry."

Her mind whirling, Rosalyn choked back what she really wanted to say. Why didn't the poison work? Had he only pretended to drink? His all-consuming gaze on her made it even more difficult to articulate her thoughts until Ursula came riding up beside them and to her rescue.

"Where's the sheriff?" the healer asked, looking as confused as Rosalyn felt.

"Called to greater matters than coddling an English Lord on his way to see justice served." Then Lachlan gave Ursula a wicked grin. "Perhaps he was certain you could handle two wayward criminals without his supervision?"

Ursula grunted in an unladylike manner, tossing her luxurious hair off her shoulder and behind her back, obviously unsettled. "You shall not be my ward," she said in an icy tone to Lachlan. "Mind your ways and keep your clothes on."

Lachlan's smile wilted and his brows shot upward in apparent confusion, but before he could say another word, she'd turned her horse and was off in the other direction.

The silence was awkward after Ursula's rude behavior, but considering what he'd done last night, Rosalyn believed he deserved the snub. Without a ready excuse to leave, too, she decided a conversation about breakfast was in order. "What did you and the bishop talk about after I left the great hall?"

Lachlan's gaze was still on Ursula's arse when he answered her. "What talk with the bishop?"

Rosalyn cocked her head to one side and her eyes narrowed when he spun around and he met her gaze.

"I ate with the sheriff and a few of the armored men." The pitch of his reply rose at the end as if in question. "I was down to the great hall well afore dawn," he finished with all his attention on her now.

"You jest. I was there for the blessing."

"Was someone baptized?" he asked with a mischievous gleam in his eyes.

"Well, it was not a hanging, I can assure you of that."

Lachlan rubbed his neck as if the possibility was too real. "I count it as a blessing that I've avoided a hanging. But nay, it must have been my brother. I left as he came in."

Luckily for Rosalyn, the castle's armorer rode up to interrupt them as the truth set in.

She'd poisoned his brother. *Damn, they are identical.*

"Can you shoot?"

It took Rosalyn a moment to come out of her fog. The armorer was speaking to her. In a voice that sounded less than assured, she managed to squeak out a paltry, "Yes, my lord."

Satisfied with her answer, the soldier rode up on her other side and handed her a quiver full of arrows and a longbow.

"Are we expecting trouble?" Rosalyn asked, holding the weapons as if she wanted to return them and at the same time trying not to let the uneasiness she was feeling come through in her tone. The trail from Berwickshire to Edinburgh was a well-traveled one.

"Never expected, that's the trouble," the armorer said, no doubt always prepared, but apparently not alarmed. "Without the protection of the Garter knights, I want everyone in the party, even the bishop, to be ready if ambushed," he said soberly. Then he nodded toward Ursula. "What about the other lass?"

Lachlan laughed. "That sorceress?" he said, pointing toward the healer. "Don't arm her, she may put an arrow through my heart." He clutched at his chest.

Rosalyn could help but laugh.

The armorer didn't appear amused, but gestured to Lachlan to follow him and the two riders moved on.

She was grateful for the interruption and pleased for an easy way to rid herself of Lachlan for now. After securing her bow to the back of her saddle, she slung the quiver over her head and settled the leather strap on her left shoulder feeling prepared. She was a good shot and was more secure about the journey ahead. Now, what to do about Lachlan? She needed a foolproof plan.

It wasn't long before the trumpeters on the parapets interrupted her plotting. Once the revelry was complete, Lord Hailes led the bishop to a grand, roofed wagon drawn by four massive chestnut destriers. Three of the bishop's men followed him to the wagon and the others joined on horseback. The priests no longer looked placid, for they were now equipped with breast plates and swords.

As she scanned those gathered at the portcullis gate, she confirmed what she'd suspected. Everyone, even Ursula, was now armed.

Lord Hailes climbed part way up the parapet steps to rise above those assembled. Then he lifted his hands in the air and addressed them.

"Holy men, lords, and ladies, a missive from Windsor arrived this morn from the realm's king-at-arms announcing only a few Garter knights are en route to Berwick for the Golden Rose transport. Most have been called by King

Henry to Warwickshire to protect his brother from a Yorkist uprising."

"God save your king and his brother," Bishop Passarelli called out.

Lord Hailes nodded. "Thank you, Bishop," he answered with a slight bow toward the holy man. "I shall send you off to Edinburgh with our retired knights and volunteers today, but will direct the Garter knights to Edinburgh after they arrive."

The bishop raised his hands. "Thank you, Lord Hailes. With God's speed, we leave you."

The restless horses stomped, pawed, and made snorting noises in response, then the bishop turned away and followed his three men into the grand wagon.

When the group began to move, Ursula rode up beside Rosalyn, her eyes wide and full of questions. Before the healer opened her mouth, Rosalyn held up her hand. "I know what you are thinking, but it was Ethan who drank our concoction, not Lachlan."

Ursula's mouth gaped as the truth sunk in.

Rosalyn decided it was time to share her thoughts as the group began to file over the drawbridge and the two women's horses fell in line with them forming a caravan on the trail toward Edinburgh. She might not have another private moment for some time.

"Ursula, I didn't use all the potion," Rosalyn admitted, tapping the wooden flask strapped to her leather belt. "Given another chance with his wine, there should be plenty here to make Lachlan sick enough to turn back."

Ursula grinned wickedly. "Then all is not lost," she said, her eyes sparking with mischief. "I, too, had another plan after seeing Lachlan arrive and sent a missive to my love." She glanced about making sure their conversation was still private, but she lowered her voice anyway. "Asking him to rendezvous with us. To escort us to the king ahead of this group."

"Are you sure your messenger will find him?"

"I cannae be certain he's even in his village," she said with a detached gaze toward the horizon.

If Rosalyn could, she would have hugged her friend. "I'm grateful," she said, her throat thick with emotion.

The healer's eyes became clear again and full of warmth. "Anything for a kinswoman. Anything." Then she nodded. "Keep that poison at the ready."

CHAPTER 8

As he rode behind the bishop's wagon on the well-traveled path to Edinburgh, Lachlan remained befuddled by the blessing.

Still, he was happy to ride along as a protector with sword and shield rather than as a prisoner with ball and chain. No doubt he'd make a much better impression with King James in that fashion, too.

Lachlan adjusted his arse in his saddle and slowed his horse to fall further back in the procession. He relished knowing he'd have time over the next two days to make some important decisions.

As much as he hated being Nicholas Luttrell's son, there were traits he'd inherited that seemed unshakeable, such as his obsession with land, lying when it suited him, and buying his way out of trouble. At the moment, his father was obsessed with Fyvie Castle and Lachlan had been willing to lie to get it. He knew a judge could be bribed, but could a king?

While mulling over how to influence King James, Lachlan

noticed he'd dropped back far enough to join Ursula, who rode alongside Rosalyn. His focus shifted to the most important decision he'd make this day: Who would warm his bed and massage his aching muscles after the long ride?

When he turned to the healer and flashed her one of his twisted, naughty grins, she ignored him. He grunted, frustrated by her cold rejection. Might the fiery redhead riding beside Ursula be more receptive?

Looking past Ursula to the Highland lass, Lachlan caught Rosalyn's eye, and she shyly returned a grin. Lachlan's smile deepened as he recounted how he'd charmed Rosalyn into a kiss more than once.

Charisma. That's one thing he had that his father didn't. Lachlan chuckled as he pondered his love of wooing the ladies. He never saw himself as the marrying kind, now or ever, because there were so many willing women out there to conquer. And Rosalyn was certainly worth pursuing, despite her sharp tongue and hatred of the English.

But Rosalyn could wait. Lachlan wanted one more go at the dark-haired sorceress.

"There's my beauty," he called over the head of his horse toward Ursula. He reined in his destrier close to her palfrey. Ursula and her horse snorted in sync.

"I am not *your* anything, Lachlan. If I had my way, you'd be gone."

"What do you mean by that, my love? Would you place a dagger in my heart while I slept?"

"Your dagger was more than an eyeful last night when I ordered you out of my bed," she snapped, then bit off an oath.

"Your bed?" Lachlan laughed. "As much as I've fantasized about joining you there, I've yet to be invited."

"You invited yourself. Don't toy with me, Lachlan."

He scratched his beard with a gloved hand absentmindedly. What was she talking about? "Toying with you is always my business, but you know I've never pushed you beyond that, my love."

"You shan't lie your way out of this one, Lachlan," she said as if condemning him to hell. "I have a witness."

"A witness to me lying in your bed? What was I wearing?" he asked, one corner of his mouth tugging his lips into a curve beyond his control.

"I shall not give you the satisfaction of describing your disgusting behavior. Rosalyn was there," Ursula said with a nod to her companion. "Ask her." And with a final grunt of disgust, she reined her horse away from Lachlan and led her palfrey into a canter. That left Lachlan behind in an uncomfortable spot with Rosalyn. It also confirmed his suspicion that his brother had no intention of winning the bet fairly. Why would it be any different now than when they were boys and Lachlan was blamed for their mother's death?

Squaring his shoulders, he shrugged off the emotions of the past and the brother who treated him as an enemy. He turned to the Highland lass, as sparring with her gave him great pleasure.

Unfortunately for Lachlan, though, the man-at-arms rode up beside them and signaled the group to stop for some rest. Before Lachlan could offer Rosalyn his companionship, she spurred her palfrey and pushed past him to follow Ursula.

Lachlan remained determined to pursue Rosalyn as he made his way to the designated grove. But as he dismounted his horse, the bishop stepped out of his wagon and waved him down.

"Lachlan, my Son," the bishop said, holding his side and walking stiffly toward Lachlan, "I need your assistance. Lord Hailes believes me to be too old to ride, yet I grow old riding in the wagon with my priests."

Bishop Passarelli looked exasperated and Lachlan understood his frustration. "Perhaps one of the women will trade places with you," Lachlan offered, then nodded toward the woods. "I see Lady Rosalyn is taking a walk. Mayhap I can convince her to ride in the wagon."

The Italian's eyes twinkled with happiness as Lachlan added, "She may be just as grateful for the switch."

Lachlan turned on his heels and watched Rosalyn walk her palfrey into the dense forest. He had an excuse to follow her, but wondered why she hadn't tethered her horse.

Glancing about, Lachlan noticed that food preparations were underway and no one apparently cared about anything else. Free from scrutiny, Lachlan walked his destrier down the same path Rosalyn took, being careful not to step on the bracken and alert her. He followed Rosalyn for a few minutes as the path narrowed and became more difficult.

Is she going to escape?

Walking in front of his horse now, and holding his right hand high to keep the branches from swatting his face, Lachlan stopped when he spotted a sizable cross trail ahead.

A short cut?

Squinting into the sun with his hand still raised to shield his eyes, Lachlan realized Rosalyn had traveled around the main trail and would be ahead of the group if that was her plan. Before he could decide whether to stop her or join her, a young lad jumped from an overhanging branch onto the path, blocking her.

Rosalyn screamed.

The lad made his intention clear. "Give me your coin, your jewels. Now!" he shouted as he stood in the center of the path and waved a thorn-covered mace.

"I have none of those things. I'm a prisoner, escaping," she answered in a shrill, loud voice.

Lachlan was close enough to know that Rosalyn was in

danger. He quickly secured his horse to a nearby tree and with sword drawn, inched his way between the shadows toward the standoff.

"Then I'll have your horse, if you have no wealth," the lad growled, giving the animal a good smack on its rump and sending it toward Lachlan. "And I'll have you for my pleasure. Take off your clothes."

Slowly Rosalyn reached under her skirt, as if to comply, but she surprised Lachlan when she drew out a dirk instead..

At first, he thought Rosalyn might succeed when she charged forward with the dagger and a rebel yell. But the attacker easily knocked the weapon from her hand with a swift kick.

When the assailant belted his mace and moved toward her, Lachlan knew he had to act quickly. Fortunately, that's when Rosalyn's palfrey reached him and he found her bow and arrows attached to the saddle. He sheathed his sword and grabbed the other weapons.

Sprinting quietly along the edge of the path, and the distance between them shrinking, Lachlan aimed an arrow at the raider.

"You will not deny me, woman," the attacker yelled, stripping the top of her dress to her waist and exposing her breasts.

Rosalyn screamed, covered her chest, then fell to the ground leaving Lachlan's target open.

Breathing hard, Lachlan stopped and drew the bow's twine tense against his cheek. The arrow quivered in the bow's nook, waiting.

Aim. Ready. Release. The arrow soared from Lachlan's grasp with a high-pitched whine and struck the attacker in the back with a solid thud. The man staggered, groaned and fell to his knees, then toppled onto a sobbing Rosalyn.

Lachlan dropped the bow and raced to Rosalyn. "Love, are you all right? Your guardian is here," he said while he rolled the dead man off her.

"Ursula?"

Lachlan laughed. "You must have taken quite the fright to think I am Ursula." His heart softened as he gazed down at her windblown red tresses and dirt smeared face. A trail of tears streaked down her cheeks.

"Can you stand?" he asked, extending a hand.

She nodded, drawing her cloak to cover her torn dress with one hand while she accepted his help with the other. He tried to turn his eyes, but he couldn't as he caught a glimpse of her soft, pale breasts and rosy peaked nipples.

"How? Where? What happened?" she asked, gazing at him like a mysterious wood nymph.

Lachlan removed the brooch from his cloak as he spoke. "My love, I promised to be your guardian, and when I noticed you'd left the group alone, I followed you . . . in case you needed protecting." He used the brooch to secure her cloak around her neck.

Rosalyn examined Lachlan's handiwork with the jeweled brooch. He had turned the cape into a coat for her.

"Brilliant," she said.

"Me?" he said, holding her gaze.

She blushed. "Well, I must thank you, of course," she said, ignoring his question, but appearing grateful.

"This was a long way to travel for a lady's reprieve and privacy."

"Was that what you were after? A peek at my privates?" she asked, eyes flashing.

Heat rose to his checks. "Never, my lady. I was far too distant to interrupt any private moments. Close if needed. And needed I was," he said, bowing slightly. "But you must know I heard you back there.

"Aye, scared for my life."

"You claimed you were escaping."

She laughed nervously. "You do nae understand. I would have said anything to save myself."

CHAPTER 9

Rosalyn breathed a sigh of relief. What had seemed so simple had gone so very wrong. She was grateful to Lachlan for rescuing her. Inside, she was still rattled to the core, wanting nothing more than to hightail it back to Berwick Castle. Even the dungeon appeared safer now than the highway.

But as they walked back to retrieve the horses, she put up a brave front, chatting about how she had been searching for a river or stream, not realizing she'd strayed so far from the safety of the group. It was an all-out lie, of course, because Ursula had planned to meet her at the short cut, and together they'd intended to sneak off from the group to join Ursula's beau, Joshua, somewhere on the trail.

Still reeling from the attack, Rosalyn reviewed their plan and knew now that escaping had been a horrible idea.

When Lachlan and Rosalyn walked back into the impromptu camp, a few travelers waved, but no one seemed suspicious of their return from the woods. Lachlan's handiwork kept her torn dress well-hidden. He offered to help her find another dress, but she declined, assuring him she was fine and promised to find Ursula.

After securing her horse to a tree, she nearly jumped out of her skin when Ursula appeared at her side.

"God's teeth, you startled me."

"Shh, keep your voice low," the healer warned. "What happened? Why did you return with Lachlan? Did he follow you and force you to come back?" Ursula's litany of questions sounded like an inquisition, but Rosalyn could sympathize with her friend's anxiety as she stood waiting for answers with her hands on her hips and eyes bulging.

"Wasnae anything like that. He saved me from being raped and left for dead."

Ursula covered her mouth, her eyes filling with tears. "My sweet girl. I shall kill the bastard myself if he hurt you."

"Nay." Rosalyn blew out the word as if it had been blocking her throat, the emotions gushing out. "But it was terrifying. After the attacker ripped my dress down to my waist, Lachlan shot one of my arrows through the man's heart. He fell dead on top of me."

Ursula gasped. "Come, we must get you changed. I'll ask the bishop's guard if we can borrow the wagon. Tell him it's women's business. I'm sure he'll agree." Ursula turned her head in the direction of the man-at-arms as he made the final call. "Let's hurry," she said, looking wild-eyed and ready to run.

Holding her arm tightly, Ursula ushered Rosalyn across the gathering space. Then, after negotiating with the guard at the wagon, she herded Rosalyn into the back of the cart like the last sheep, clicking her tongue and pushing her arse.

"Stop prodding me, weren't not on a sheep farm," Rosalyn complained as she gathered her skirts and stepped into the bishop's inner sanctum of the grand covered wagon.

Rosalyn gasped in awe as she gazed at the various books,

soft gold-and-white floor pillows, and assorted rosaries within the room. Her eyes were drawn to the ceiling as the healer pointed above.

"Lavender, fenugreek, and sage," Ursula said with a tinge of surprise in her voice. "Fenugreek is not found in England or Scotland." Ursula sounded impressed and appeared ready to poke through the bishop's belongings if Rosalyn didn't get the healer back to the task at hand.

"Mayhap when we settle in for the night, you can ask more about these concoctions, but for now—"

"Oh, lass, I shouldnae been so distracted," Ursula said, refocusing her gaze on Rosalyn's makeshift coat. "I'll be back in a moment with a new dress for you," her friend promised and rushed past Rosalyn in a fury and out of the wagon.

Feeling safe again, Rosalyn thought back to the moment the attacker ripped her dress. She slid down to her knees among the soft pillows and rested her head on one.

Content in the bishop's sanctum, she fought back tears. She knew if Lachlan had not been there to save her, she would have been raped. How lucky she was that he had followed her, no matter what his reason. Even if it was to spy on her, or who knows what else, he was an honorable and brave man to have killed the attacker. In the Macpherson family, when someone saves your life, you are indebted to them until you return the gesture. That would complicate things, for the very man she had attempted to poison had saved her life.

"Comfortable?"

Rosalyn yelped when she looked up and found Lachlan peering at her.

"Ursula said you'd be decent." He paused. "I'm not being perverted," he said, color rising on his cheeks for the first time in her memory. "She asked me to deliver this." He pitched a soft bundle over the gate to Rosalyn.

She caught it and tossed him a grateful grin.

Lachlan gave Rosalyn a long, thoughtful look and said, "Happy to see you smiling after that attack."

"Thank you for being my guardian." Rosalyn choked back the emotion that nearly bubbled to the surface.

He nodded, turned to go, then whipped around just as quickly. "Almost forgot," he said, looking a bit embarrassed. "Bishop Passarelli heard that you took a tumble in the brush," he said, winking, "and he insists you ride in the wagon for the rest of the day."

When Rosalyn protested, Lachlan held up his hand. "Disagree all you want with me, but the bishop insisted. He's a man of God and you can't argue with God's will."

She contemplated that for a moment, then shrugged her shoulders. "Then I cannae refuse."

Lachlan chuckled, nodding in agreement, then turned and left her alone in the wagon.

Rosalyn heaved a grateful sigh as she removed the makeshift cape Lachlan had fashioned into a coat, then stepped out of the torn dress. Grateful for a change of clothes, she slipped a comfortable linen shift over her head.

God's will. What did he have in store for her? Life with Lachlan was getting complicated. Somehow, she hated him less than yesterday.

As Lachlan strutted across the clearing toward Rosalyn's palfrey, he hummed a little tune. The redhead was no longer angry with him. In the bishop's wagon, she'd behaved like coy cat, seemingly approachable. But as Lachlan considered the comparison further, his cocky grin disappeared when he remembered cats are also unpredictable, capable of clawing your eyes out.

Reaching her palfrey, Lachlan came to a reasonable conclusion, deciding it would be prudent to keep a good distance between them the next time they spoke. That anger of hers could spark at the slightest provocation and she also was dangerous with her dirk.

As he pondered her redeeming qualities and readied her mount for the bishop, Lachlan noticed Rosalyn's flask dangling from the saddle. Because he had followed her into the woods and not eaten or drank for hours, he was famished.

"Well, at least I could have a drink while I wait," Lachlan muttered.

Tugging at the ties, Lachlan easily released it from the saddle and popped off its cork. With a long swig, he guzzled the liquid. "*Hmm.* Not mead at all. Perhaps it's wine from northern Scotland," he whispered as he secured the flask to Rosalyn's saddle.

"*Bene! Eccoti,*" came a familiar voice from behind. "*El'eroe!*"

Lachlan spun around to greet the bishop. Did he just call him a hero?

"You are doing God's work," the holy man said, switching back to English. "The lass is lucky to have had you as her savior," Bishop Passarelli continued, walking up to receive the palfrey's reins. "*A chi bene crede, Dio provvede.*"

As Lachlan struggled to understand, the bishop offered the translation. "He who serves God has a good master."

Lachlan nodded and grinned at the smiling bishop. He was cherub-like except for the graying hair.

"Are you feeling *bene?*"

There was that mix of English and Italian again. Lachlan had studied Latin in school, yet he was not as familiar with the Roman language. But it was the look of concern on the bishop's face, not the snippet of Italian, that prompted Lachlan to scratch his beard.

"This morn, after I gave you the blessing, you drank the wine and not long after started to shiver and broke out in a sweat. Then you left to rest," the bishop said, still eyeing him with concern.

Ethan. He'd been the one at the table that morning for the blessing with Rosalyn. Now it made sense. No doubt his conniving brother did nothing to correct the misunderstanding.

Lachlan cleared his throat and squared his shoulders before he responded. "But of course I'm well. Here I am," Lachlan replied in a cheery tone. Although now that he thought about it, he did not feel well. His skin felt clammy and his mouth dry, as if he had grabbed some trail dirt and eaten that instead. *The wine?*

"If you are *insistere*, let's ride together. As I told you before, it's rare my position allows me a moment in the saddle." The holy man shook his head. "Such a waste. My father sent me to a prestigious riding academy and now I'm told to ride like an old man in a woman's wagon."

The bishop stopped for a moment and looked at Lachlan, who saw a glint of mischief in the bishop's eyes. "Let's have a race," the bishop said with childlike enthusiasm.

Wanting to give the bishop a chance to relive his youth, Lachlan nodded as they mounted their horses.

"To the fallen tree," Lachlan challenged, pointing to the toppled oak about two hundred paces off the trail.

"And back," the bishop responded.

Lachlan turned around in his saddle and quickly surveyed the camp, grateful to find most of the men still laughing and drinking near the supply wagon. He nudged his war horse into a canter and led the way to the trail's edge.

"On my mark," the bishop said barely loud enough for Lachlan to hear. "Ready, set, race!"

Lachlan dug his heels into his horse. The destrier shot

forward. But the bishop's horse was faster and soon, led by a length.

Kicking his spurs, Lachlan's horse pulled ahead as they raced toward the tree, the wind whipping Lachlan's cape wildly behind him. He hadn't been challenged in a long while. It felt exhilarating.

They reached the fallen tree, the bishop rounding the old oak first. But Lachlan was close behind.

As they approached the camp, cheers and shouts filled the air. The race had become a spectacle.

Lachlan kicked his warhorse's flanks again and drew head-to-head with the bishop, his mount snorting with competitive zeal.

The riders rushed toward the finish line with Lachlan in the lead. But just as Lachlan anticipated victory, his vision blurred and his mind spun. He grabbed the beast's mane and dug his fingers into the coarse tufts to anchor himself.

They were almost there. *Closer, closer.*

Then everything went black.

CHAPTER 10

When the soldiers carried Lachlan's limp body into the wagon, Rosalyn didn't know what to think.

"Make way, make way." Ursula's demanding voice could be heard from behind the men as they eased Lachlan onto the floor near Rosalyn's feet, his skin slick and pale.

Lachlan groaned as Rosalyn tried to make him comfortable. Propping his head on a pillow, his eyelids fluttered. The men had removed his armor and his shirt. Lachlan's charming mouth trembled, as did his entire body as if it was buried in snow.

"Be quick about it, men. Out of the wagon. I'm in charge now," the healer barked, like a commander, making the retired knights rush out and follow her bidding.

Motioning to Rosalyn for help, she forgot her own worries and scrambled to her feet.

"What happened?" she whispered to her friend.

"Our plan is working," Ursula bragged and revealed Rosalyn's flask tied to her belt.

Rosalyn clamped down on her lip, biting it to stop from

gasping. *The leftover poison?* Apparently Lachlan had found her flask.

Once Lachlan appeared settled, Ursula mouthed directions for her to move to the back of the tent.

As they huddled in the corner next to the long row of rosaries, pangs of regret washed over Rosalyn. "You said the plan is working, but this isnae the plan," Rosalyn whispered.

The healer's eyes narrowed. "This is the plan," Ursula whispered more harshly, then nodded toward Lachlan without taking her hard stare off Rosalyn.

"That was before he saved my life." Her words were choked with emotion.

When Ursula's eyes grew as wide as saucers and her lips hardened into a thin line, Rosalyn hesitated, wanting to come up with a rational reason for her change of heart. Finally, she said with a sigh, "'Tis complicated."

"Surely, 'tis complicated. Poisoning someone 'tis complicated." Ursula let out a huff.

"Well, it needs to be undone."

"Cannae be undone."

"No antidote?"

Ursula crossed her arms over her chest.

Rosalyn did the same, but looked up into the ceiling of the bishop's sanctum, instead of into the harsh, judging eyes of her friend. Herbs of all kinds hung from the sturdy rafters above their heads. No doubt there was a concoction Ursula could make that would at least ease the symptoms. She lowered her eyes, ready for battle, but then a commotion at the entry made her spin away from confrontation to find out what was causing all the noise.

"*Scusami!*" The word rung through the wagon as a white linen hat framed by graying curls popped into view. In a few short moments, the bishop had climbed into his sanctum, straightened his robes, and was looking to the two of them for an explanation.

"Your Excellency," Ursula said, speaking first and bowing her head in respect.

Rosalyn bowed low, too.

"Rise, young maidens. No formalities needed here," he insisted, sweeping his hands in a wide arc. "What ails *el'eroe?*"

They both looked at each other, then back at the bishop.

Ursula gasped. "Hero?"

"Saving the life of the lovely Rosalyn with God's guidance. *Si, el'eroe,*" the bishop said with pride, looking down at a groaning Lachlan.

Rosalyn turned away from Ursula to hide her smug smile. Yes, until today, Rosalyn would have joined Ursula in poisoning Lachlan with no regrets. Up until then, he'd been only her advisory, conceited and self-serving, intent on taking Fyvie from her. But her feelings had changed.

Rosalyn glanced over at Ursula when the silence lingered too long, but it appeared her friend's reticence had her tongue, so Rosalyn answered. "Aye, bishop, he is my hero and it's our turn to save him. I believe he's been poisoned." Rosalyn clasped her hands together in a pleading prayer. "I can only hope Ursula will give him an antidote."

She was close enough to the Highland lass to hear her sigh. Then Ursula tossed her an I-will-get-even-with-you glare that the bishop couldn't see, before she sweetened her tone. "But of course, Your Excellency," her friend said tightly. "I will do everything in my power, but I am in need of a few special herbs." She stopped and stared up into the rafters as if searching and not finding what she wanted.

"I suspect you'll be needing valerian and horehound. Perhaps even a dash of sage," the bishop offered with a warm smile. "You shall not find them with my common herbs," he said, walking toward the chest. Once there, he threw back the lid and began tossing silk bundles to the floor. Altar coverings or ceremonial robe adornments, she wasn't sure which, but he treated them like common kitchen linens as his search intensified.

Finally, he let out a little shriek of joy after finding what he wanted. With great care, the bishop lifted up an ornately carved ivory box, then cradled it in his arms like a baby ready for christening, taking it to the makeshift altar.

Once the holy man opened the treasured box, he got busy sorting through its contents like a young boy again. Brightly patterned silk sachets where tossed onto the altar while he dug around inside for something special.

While the holy man's search continued, Rosalyn shrugged her shoulders in response to Ursula's irritated gaze. She didn't dare interrupt the bishop's search. But finally, after a triumphant shout, the bishop held up a red silk pouch covered in gold embroidered stiches and Rosalyn released a grateful sigh of relief.

"*Si, signora. Si,* I have what you seek," the bishop said with pride as he turned and held up the satchel like a prized fish. "Come, come, join me."

Now it was Ursula's turn to shrug her shoulders when she surrendered to the giddy glee of the holy man and his resources. Following the bishop to the altar, Ursula and Rosalyn knelt on either side of him.

"*Si,* here are the herbs you will need," he said in a victorious rush, thrusting the red silk bundle into Rosalyn's hands. "As the chosen one, you also have the power to heal. You always have. You will know what to do. Believe in yourself," he said as if to help manifest her confidence. Then he rose, made the sign of the cross over his heart, and began to pray in Latin.

As Rosalyn waited for the bishop to finish his prayer, a new plan began brewing in her head. Plants and flowers, learning their vocabulary with her grandmother, that had been her life's classroom. And even in the short time she'd spent with Ursula, Rosalyn had learned much more.

Was it the bishop's prayer, or the confidence he had in her? Either, or both, somehow Rosalyn was certain, even without Ursula's assistance, she could save Lachlan. The debt could be repaid now. Then, she'd be free to fight for Fyvie.

Before the prayer was finished though, Ursula nudged her ribs, forcing Rosalyn to open her eyes.

When the healer extended her hand, Rosalyn shook her head.

Ursula huffed, narrowed her eyes and reached for the parcel.

With her own huff, Rosalyn swatted Ursula's hand away and tucked the precious cargo behind her back.

When the bishop finally finished, he walked directly to the wagon entrance and quietly disappeared without another word to either of them.

They watched him leave in silence, then spun to face each other.

"What do you intend to do with the herbs? Throw them out?" Rosalyn accused.

"You want Fyvie Castle back, donna you now?" her friend bristled, her brogue returning.

"No. Well, yes, without hurting Lachlan."

As if he was listening, Lachlan let out a loud groan, then began babbling between shouts of obvious pain.

Rosalyn tensed her entire body as if she would could somehow absorb some of the hurt. She wrapped her arms tightly around her middle and began to twist back and forth.

"You arenae hurting him. You didnae take a weapon to his flesh."

"Nay, but I am still responsible for this," Rosalyn said,

pointing at his flailing limbs and sweating brow. "He looks like he's burning from flames we cannae see."

Ursula's face hardened, statue-like in its inflexibility. She blinked a few times and then finally spoke. "I willnae be the one to make the decision for you," she said, trembling from either anger or exhaustion. "This is your battle to win or lose. Your patient to heal or not. Do what your heart tells you is right. I will support your choice, but it will not ride on the back of my conscience."

Then with final huff and flick of her waist-length hair, Ursula spun on her heel, and without another word, she climbed out of the wagon.

Rosalyn let out the breath she was holding. She could not explain the total change of heart, but the man who lay writhing in perspiration and pain was her responsibility now. Even if his intention had been to spy on her in the woods, in the end, he had committed a selfless act. He'd have much to gain if she'd been killed.

When Lachlan's groan brought her back to the present, she dropped to her knees by his side. Reaching across his bare chest covered in dark, curly hair with the intent to capture a pillow and make it her ally, she stopped abruptly when her chest brushed his.

In that moment, she had the urge to let her cheek rest on his taut chest muscles. She set her ear to his heart. When the steady beat reassured her, she let out a little sigh.

"What type of healing are you providing, lass?"

Rosalyn sucked in a sharp breath and jerked her head up. But she wasn't fast enough. Before she could move away, he'd wrapped his arms around her back and he trapped her to his chest.

CHAPTER 11

osalyn closed her eyes, trying not to panic, and took in a long, calming breath, until Lachlan squeezed the air right out of her and she started gasping.

"Just a little lower, my love. With this kind doctoring . . ."

"Let me go," she demanded, interrupting whatever suggestive words he had for her. She squirmed against his hold. "You don't understand."

"All I know is that one moment I'm winning a horse race against the bishop, and the next you are in my arms." He gave her a kiss on the top of her head. "You are a gift from God. The bishop knew what I needed to be right again."

"God's teeth, you are not right in the head," she said, her tone more irritated than she meant. "God would not punish me to make you whole."

Rosalyn wasn't sure if it was her words or her wiggling that had the desired result, but after a few moments of pushing against him, she broke free.

Rising up from Lachlan's chest, Rosalyn smoothed her tousled hair away from her eyes, then with a *tsk*, she adjusted her bodice back in place. But when she peered down at him, wondering why he'd given up so easily, Rosalyn was greeted by a placid Lachlan, looking very much asleep.

She wanted to slap him and tell him to quit pretending. But then she noticed his heavy breathing and his relaxed angelic expression.

Lachlan angelic? A hero? No wonder Ursula had looked at her as if she'd joined the ranks of the jesters. Where had her sensibilities gone? Was it his disarming smile?

Just then, the wagon jolted forward and began to move, rocking her onto his chest again. As much as it flustered her, this time he did not grab her. Instead, he lay still, her body rising and falling rhythmically with his breathing. This time she was able to move away at will.

The poison. No doubt it was giving him some lucid moments between bouts of delirium. As she gazed down at the peaceful, sleeping aristocrat, she was reminded of her dislike of everything English. Could she make an exception for Lachlan? Was she going all soft on him because of his one kind gesture? But she sobered when she considered the consequences of her actions without his intervention.

For now, she would try to like him until he did something to change her mind. At least until she saved him.

Rocking back on her heels, Rosalyn touched his forehead to check for fever. She was grateful to find him cool now, but she was still concerned. Ursula had said she'd made the poison strong enough to make him sick, not kill him. Could she trust her?

Rising, Rosalyn headed to the low altar and busied herself preparing the herbs, thankful that she was able to do this alone and not under the eagle-eyed scrutiny of Ursula.

Besides the herbs, it didn't take her long to find the other items she needed stored neatly under the altar's skirting: a pestle and mortar, and a flask of water. She unwrapped the bishop's herbs from the red silk and laid them out.

Taking pinches of valerian, horehound, and sage, she placed them in the mortar, then added a few drops of water. Using the pestle, she formed a sticky paste. Once satisfied with the concoction, she headed back to Lachlan's side, on a mission to save him.

"Lachlan," she whispered, "wake up."

He groaned and flipped over on his side facing her.

"Lockie?" She tried the nickname he'd asked her to use, hoping it might illicit a better response.

"Ursula?"

Ursula! What?

"Yes," she lied. "It's Ursula. I want you to eat something."

"Eat? No!" He almost shouted the response.

Hmm. What to do if he refused the antidote?

Time was her enemy now, and she couldn't wait until his constitution changed. She glanced about the tidy wagon trying to figure out how to feed him the herbs. Nothing. No bread or fruit to use as a serving tool. Stumped for a moment, she relaxed her breathing and began to sort through what might make Lachlan open his mouth.

Finally, deciding saving his life was more important that her squeamishness, Rosalyn scooped up some of the paste on to her middle finger, then she lay down on the floor facing him.

Because his arm was draped under his head, she was able to scoot right next to his chest and get close enough to suit her needs. Once situated, she said a little prayer, asking God to let the herb and his power save Lachlan.

Following a reluctant sigh, she whispered, "Here, suck on this." With her palm up and middle finger cocked back filled with the antidote, she gently placed her free index finger to his mouth. Tracing over his top and bottom lips yielded the desired results, allowing her to slide her index finger into his warm mouth.

"Mmm," he groaned in a pleasant way.

Immediately, something in her core fluttered and pulsing heat surged through her groin. She almost withdrew her finger, but Lachlan had a strong hold. Groaning even more, he took his free arm and draped it over her waist. Rosalyn's eyes widened and her heart began beating wildly. He wasn't holding her down, but she felt trapped. Images of a naked Lachlan in Ursula's bed filled her head, his erect cock rising before he did.

With flushed cheeks, she couldn't help but glance down at his crotch. *Oh, no, it's happening again.*

Before she had a chance to figure out another way to feed him the paste, his hand slid up the side of the linen dress she wore. The covering was more like a sleeping garment than a traveling frock. She was surprised for a moment when his hand tickled her and she giggled out loud, diffusing her panic for a moment, until his hand was on her breast and he groaned with pleasure.

That moment, between panic and clear thinking, was then she made the decision to sacrifice her dignity and save him. So she returned the groan. That fueled him further, and he slid his hand underneath the neckline of her dress and began to rub her nipple. There was nothing to slow him. No ties to undo. The surge of passion was like nothing she'd ever felt before. She froze, wanting to hate what was happening, warring with herself not to fight the wonderful sensations that rippled through her.

But like a warrior of healing, Rosalyn had to set aside her feelings and continue her mission. Knowing she'd had his full attention now, she quickly pulled out the index finger and replacing it with her paste-filled one.

At first, she worried that he'd refuse the paste. It had to be bitter and downright nasty. She held her breath as he kneaded her breast, hoping he'd swallow the remedy while she swallowed her pride.

"Um, you taste divine," he mumbled between sucks on her middle finger and rubbing his thumb over her hardened nipple.

She let out the breath she was holding, thrilled that he was taking the antidote, but also exhilarated by the sensations surging through her. A tiny ribbon of sweat began to trickle down between her breasts. Moist heat and a primal throbbing was growing in her groin. What was happening to her?

With eyes still closed, as if his strength returned, Lachlan released her finger and caressed her cheek. Ever so gently, he put his hands about her waist, and with little effort, he rolled on to his back taking her with him.

Rosalyn came to rest on his dark chest curls. They tickled her nipples through the linen. She giggled. But her next inhale was cut off when Lachlan's hands moved to grasp the back of her neck and he collapsed the gap between them, crushing her against his chest while his lips claimed hers. A kiss even more possessive than the one he'd stolen in the dungeon.

As her heart sped up, beating hard against his chest, she wondered if he could feel its frantic rhythm, wanting to return the passion he incited. Rosalyn had never been with a man like this before. Well, she'd never been with a man.

She was a virgin, for God sakes.

What was she willing to do to heal him? How far would she go? She was in a provocative position and he still was thinking she was Ursula.

At least the herb concoction appeared to be working. Perhaps too well. As Lachlan's kisses fueled her desire, she found herself hating him less. His hands roamed over her back, her arse, exploring her curves while she lay on top of him.

But just as she was ready for more, his kisses slowed and his movements did too. When his lips released hers, he rolled her off his chest onto her side next to him.

Did she want this to stop?

Now that the passionate connection was broken, she opened her eyelids a crack, peeking at his face from under her lashes. His eyes were still closed and his breathing slowed. Color had flushed his cheeks and he no longer looked sickly.

Was it her willingness to join him in a romp or the herbs that were working to bring him back? She'd like to think a little bit of both as Lachlan reached out a lazy hand to find her lips and traced them as she'd done his. She nipped at his middle finger, inciting another groan from him. Rosalyn was surprised how right it felt to be with him, when it shouldn't. She, an unmarried virgin, and he, well, no saint.

Just then, she made the mistake of letting her gaze drift to his crotch. *Oh, my!* The bulge was still there. She'd have to stop looking. But she was a curious girl. Interested more in practice, than theory. She'd been told it was painful for a man not to release his seed when erect, as Lachlan was right now.

Her curiosity trumped caution, though, as she began to stroke his chest, twisting her fingers around his dark curls. Slowly, she moved down to his waist and loosened his belt. He moaned slightly, but didn't move. His breathing grew steady. Now that her heart had slowed to a normal beat, she noticed how the gentle rocking of the wagon made her feel as if she were in a safe cradle. Lachlan must have sensed it too for he wore a serene expression.

After letting the belt fall away, she tugged at the heavy linen fabric until she could slide her hand down inside his breeches. Yes, she did. As if on a treasure hunt for a prize, she walked her fingers down his midsection until the top of her hand found her reward.

Grasping his shaft firmly, she began analyzing the human reaction with her scientific mind. Amazed by the male anatomy, she stroked the shaft up and down with a firm grasp. Every so often, she rolled the palm of her hand over the top, following the instructions she'd been given by those with experience on how to please a man. Although she'd listened, she wasn't sure she'd remember until it was time to act. But this felt right. Natural.

Lachlan groaned with pleasure as she stroked him. She had control. This man was under her spell. She held the power to make him beg.

Just then, his shaft began to quiver and he shouted, "Now, faster."

She responded and in a matter of seconds, he had his release.

But when his eyes flew open, his handsome face twisted into a puzzled expression.

"You're not Ursula!"

CHAPTER 12

"*R*osalyn?" *What just happened?* Lachlan's head was spinning. Last he'd remembered, he was talking with the bishop about his riding academy, and now? There was Rosalyn, flushed cheeks, her red hair spilling about her shoulders, and her hand on his, well . . . *Am I dreaming?*

"My lord. This—I . . . you see—"

"I clearly see your hand is in my breeches."

"'Tis not." The lass's face turned a bright red shade and she yanked her hand out.

"What were you about?"

She stared at him, her lips parted as if to speak, but nothing came forth. She looked so beautiful. Her breasts made taut peaks under her dark blue dress.

"Why did you stop?"

"There's more to be done?" she asked in a whisper, her eyes full of concern. "I do not want you to be in pain." She leaned forward, looking at him quizzically, as if he had a big wart on his nose.

He chuckled deeply. "Pain, no. But men don't want to be

taken to the precipice of pleasure and then pushed off the cliff. I'd rather have someone to hold on to me and keep me safe." He raised his arms in her direction.

She shook her head. "As long as you are not in pain, I will keep my distance," she said as she stood and turned her back to him. "I am here to heal you, not love you."

Even though she said the words so softly, he'd heard them, but he refused to let her keep her distance. "Did you say you are here to love me?"

Rosalyn coughed. "I gave you some herbs to help you feel better."

"I can assure you, it was not the herbs that made me feel better. Were you rubbing them on my cock? Is that what you were doing?"

She kept her back turned, but her shoulders tensed and her hands fisted at her sides. "Healers do what they must. Even if it means sacrificing their dignity," she said with clenched teeth as she turned to face him.

"Well then, I'm grateful for your sacrifice. When do you suppose you'll need to do that again?"

Her eyes shot daggers at him. "Sir, my intentions were pure. Stop asking me questions." She crossed her arms over her chest, exasperation in her expression.

He patted the pillow. "Come, sit by me and make sure your good deed is working." When she recoiled at his words, he coaxed her with a promise. "I shall not touch you and you can ask me all the questions you'd like."

A smile crept up one side of her face.

"Come, I promise," he said, patting the pillow again. "I won't bite either."

She bowed her head shyly and shuffled to his side. In a tomboyish way, she plopped down on the pillow beside him.

"All right then," she said, settling into a comfortable pose with her legs crossed beneath her soft blue dress. "Why do you want Fyvie?"

He let out a long sigh, his smile and enthusiasm for her questions deflating. "Why do I want Fyvie?" he asked, staring off to the rosaries hanging along the wall, reminding himself that he was in the place where the bishop was making his home and lying would be more difficult with a makeshift altar in view. Even God's presence seemed to linger about the place making what had transpired, although briefly in his opinion, blasphemous. He chuckled thinking about it.

"Why do I want Fyvie?" he repeated, as if digging deep into his soul for the real answers, not the ones he'd learned to accept. "Well, for one, my father wants me to have it." *That is true.*

"Go on," she said with a softened expression.

"For you to know why my father wants me to have it, means you'll need to know more about my father." He turned his head and gazed up at her from his position on the floor. "I certainly don't want to bore you with family drama."

Rosalyn nodded patiently before saying, "We are tethered here together, not physically as in the prison, but bound here until we make our final destination. I have nothing else to do but humor you while you are awake."

"And when I'm asleep, will—"

"No, I'm asking the questions now," she reminded him.

"Where was I then?"

"Your father."

"Ah, yes," he said, stalling, knowing he had to omit his father's name or the ruse would be over, but he'd tell the truth. "My father, third cousin to King Henry VII, Earl of Dunster. My notorious father."

"Notorious?" Her eyes grew wide and childlike, as if she was listening to a bedtime story.

He grinned wickedly. *My bedtime story.* "I come from a line of notorious men, Rosalyn, many treasonous."

Rosalyn's eyes grew even wider. Her pretty, pouty mouth pursed, as if ready to ask another question, but he beat her to it.

"And why you may ask? For land. For castles like Fyvie. To conquer other lords." He lowered his voice. "To steal from the Scots."

She covered her mouth, but a disgruntled grunt escaped anyway.

"Highlanders and Lowlanders," he continued, "but Fyvie has always been special. I was told after your da's death, the castle was given to a woman named Victoria. She was married to my father until he found out that she was a Scot."

Rosalyn gasped.

Lachlan ignored her outburst. "She lied to him, to get to his wealth." When Rosalyn looked to object, he amended his response. "Or so he said."

But then she jumped to her feet anyway. "That Victoria is a Macpherson, one of my kin!" she shouted.

"Lass, will you seek out a weapon and slay me now?" Lachlan asked, chuckling at her ignited anger. He'd never known a woman who was set off so easily. Short-tempered, but beautiful in every way. Her hair, her eyes, and her skin, were shades of burnt red, charred amber, and warm gold. The colors of a glorious bonfire.

"I've yet to decide on your fate, but if what you say is true, Victoria came into the castle after my da was killed, because I was not of age yet to keep it. But then Nicholas Luttrell stole it from us all." Rosalyn stared past him to the altar, but as if gaining strength from God, she fisted her hands and shook them at *him*. "Fyvie Castle belongs to the Macphersons. I want it back," she said defiantly, her legs spread in a wide stance, her arms crossing her chest.

Lachlan studied her. So far he'd managed to keep his family name from the conversation. Rosalyn must *not* have known Victoria and Nicholas had wed or she'd have called him out by now. As much as he knew, Victoria had remarried shortly after their annulment, then disappeared. Truth be told, Lachlan could swear Rosalyn's Victoria had been killed by his father, but perhaps not.

At least now he'd figured out the only way to win Rosalyn over was to accept her family's plight. "Yes, my love, I understand your wish for the castle to stay with the clan. But you know as well as I, your family was no longer in control of the land and you would have lost it to a rival clan. Now which is worse?"

She let out a loud unladylike *harrumph*. "You didnae know anything about my da, nor my clan," Rosalyn insisted in a childlike voice.

That was true. He knew only a little about the chieftain who'd been Rosalyn's father, and Lachlan had expected a challenge from a Macpherson family member, just not from his daughter. But if she'd looked then, like she did now, he never would have forgotten her.

"Would you tell me about your da?"

She shook a finger at him. "Now, donna be asking the questions again," she warned, her face puckering with anger.

Then Lachlan remembered she'd reminded him of a cat, making note of the length on her fingernails. "No, no, you ask the questions. Sit," he coaxed.

Returning to the pillow beside him, she considered him with a wary stare. "Who is this Victoria Macpherson to you?" She tilted her head as if trying to get clarity. "Your mother?"

Lachlan shuddered when he thought of the last words his father had said about Victoria. *"That witch will pay for her deceitfulness."* He'd spoken many times of a score to be settled between himself and her son, a Knight of the Garter. But

Lachlan wanted to reassure her there was no animosity between himself and her family. "Victoria? My mother? Nay. My father had the marriage annulled after only a few months. The castle must have stayed with Victoria, but my father wants it now."

Rosalyn studied him closely. "Praise Mary, we aren't cousins," she said with an odd look on her face.

"Because when we have children it won't be blasphemous?" Lachlan asked, looking to rile her and steer her away from her questions about Victoria, and his efforts paid off. She huffed when he finished. "Even in my grandfather's day, cousins married," he reminded her.

"Not first cousins. Nay, if you were my cousin, I couldnae argue with King James for my land."

"Your land, through forgery," he claimed, annoying her again.

She gave him a wild-eyed glare. "You're suspected of forgery too," she challenged.

"But even then, my crime would not be as serious as yours."

Her beautiful, pouty mouth puckered, her amber eyes narrowed into slits, and she jutted out her chin in defiance. "Why is that?" she dared ask him.

Of course, he'd been an idiot to leave the king's seal at Berwick. But when he'd contemplated it further, he began to wonder how he'd have proven it belonged to her.

Perhaps she'd even dropped the satchel on purpose knowing someone in the castle would find it and she'd be rid of the evidence. But the jewel? That made him pause. No, she would never put the red gem in jeopardy. But at least now he had a plan.

"Because with the proper evidence, you'd lose your pretty head."

CHAPTER 13

Rosalyn balled a fist. Lachlan had rattled her before. Actually, every time she'd been alone with him her body became flooded with competing sensations. From loving to loathing, from adoration to angst, from trusting to tyrannous, no matter the circumstances, her heart would race and her anger spark.

Now, he was threatening her with evidence. Could he have found her pouch and kept it? Ursula had said she'd asked him about it. He was in the room. God's teeth, he'd carried her there. How long had she been unconscious before others had joined him? He could have searched her body. He could have . . . she shuddered to think and stopped herself, then turned her attention back to Lachlan.

"Evidence? Show it now," she demanded, rubbing her neck absentmindedly.

"I didn't say I had the evidence. I'm speaking hypothetically."

"Speak plainly, instead," she said, never more angry with him for putting on airs and being secretive.

"The Golden Rose."

"You donna have the Golden Rose." She shook her head in disbelief, knowing her time spent with the bishop in the chapel made it clear that the Golden Rose would be anything but evidence against her.

"Yes, I do," he said, pointing to something behind her.

She spun around to look. If it was here, she hadn't noticed. Her eyes scanned the room and finally settled on a shelf behind the altar.

"Why is it displayed and not under lock and key?" He voiced what she'd been thinking.

"Perhaps the bishop believes he's traveling with English men he can trust." Crossing her arms over her chest, she turned around to face Lachlan. "But he's a fool if he turns his back on men like you."

Lachlan snorted and leapt up from the pillows as if he'd never been ill, and to her relief, secured the belt on his trews before he made his way to the rose.

Faking it? Faking an illness to spy on others, on her, to gain entrance to the bishop's sanctum?

"It's beautiful, you know," he said in a low voice, then he turned to look at her and paused. His gaze softened and the corners of his mouth turned up into that wicked grin. "But not as beautiful as you."

Rosalyn coughed. "The healer needs no compliments to do her work. I wouldnae do anything more or less for you because of your flattery," she promised him.

He picked up the vase and began to walk toward her.

She shook her finger at him and stood. "You should put that down. What if the bishop came in now and found you fondling his rose?"

"Ye, who throw caution to the wind, should not be so righteous. What if the bishop had come in and found you fondling my cock?"

Rosalyn burst out laughing at the thought, although she

should have been mortified. Yes, that would have been dreadful and she hadn't considered it when she was lost in the moment, when her heart had been thundering in her ears, when she'd never felt more alive in her life.

"I know about the rose. It's been blessed. You could tarnish it." Once she'd said the words, she couldn't take them back and she didn't mean to be so uncomplimentary, but perhaps that's what she really thought. Although it was Lachlan's turn now to laugh loudly.

"Me tarnish an artifact made of precious gold?"

As an alchemist, Rosalyn knew there were a number of ways to tarnish gold, but she wasn't about to list those for Lachlan, nor did she want him to know the depth of her education.

"The Rose belongs to the King of Scots. You should look, not touch," she insisted, but Lachlan ignored her anyway, walking to where she stood.

"You shouldn't—"

"Shh!"

"Donna be shushing me—" she started.

"If you are going to lecture me, at least tell me what you know about the Rose. I heard the bishop invited you to a special ceremony."

"I am the chosen one."

Lachlan's eyebrows arched up.

"'Tis what the bishop told me," she amended and held her head high. "I am the one chosen to deliver the Golden Rose to the king. It must be a Scot, and the bishop said I am the one." *There.* Perhaps now Lachlan would reconsider using evidence against her, if he had any, because she would not only be endeared by the Bishop of Imola, but also by her king.

"Then I will be in high regard for saving the life of the *chosen one.*"

Is he mocking me?

"Rose?"

"Why do you insist?"

He rolled his eyes. "The Golden *Rose,* not you, Rosalyn. You promised to tell me about it."

She huffed. "Aye. You heard what the bishop said at Berwick, unless you were not listening, but flirting with the women at your table." She paused and stared at him, but he returned a coy smile in answer to her suspicions.

"Then I shall remind you that the Golden Rose was blessed by Pope Innocent VIII and sent to Scotland as a gift to King James in recognition of—"

"Yes, yes, I know that part," he said, interrupting her. "What's its worth?" Lachlan asked as he held the rose up. "Are these jewels?" He picked at a red ruby nestled on one of the rose petals.

Rosalyn's jaw dropped and she blinked rapidly. "It's priceless." *Is he that ignorant?* When he proceeded to start scratching at one of the leaves, she smacked his hand away.

"Why would the pope send a gift with jewels made of glass and roses painted in fake gold?" she asked, gazing at the vase full of ten beautifully crafted delicate roses, complete with thorns and stems.

"To keep men like me from coveting it."

She took her gaze off the rose and gave him a sideways glance. "Not only is it made of pure gold, all the stones are real—precious rubies, diamonds, and emeralds."

"Will this turn lead into gold?" he asked, tipping the rose sideways.

Is he joking? She blinked hard, and held back what she really wanted to say. "Nay, be careful," she warned, wanting to grab the precious cargo from him. "That tall rose in the center holds musk and balsam oils used to bless the rose. You will nae be wanting to tip that over and spill out the Holy Spirit."

As he righted the golden bouquet, Lachlan's gaze caught hers over the top of the highest rose, the one that held the oils. His mischievous, unblinking stare made her heart miss a beat. Was it because she was worried he'd do something idiotic again or something more disturbing?

"Here chosen one," he said, breaking the long silence. His grin lit up his face as he shoved the precious Golden Rose toward her. "You take it." And just as she reached for it, he let it drop.

Rosalyn screamed and her heart dropped too. "Got you!" he shouted and burst out laughing.

Yes, she thought he'd dropped it, when only he pretended to. With a jester-like cock of his head, Lachlan turned on his heel, then strutted to the altar.

But just when he was setting the Rose back in its rightful spot, the wagon screeched to a halt and tossed him forward. This time, he almost dropped it without pretending. Once he regained his footing, Lachlan gingerly set it back in the sturdy box meant to keep it from tipping.

After a few moments, the curtains of wagon rustled and Ursula popped her head through with a murderous look on her face.

"I was riding with the driver and I heard a scream coming from here. I held the soldiers back because I said I would take care of whatever was happening." She gave an exasperated glance about the wagon. "What's happing?" Her eyes darted to Rosalyn. "Did you scream?"

"Ursula, assure the soldiers that there's nothing wrong. I thought I saw a rat." She glared at Lachlan for an instant, then gave Ursula her attention. "But I think I made a mistake."

Ursula looked relieved, and she disappeared as quickly as

she had come. In a few short moments, the wagon started up again.

"I hope you are proud of yourself," Rosalyn said in a scolding tone. "Now, the entire party will be wondering what's going on inside this wagon."

Lachlan glanced at the Rose, safely back in its place, then walked to the opposite wall where the rosaries hung and began pushing against it, rocking the wagon slightly. He turned to look at her over his shoulder. "I can make them wonder even more."

"And if you do that again, Lachlan, I shall scream even louder than before. Donna test me."

He stopped, but still stared at her. His eyes began to narrow, his gaze smoldering. Was he angry with her defiant response?

Slowly, he turned and stepped forward with a swagger. The closer he came, the more intense his gaze. Once he reached her, his lips parted and his head raised slightly as if superior to her. Without a word, Lachlan reached one hand under her chin and turned her face toward his. With the other hand, he grasped her firmly around the waist and pressed her to his groin. When she gasped, the corners of his mouth switched. He took the hand from her chin and raised it up above her head.

Her instincts told her to twist away. Cringing, she raised her elbow to serve as a shield.

But he didn't strike her. Instead, he grabbed her elbow and in one swift moment, pinned both her arms to her sides. When he leaned toward her, his breath swept across her face, a mix of wine and herbs. Sweeter than she'd imagined after he'd taken the concoction.

Rosalyn's chest heaved from her rapid breathing. What was he going to do? She was about to ask him outright, but just as her lips parted to speak, his mouth claimed hers and he drilled his tongue inside, twirling it and causing her to forget her question.

When his hands grabbed her arse, her eyes opened wide, prompting her back to clear thinking. While kneading her bum, Lachlan bunched the linen fabric efficiently up her back side. Before she realized his intention, his hands were under her dress.

That dream of being wrapped up with Lachlan in bed resurfaced. His movements intoxicating. But as much as this felt right, it was wrong. She shook her head to clear it from Lachlan's effect.

Surely, his inclination to take liberties with her was intensified by the poison. Even if she could rationalize his bad behavior, she did not intend to fall victim to bad judgment.

With his strength and strong hold, she needed a clever intervention to escape his groping, something other than screaming.

So instead of fighting, she began to give in to his kisses. Then she reached her hands behind his back to fondle his arse. What a muscular delight it was. *No, do not enjoy this.*

Lachlan responded with a deep groan and started grinding his hips against hers. Just as she was about to give him something else to think about, she discovered a bump under his belt. *Odd.* She reminded herself she was groping his arse, not his crotch.

She reached under his belt and tugged on the item. To her delight, it came loose into her hand. At that moment, she also raised her knee, and with a mighty effort, she thrust it between Lachlan's legs.

Immediately, he released his hold on her lips and thighs. Then Lachlan grabbed his cock and screamed like a girl.

"Now, let's see what they think has been going on in

here," she said, hiding the pouch in her skirts. "My work here is done. You are fully recovered."

And with that, she turned her back on Lachlan and held on to the wall as the wagon came to another abrupt halt. Ready to join the driver and Ursula, Rosalyn escaped through the curtains, having had the last word.

CHAPTER 14

*L*achlan woke disoriented. As he glanced about his surroundings, he was reminded of a church. Covered with ceremonial urns and silks, a makeshift altar ran the length of one wall. Rosaries hung on another. But then he remembered the poisoning and Rosalyn's passionate mission to save him. Still baffled by some of her actions, the darn girl had left him aroused and wanting more. He wasn't sure if it was the herb mixture or his partially satisfying and equally frustrating romp with her that made the difference.

After shaking off his grogginess, it dawned on him it was a new day. In no time at all, he was dressed and out in the camp mounting his horse as if he'd never been ill.

Lachlan circled the camp's perimeter, but stopped short when he discovered another party had joined their group.

Drawing his horse flush with the bishop on the outer circle, he leaned toward the holy man hoping to get some answers.

"English or Scot?"

"Not Roman." The bishop chuckled. "The men identified themselves as Knights of the Garter. Do you know them?"

"Ah, the noble Knights of the Garter," Lachlan said, thinking back to a time when he was recruited. "The legendary order founded by King Edward III. They are quite revered," Lachlan said in a condescending manner.

"You do not sound impressed."

It was Lachlan's turn to chuckle. "I have some history with the group and it did not fare well. Though I'm not familiar with any of those men."

The bishop coughed politely. "I do believe they were part of the promised escort, though you and the other men have been quite efficient."

Of course, the Garter knights were to be the original protectors. Lachlan paused. That did alter his plans somewhat. His hope was to arrive at Edinburgh Castle, the hero, having led the bishop, the Golden Rose, and the entire party safely from English soil to Rosalyn's Scottish homeland.

But just as he was about to look for the lass, one of the rider's caught his attention. A mounted nobleman without a Garter banner. As Lachlan squinted into the sun to get a better look, the man raised an arm and began to wave.

Lachlan spun in his saddle to look over his shoulder. *Who is the rider signaling?* But when it was obvious he'd been the mark, Lachlan turned back only to find the rider approaching. The wicked grin, a mirror to his own.

As the sun's rays cut swaths of bright beams through the dense trees, his brother rode through splashes of light and dark until he reached them.

"Brother, good to see you."

"Why are you here?" Lachlan demanded when his brother reined in his warhorse short before them.

The bishop made the sign of the cross. Clearing his throat,

he offered, "One of these men appears to know you after all. *Scusami.*" Then the holy man dug his heels into the sides of his steed and steered his horse toward the front of the caravan.

After the bishop was out of ear shot, his brother spoke first. "No words of endearment?" Ethan asked, cocking his head to one side, his sarcastic tone ripe.

"Last I heard, you were posing as me. I thought you traveled to Somerset, to see our father."

"Last I heard, you were poisoning me."

"What?"

"Do not pretend," Ethan spat, breath hissing through his teeth. "I know your plan. Sideline me from making my report. But Father came to Berwick to see for himself. And he wasn't pleased. You know what that means?"

Disgust rising from within, Lachlan glared at his brother. The same features, the same father, the same blood, but in Lachlan's eyes they were more like mortal enemies.

"That you will do everything in your power to make yourself look good and make me look like an arse." He was angry, and if they weren't both mounted, he'd have punched him in the face.

"Turn around, Brother," Lachlan said slowly, working hard to keep his voice level. "Go take my place in Berwick with the ladies. Tell them you are Lachlan and enjoy the fruits of my bed."

His brother laughed louder than necessary. "What? And disobey Father? That's a death sentence, Brother."

"Perhaps only one of us will survive this battle for Fyvie," Lachlan threatened.

"From your mouth to God's ears," Ethan replied, his disgust apparent.

"If we are choosing allies in that arena, I already have the bishop in my stead."

"You are too impressed with yourself to remember that he's already blessed me."

"The devil owns your soul. No blessing will save you."

"Gentlemen!" Rosalyn's sweet voice cut through the arguing. "Stop acting like spoilt children and prepare to disembark."

Lachlan's gaze darted from Rosalyn to the Garter knights, who'd stopped to gawk at their squabbling.

"Brotherly banter, I assure you." Lachlan's swung his gaze to meet Rosalyn's again. "Don't you fight with your siblings?"

"Not in front of noble knights and men of the church," she said in a condescending manner, *tsk*ing him after.

"Well then," Lachlan said, clearing his throat, "we've just shown you how it's properly done." He glared at his brother and guided his horse forward, kicking the sides of his destrier.

"Come, Rosalyn, it appears I may join your efforts and help you win Fyvie Castle after all." He kept his eyes on his brother as his horse fell in step beside hers. "If it means defeating my father and brother at the same time, it may be worth the sacrifice," he muttered to himself.

Rosalyn sucked in a sharp breath, making him turn to her. Hope gleamed in her eyes.

What's one castle, when I have the means for many more? Perhaps his efforts would be better served joining forces with the Highland lass than fighting for it in her homeland. His brother had a way of altering his goals and ultimately, spoiling his good fun.

Once the party was underway, it wasn't more than a half days ride until the group, led by the Garter knights, finally thundered across the drawbridge, passing under the jaws of the iron portcullis gate, and into the grand walled fortress that guarded the King of Scots.

First a golden rose to deliver, then Fyvie Castle's fate to be determined. Lachlan was anxious for both.

* * *

THE LAST HOURS of the day's ride passed quickly enough for Rosalyn after the soldiers had announced Edinburgh was near.

And when her king's castle finally came into view, her pride of being Scottish had never been stronger.

Once they'd been properly welcomed, Rosalyn was led by soldier escort through the halls of King James's castle, grateful to be a guest and not a prisoner.

Her life had taken precarious turns since she'd left Aberdeen. Not sure of who to trust or what to cling to, except for her love of her family, it was her determination to regain control of Fyvie Castle that saw her this far.

Through no fault of her own, Rosalyn had traveled through most of England and back to Scotland on her own without an escort. Although she'd left Aberdeen with her Uncle Angus, he'd fallen ill on their way to reclaim Fyvie. Traveling wool merchants from her home in Aberdeen had seen her safely to Berwick-upon-Tweed where she'd expected her uncle to rejoin her. But he hadn't. Until today, finally back in her homeland, Rosalyn had been vulnerable without a chaperon.

Now that she was settled in the chamber next to Ursula's, Rosalyn fell backward onto a freshly threshed bed and closed her eyes, recounting the words Lachlan had said earlier that afternoon. Could she begin to hope that the jealousy and competition between the twin brothers could work in her favor?

A sharp rap on the door interrupted her thoughts. Just as

she raised her head to ask who was there, Ursula slipped into her chamber like a thief.

"The plan?"

"He's on our side," Rosalyn replied, hardness entering her voice.

"What?" Ursula asked, crossing the ornate rug, stepping softly as if she was still trying to steal her way in to the chamber.

"Lachlan is on our side. He wants to help me fight for Fyvie," Rosalyn declared breathlessly, hoping there was some sincerity in his offer.

"Why would he help you?" Ursula asked flatly, seemingly unimpressed with Rosalyn's enthusiasm.

"Because he hates his brother and father more than he wants the castle. I suppose there's more, but I am certain his brother is a bigger threat than I am," she concluded with a huff.

Ursula eyed her like a traitor. "Remember, lass, I've known the man longer than you and I wouldn't put much stock in his willingness to look out for you before he looks out for himself. What makes you so sure he and his brother aren't playing you for a fool?"

Rosalyn hopped up from the bed, anger flaring, cheeks heating as she moved toward Ursula. "Because I saw the go-for-blood look in their eyes. Because I heard the bitterness of competition in their voices. Because I could feel the hatred radiating between them." Rosalyn's hands fisted at her sides.

Ursula took a measured step back as Rosalyn began searching inside her skirt pocket for the furry pouch. When she found it, she held it high above her head like a victory trophy. "And because I found this," she said, gloating.

Ursula remained silent, but crept closer when Rosalyn lowered the prize and began to loosen the thin, leather tie that held her precious pouch closed. She strode over to the bed and dumped the contents out onto the fur coverlet.

Ursula followed, then stood, curiously quiet beside her as Rosalyn began spreading out her precious cargo.

"Tartan. Key. Stone." Rosalyn sucked in a sharp breath when the item she wanted wasn't there.

"Where is it?" She turned to Ursula as if she'd know.

Ursula shrugged. "What are you missing? Is this the pouch you'd lost at Berwick?"

Rosalyn nodded frantically, tears welling in her eyes.

"Where did you find this?"

"In Lachlan's breeches," she said, sniffling.

Ursula burst out laughing. "You were searching Lachlan's crotch in the bishop's quarters and found this?" The healer's eyes bugged out of her head.

"That sounds horribly wrong. Please understand I was held in his tight embrace. He was kissing me and I wanted to get away." She sighed when she realized Ursula was holding back another laugh. "I—He does not know I have it," she said with an exasperated sigh, sitting down on the bed next to her precious belongings.

Ursula joined her and put an arm around her shoulder. "Now, calm down and tell me everything from the beginning," she said in a soothing voice.

Rosalyn sniffled and laid her head on Ursula's shoulder. Seeing some of her most beloved treasures made her yearn for her mother and family.

"These are precious mementos. An important part of my life. My story. My family. I always carry them wherever I go."

Ursula unwound her arm from her shoulder, then reached over her lap to take hold of the red stone.

"Do you recognize it?" Rosalyn asked, brightening.

"Is this what I think it is?"

Rosalyn nodded excitedly, forgetting some of her trepidation about the missing stamp.

Ursula stared at her in awe. "How do you come by this?"

"'Tis been in my family for generations. It has been hidden. Sadly, many have died protecting it."

"If it wasn't missing, Lachlan must not know the stone's value."

Lachlan. The missing stamp. Her fears began swirling. A cloud of dread hung over her now and Ursula must have sensed it.

"Tell me more. Start at the beginning," Ursula asked her, reaching over to swipe a tear off her Rosalyn's cheek in a loving way.

Rosalyn heaved a sigh. "Yes, these tokens are all precious to me. The tartan. The stone . . ." She stroked the metal keepsake. "The key—" She lowered her voice. "to Fyvie's secret treasure chest."

"Pray tell, the token you are missing is as precious as these?"

"I'm missing evidence that will save me or damn me. And if Lachlan still has it, I'm not so sure he'll want to save me."

CHAPTER 15

*B*eing back on Scottish soil made Lachlan a little uneasy as he lay on the massive chamber bed staring at the ornate ceiling the next day. Not that he expected foul play under the roof of King James at Edinburgh Castle, but he'd seen enough mysterious disappearances and unexplained deaths to keep his chamber locked and his sword in its hilt. Even more so while he stood in the way of his brother's ambition.

Ethan was destructively greedy like his father and Lachlan hadn't been successful in convincing his brother to let him secure Fyvie while Ethan played at Berwick. He'd promised he'd give his brother the credit. Ethan would take it anyway. Now, Lachlan must choose who he'd support when he appeared in the court of King James.

The lass wanted Fyvie desperately. And at first, he hadn't cared. Not a whit. But despite his wanting to remain detached when it came to women, this one was proving difficult to ignore.

He'd come to enjoy being pursued by the ladies of the court. Flowers in his room. Promises of trysts and late-night rendezvous. Whether well-seasoned or virgin, matron or maiden, Lachlan had welcomed them for flirtatious fun, but never, ever cared for one enough to settle. He loved women too much and it would be a crime to commit to only one forever. *Wouldn't it?*

Then why was this lass so special? This one whose torch flame-colored hair was as hot in hues as her temper was short.

The dilemma. What would he gain if he helped her while he undermined is brother and father? Admittedly, his thirst for land was as much to quench his desire for power as it was his father's. And oh, how he hated the man his father had become. Yet, land was key to the kind of wealth and prestige he yearned for. The title was less important.

What would he lose if he stole the land from her?

The persistent knocking at his door finally broke through his thoughts, requiring him to answer door instead of his nagging questions.

Lachlan raised his head off the pillow, "Who calls?"

The door slowly creaked halfway open, then stopped. He'd forgotten to lock it. Even though he was dressed for the day, he'd been held in his chamber, waiting to be called by the king.

When the silence grew too long, he jumped up from the bed, still wearing his sword and grasping its hilt.

But once a curly mop of graying hair appeared through the doorway, Lachlan relaxed his grip.

"*Scusami, perdono,*" the bishop said shyly. "I meant not to make a suspicious entry, but one of my clergyman stepped on my robe in front of your door." He chuckled, throwing his hands up and shrugging his shoulders. "They follow me too closely, you know," he whispered, shutting the door behind him and leaving his entourage in the hall.

The bishop's face grew serious as he walked into the

chamber. Lachlan pointed to a sitting area by the hearth and the bishop followed him there.

Once they were seated, the holy man closed his eyes. "Let us pray," he started. "Dear Lord, thank you for Lachlan's guidance and Your Holy Grace in delivering us to the King of Scots safely. Only Your blessed gift, the Golden Rose, is missing and I seek Your assistance in bringing it back to its intended owner. Amen."

Lachlan's eyes shot open as soon as the bishop finished his prayer, realizing he was the last one, other than the bishop and his men, to have been in the presence of the Rose.

Bishop Passarelli's kind eyes studied Lachlan, but he did not speak right away. Did the bishop think he had something to do with its disappearance?

With a steady gaze and an unexpressive face, the bishop said, "The Rose is not the only thing missing, so is your brother."

Lachlan's shoulders stiffened. "Ethan is missing? Pardon this blasphemous insinuation, but perhaps he's with a wench somewhere in the castle?"

The bishop's right eyebrow raised slightly. "No need to look for him in the church's chapel, you say?" He gave Lachlan a broad grin, but that quickly faded. "His horse is gone too. Do you know his plans?"

Lachlan studied the holy man's face. At first impression, it appeared Ethan's whereabouts would be more closely associated with the missing rose than Lachlan's.

"I told him to go back to Berwick Castle. Perhaps he took my advice."

"You two were arguing yesterday."

"'Tis how we communicate."

"Why did you want him to leave?"

"Because he threatened me."

The bishop leaned back in his chair and steepled his fingers.

Lachlan mirrored him. And silence ensued.

Finally, Lachlan knew what he had to do. He just needed the bishop's permission.

"I will find the Rose," Lachlan pledged to the bishop then pounded his chest for emphasis. "I vowed to see it delivered safely to Edinburgh Castle, with the plan to place the blessed award into the hands of its king. My promise is more important than anything else before me."

The bishop's gaze softened. "Yes, your honor is important to you," he confirmed, "yet, you have another challenge before you that questions your honor." The bishop paused then continued. "Your dispute with Rosalyn. How will that be settled?"

Yes, how will that be settled? He had been distracted by the bishop's news. The Rose was to be his barter.

It took him a few moments to collect his thoughts, even more difficult with the bishop waiting. Even though he wasn't always honest, he refused to lie to the holy man.

"The future of Fyvie is uncertain, but my service to Rosalyn is unwavering." Lachlan gave the bishop a nod. "After speaking with my brother yesterday, I entertained the idea of joining forces with her, to find Fyvie's ownership in her favor. Yet, even if I did, I know my father. He would tear it from her hands. And if I know Rosalyn, it would be the death of her."

"What do you propose?"

"I'm at odds, Father," Lachlan spoke honestly, his gaze dropping to his boots. "I'd hoped to win the favor of the king, as I said, with the delivery of the Rose and its party in good stead. Then have the castle in Aberdeen awarded to me as a gift of honor."

He stood and began to pace. "After that, arguments for or

against property ownership I'd hoped would be avoided. Perhaps that was foolish," he said, his gaze meeting the bishop's.

"No, my Son, your intentions weren't foolish, but perhaps your hope for an easy resolution was." The holy man got up and started toward Lachlan.

"The outcome is not in your hands anyway." The bishop rested his hand on Lachlan's shoulder, the holy man's long, flowing sleeve draping over most of Lachlan's arm and chest. "It never is."

Giving his shoulder a light squeeze before he released it, the bishop turned to go. "The king wishes to settle Fyvie and your fate before dinner. It was he, who asked me to pay you a visit and make an assessment. I have what I need. I will see you in the great hall later this day," he promised. Then the bishop silently glided out leaving Lachlan wishing he'd brought the king's seal with him.

* * *

EXHAUSTED from the journey and the constant worry over the looming court proceedings, Rosalyn had slept til midday. Told upon waking, to wait in her chamber until the king was ready to hear her plea, she had eaten alone. Thankfully, Ursula convinced the guard outside Rosalyn's door to give her access and the healer helped Rosalyn pass the time as they concocting an herbal remedy that promised courage.

Perhaps the exercise had been only a distraction, for Rosalyn felt anything but courageous when she was finally ushered into the great hall later that day.

Her knees wobbled beneath her, just as they'd done the day she met Lachlan and argued her case for Fyvie before an English judge.

Even though she was on native soil before her king, there was little to make her believe her situation had improved.

Even more disturbing, the bishop had stopped by her room to tell her the Golden Rose was missing and asked if she had any idea who might have taken it.

She wanted to say she was suspicious of Lachlan, for the disrespect of the holy artifact and his cavalier attitude toward it. What was more damning, though, was the fact that he'd been the last one, outside the bishop and his men, to see the Rose before they arrived at Edinburgh Castle.

She was hoping that any of those points could help her with a better chance of winning Fyvie. But as she pondered the circumstances, she began to put her fear in check. For even if he held the missing king's seal, his integrity could be in doubt. Lachlan couldn't prove the seal had been in her possession. In fact, for him to have it, could play to his detriment, giving the king reason to assume he'd stolen it and the Rose to forge his claim.

As she approached the king's dais, passing the curious courtiers, she still trembled. The king was an intimidating figure, wearing a black bear skin around his shoulders, his blond mane of hair held in place by a gold encrusted crown decorated with massive precious stones. The light shining in through the windows from the late day sun reflected off the jewels creating a halo of light about his head and making him appear God-like.

"Come forward," he beckoned.

She glanced nervously over her shoulder only to realize he was talking to her. Rosalyn lowered her head as she started forward, glancing under her lashes from side to side. Could Lachlan have forsaken his claim after all? She could only hope.

"Hear ye, hear ye," the court official announced. "We

bring to order a dispute of Scottish property, one Fyvie Castle in Aberdeen."

Although it was the highest court in the land, the king's court was the least formal. The king was the king, and his word was final. There was little need for anything other than His Majesty's presence and a court bailiff to call to order. The onlookers were there merely for sport.

"The court calls Rosalyn Macpherson to speak. Come forward."

Rosalyn shuffled her feet. She was already as far forward as she dared, but she dove down on one knee and bowed her head low before her king. "Your Majesty," she said breathlessly.

"Rise, Rosalyn." His stern expression relaxed. "Be at ease. This is your court. Your voice will be heard."

She couldn't help but glance over her shoulder for Lachlan, who to her surprise did not appear to be in the great hall.

"Who are you looking for, lass?" the King asked, and she turned around to face him, her face flushed with embarrassment.

"The English man who disputes my claim," she said softly.

"I will hear his plea later. I will speak to you first. Without him."

She nodded, pleased with the circumstances for now. Last time Lachlan had made a mockery of her.

"Yes, Your Majesty." She smiled as she rose.

As the King of Scots leaned forward, one hand on his staff, the other on the arm of his massive throne, the great hall's twittering halted when he asked, "Why should I award any property to a woman?"

CHAPTER 16

*R*osalyn sucked in a shaky breath. She wanted Fyvie Castle more than anything. It had been in the family for generations. Her da had fought for the clan, and with his dying breath had said to those with him, *"Tell Rosalyn to stand by Fyvie, no matter what comes. When she is of age, make her laird."*

As much as she wanted to crumble before her king, she couldn't, especially when she considered her da's dying wish.

"My lord, I'm not any woman. I'm a Macpherson, daughter of Dengas Macpherson, once Laird of Aberdeen. With no sons in the family, my father asked in his dying will that his property be entrusted to me."

"I understand property law, lass," King James said in a softer tone, handing his staff off to the bailiff, then easing backward into his massive throne.

"Dengas Macpherson?" When the King said her father's name, his eyebrows knotted together. Then after a short pause, a look of recognition emerged. "I knew your father. He was loyal to me, and his death brought me great sadness."

Rosalyn was relieved to hear that her da had been in good

standing with the King. Perhaps he'd reconsider his initial concern about her owning property.

"As King, however, I have the prerogative to interpret the laws to my liking." He paused. "Or rewrite them entirely with good reason." He leaned forward again, this time with both hands gripping the arms of his royal throne. "Although I'm tempted to consider female ownership of property outside of titled families, the British Empire will nae support it. However, if you are able to find a man willing to take your name, the Macpherson name, I can choose to award the land to you and your husband."

My husband?

Of all the possible outcomes, including losing her head for the deception, Rosalyn was shocked into silence as she considered his decision. Perhaps having an amiable husband, one who would let her rule, could help with her dilemma.

She finally found her voice. "How soon, my lord, must the man be found?" she asked quietly, dreading his answer.

"Well, immediately, of course." He gestured about the great hall. "There are many eligible men."

Her anger flared and she swore inwardly, frustrated that the solution to her problem couldn't be the one she wanted.

"Immediately? That won't do."

The King cocked one brow.

"That won't do unless I have a volunteer," she quickly amended, swallowing her anger, now willing to take what the King had offered. At least this decision allowed her to keep Fyvie from Lachlan. With some vindication, she spun around and scanned the room. Surely, amongst the throng there would be a man she'd find agreeable. She needed a business relationship, not a soul mate.

There were a few dry coughs and many downcast eyes, but then one man in the back of the hall shouted, "I'll take her hand in marriage."

She strained her neck and stood on her tiptoes to get a better view of the volunteer. But it wasn't long before he strode proudly forward into her line of sight and it was then that her worst fears were realized.

Lachlan? Isn't he supposed to remain in his room until the King calls for him? But when did he listen to orders?

Before she had time to protest, Lachlan had reached her. After a short bow of respect to the King, he gave her that mischievous grin of his, and took her hand. Then he gazed deep into her eyes and said, "I'll marry you, Rose. 'Twill be my pleasure."

Rosalyn jerked her hand free of Lachlan's grasp, then strode toward her king. Now more afraid of the consequences than her leader. "Nay, Your Majesty, this one willnae do."

The monarch leaned forward, chuckling and crossing his arms to cover his belly. Finally, when he raised his head from a crouched-over position, he smiled at her with amusement. "Lass, your da would either be proud or mortified at your behavior today. First you tell your King that you arenae satisfied with his decision and then you tell me that the man who is willing to betroth himself to you, isnae suitable."

"Well, my da always encouraged me to speak my mind, with all due respect, Your Majesty," she offered with a curtsy. "This man is English," she said as if he'd understand, pointing to Lachlan. "And he wants Fyvie. He's the one who contests the ownership."

This made the King double over even further with laughter. "Of course, if you want me to toss him in the dungeon for disobeying me and attending the hearing before called, I can, but rarely do I find the solution in my court so easily solved," he choked out between chuckles. "You'll be wed on the morrow. Case dismissed." And with those final words, the King stood and shooed them away with a pompous wave of his hand.

Collecting his staff from the bailiff, King James proceeded to walk through the great hall, stopping to chat with courtiers until he finally made his way out of the room and the rest followed.

Still in shock over the verdict, Rosalyn stood next to Lachlan while the servants began readying the great hall for dinner as if the two of them were no longer present.

She dropped her gaze to her feet, unsure what to say.

Lachlan raised her chin to bring her gaze level with his. "We'll both get what we want."

She fisted her hands at her sides. "You and the King will both get what you want. Not me," she said, then made an unladylike *harrumph* sound.

Before she had time to protest, Lachlan gathered her up into his arms, as if ready to carry her off, his lips just inches from hers.

"Being married can have its benefits. You can sleep with me legally now rather than sneaking around," he said coyly, his meticulously groomed beard brushing her cheek as his lips inched closer. His pitch-black eyes and hair gleamed in a way that mesmerized her. A pleasant concoction of musk and rum wafted about him. Her herbalist senses were on alert. She barely could contain herself, wanting to let her nose drift to his neck and work its way up to his ear.

Marry English?

Coming to her senses, she yanked back from his clutches as if he'd set her arse on fire. "Ye will take my name?"

"I hate my surname," he admitted with a sincere reply. His normal cockiness fading. "I no longer wish to be a Luttrell."

"A Luttrell?" Her heart almost stopped beating. "Put me down," she demanded.

As Lachlan followed her order, his face lost all color.

Before he spoke, she could see in the depths of his eyes an emotional struggle taking place.

"Not Lachlan de Leverton, but Lachlan Luttrell?"

"Tomorrow I will be Lachlan Macpherson." He plastered a placating smile on his lips and looked about the hall. "I cannot speak of this here."

Rosalyn sighed. At least she agreed with him on that. Even though the servants seemed to be keeping their minds to their tasks, voices carried easily in the high-ceilinged great hall.

"Come," he said, taking her hand and bringing her in tow behind him in a protective way. "Follow me, and I will tell you all."

Conflicted but curious, Rosalyn set aside her initial disgust over Lachlan's outburst and followed him down a labyrinth of Edinburgh Castle corridors until he stopped abruptly in front of the castle's chapel entrance.

"In here," he said and almost shoved her inside the small, private chamber.

Rosayln turned around as he came in behind her. She was about to start into her reasons why they had no right to be in King James' chapel when Lachlan put a finger to her lips and said, "Shh!"

She swallowed her words for a moment while her fiery response began to smolder like warm embers inside her belly as she began to think of Lachlan as a protector and not a predator.

Rosalyn held her breath, as if his finger against her lips kept her boiling air inside and her diatribe of words from spilling out. Then he grinned when she nodded and he ushered her to a seat in the first pew of the small, but glorious stained-glass refuge.

Although her heart had been pounding ever since she stood before her king, Rosalyn tucked her skirts in around her and settled down next to Lachlan in this place of God, hoping the blood pumping through her veins would slow. After a few deep breaths, a sense of calm swept over her as if God himself had waved his hands and blessed this moment.

"We'll be married here tomorrow," Lachlan said softly. A warm glow in his eyes made those internal embers cool even more.

Married? The idea seemed foreign to her. Somehow, in all her twenty and one summers, Rosalyn had not imagined herself married. Perhaps it was because she'd always been protecting something. Her mother. Her sister. Her land. Her castle. Even herself. She'd never daydreamed of a picturesque church with a handsome groom smiling at her while she said her vows before family, friends, and God.

Instead, her dreams had been full of adventure, foraging for new herbs, visiting foreign lands, healing travelers on the road, keeping the wool trade alive for her da. And regaining control of Fyvie after Nicholas Luttrell had stolen it from her family.

Luttrell. Lachlan's *father* was one of the most hated men in all the realm. Nicholas Luttrell. She should have realized it when Lachlan had spoken about his father and Victoria before.

From deep in her being, Rosalyn couldn't bury the past yet. Even if it was painful, she needed answers.

"Your father banished my family from Fyvie after my da's death," she declared.

"Nicholas Luttrell impregnated my mother, but he's never been a father to me. He's been a murderous bastard as long as I can remember. If he threw your family out, you must believe me when I promise you I had nothing to do with that." Lachlan gazed into her eyes with a sincere pleading she'd never seen before. "I'm so sorry, Rosalyn," he said, putting her hand to his lips and kissing the top softly.

"Remember I told you my family is full of notorious men. Some murderous like my brother. He took my mother's life. But I'm different. You'll have to trust me," he insisted.

When she looked into his eyes and saw the pain there, she knew she had to believe him—believe that there could be a Luttrell with some honor and goodness inside.

She sighed, willing to agree to the marriage for now because it took her one step closer to home. Then, if he proved worthy, she'd decide if he was for keeps.

"Granted, if we're to be married for convenience," she said, ready to negotiate, "then we must establish some rules."

CHAPTER 17

"Rules? No, not now, not ever," Lachlan said, still grinning. "I never live by the rules and I'll be damned if I start as a married man."

"You shall start married life as a damned fool if you donna, Lockie Macpherson."

The look in Rosalyn's eyes was as intimidating as any warrior. He leaned back against the pew and studied his betrothed. *Marriage?* Another device to get what he wanted. No doubt she was thinking the same.

"I will ask the bishop to bless me. Then I can't be damned, whether I follow your rules or not."

"You are not marrying the bishop."

Lachlan laughed, diffusing his discomfort and his initial resistance to being restrained. "God's teeth, let me hear the rules, then I shall decide if I'll abide by them."

Rosalyn scooted a little further from him on the pew bench and crossed her arms defensively over her chest. "First rule, you abide by all my rules." She cocked her head to one side and waited for his reaction.

Lachlan couldn't help but release a loud grunt, but kept his mouth shut, for now, while he waited for the rest.

"Second rule, separate sleeping chambers."

She paused, allowing him to respond. As her husband, he had the right to visit her bed anytime, giving him a workaround to get what he wanted.

"Agreed," he said stoically.

Her right eyebrow raised in response as she kept her gaze steady. "Next rule, no one in my family or anyone in Aberdeen should be told of our . . . this . . ."

"Arrangement?" he suggested.

"Yes, that's it. Our arrangement."

"'Tis an arranged marriage, after all. Isn't that what they call it?" He snorted loudly.

"Shh!"

"Only God can hear us in here."

"I don't want God to hear that."

"Then you should have picked another spot."

It was her turn to snort.

"I will agree to keep our marriage a secret, but I don't think that qualifies as a rule."

Sobering quickly, she ignored his comment and squared her shoulders. "And finally, I will remain a virgin as long as I wish."

He straightened. "The king will require consummation of our marriage, and proof. I'm sorry, Rosalyn, but you can't make that rule."

She bristled, her pale, creamy skin turning a light pinkish-red. While Rosalyn held his gaze, she smoldered with ire.

He wanted to tell her she couldn't get angry for something that he had no control over, wanting to explain the laws of marriage, but he didn't. Because he had no intention of abiding by that rule, even if the king agreed. He planned to take her as quickly as he could woo her. And frankly, he would take her virginity right now if he could. The law would be in his favor, Lachlan rationalized, as he waited for her backlash.

Even before Rosalyn spoke again, her entire body shook. "I will speak with the king about that," she said in a huff, standing, then coming close to stare down at him. "Do I have your agreement?"

Lachlan reflected for a moment. Damn her rules. Yet he was certain the marriage would solve the land dispute and keep his father's wrath at bay until the senior Luttrell discovered Lachlan had abandoned the family's surname. But that was another battle. For now, Lachlan needed to tie the knot.

"If the king agrees, then so shall I," he promised, standing and taking her hands in his. Now it was his turn to stare down at her. "Any arrangement calls for sacrifice, and I'm sure we'll both make concessions for Fyvie."

"For Fyvie?" she whispered.

"For our future," he corrected. Then he wrapped his arms around her and nestled her hips up against his groin. He slid his hands down her sides and with a gentle rocking motion, ground her body across his bulging cock.

When her eyes widened as big as teacup saucers, he bent to kiss her neck below her ear and chuckled into her skin. "Are you certain you want separate beds?"

* * *

Rosalyn took in a sharp breath, feeling lightheaded and in need of air, like the day she'd fainted at Berwick Castle. But before her head began to spin, she ducked out from under Lachlan's embrace. Taking quick steps, she hurried toward the chapel door.

Tossing back her head and forcing a cheery countenance,

she said, "See you at the wedding tomorrow." Then she slipped through the door, leaving Lachlan at the altar.

Her heart wouldn't stop fluttering as she rushed down the corridor wanting to get away from Lachlan and find Ursula. Rosalyn had so much to tell her. And then she'd need to talk to the king.

As she continued on her way from the chapel, the magnitude of marriage weighed heavy on her. What would her da think of her marrying an Englishman? Was he turning in his grave?

"Oh, my!" Rosalyn stopped in her tracks.

"Where are you going in such a mad hurry, lass?" the bishop asked.

She realized that her breath was heavy and she was perspiring. Had she run this far unaware?

"My dear, has someone threatened you? You look like you've seen a ghost."

Rosalyn nervously smoothed a few stray strands of hair from her forehead and forced her lips into a smile. "Your Excellency, oh my, no. I was just in the chapel."

The bishop chuckled. "Are you sure the ghost wasn't a holy one?"

The quip caught her off guard and made her laugh along with him, allowing her to slow her heart and her mind.

"Bishop, I-I-I am to be married," she finally said, not knowing any other plain way to tell him.

His eyes widened as well as his grin. He clasped his hands together with gleeful acceptance. "Wonderful, yet surprising news, my dear." Then he paused as if waiting for her to tell him more.

She hesitated.

He turned his head slightly, raising both brows. "Who's the lucky fellow? Do I know him?" the bishop prompted.

"Yes, well, it's Lachlan," she said, flustered. "He volunteered."

Scratching his beard, the always-jovial bishop sobered for a moment at her revelation. "Let me understand, lass. A man you hate, an English man who's been after your land, volunteered to marry you. And you accepted?"

She nodded rapidly, trying to blink away the tears that were welling up. It sounded crazy, she knew, but it had all made sense a little while ago.

"It was the king's idea," she offered, as if that would make it all sound more right than wrong.

"Oh, of course," the bishop nodded as if he was still in a fog over the situation she'd just described. "It was the king's decree."

She blushed. "Not his decree, but his, well—" she stopped and wrung her hands. "He ordered our marriage in court as a solution to the dispute over Fyvie."

The bishop stilled her hands with his gentle touch. "My dear, even in my home country of Italy, I would interpret the king's insistence on your marriage a decree."

She shrugged. "'Tis a solution, your Excellency," she said, hoping she sounded happy.

"God's will and the king's will are often the same," he said, then brightened. "Congratulations are in order. I would be honored if you'd allow me officiate," he said with a slight bow. "Of course, with both yours and the king's permission. For an English and Scottish union, perhaps a neutral party will be best."

Rosalyn bowed over the top of their joined hands. "I couldn't be happier." She raised her head and grinned at him. "Thank you."

He squeezed her hands. "I shall be off to the king to discuss it." When the bishop released her hands, Rosalyn hung on and gave him a tug.

"Your Excellency, I have one more favor," she said, feeling her cheeks heating up. "I need a promise from the king that I remain a virgin after my vows." She paused, embarrassed by her frankness. "You understand," she added with a shrug.

It was the bishop's turn for his cheeks to flush. "Lass, I'm an influential man, but that is an unusual request. I shall promise to do my best."

Rosalyn smiled shyly when she finally released his hands. It was the best she could hope for and no doubt he'd have more influence over the king than she could. At least that's what she hoped for.

Getting her bearings first in the corridor, Rosalyn rushed down the hallway and soon made the turn toward the women's chambers. In a matter of moments, she was briskly knocking on Ursula's door, anxious to ask the herbalist to stand with her on the morrow.

A cautious Ursula cracked the door open far enough only a fly could navigate. When she recognized Rosalyn, the cautious healer opened the door enough to draw her in before the door snapped shut like a trap.

"Is it true?" the healer asked, her black eyes bulging like a bug's.

"Is what true?"

"That you've abandoned our plan. What will I do now?"

"I, um, the plan has simply changed. You are still a part of it."

"As the fool who will stand by and watch you throw your life away and marry your enemy?" She put both hands on her hips.

Of course Ursula was upset. The woman was reactionary before logic set in.

"Let me make a soothing concoction for you," Rosalyn offered, gliding toward the potion-filled cabinet past Ursula, who looked more sorceress than advocate.

But when Rosalyn reached into the cupboard, Ursula caught her elbow and spun her back around.

"I donna need a soothing concoction. I need a potion to bring you back to your senses. What are you thinking to marry Lachlan de Leverton?"

Rosalyn sighed inwardly, not wanting to tell her friend who the real Lachlan was. That would make her head spin even faster.

Then she remembered the bishop's words. "'Tis the king's decree. I cannae fight our ruler." When Ursula gave her a look she was unconvinced, Rosalyn defended her decision further. "The bishop told me 'twas God's will to be done."

That made the healer laugh, and she released Rosalyn. "Go ahead and make that concoction. I am sure I will need it after all."

CHAPTER 18

*L*ight streamed in through the window as Rosalyn groaned and flipped over. She and Ursula had stayed up gossiping like sisters well past the time the fire had dimmed to embers in her chamber.

While her thoughts swam through the early morning haze between her ears, her heart skipped a beat. Eyes blinking rapidly, she sat bolt upright.

"'Tis my wedding day!" she shouted as if to wake herself up from the fog.

Glancing around the vast guest chamber, Rosalyn felt her clarity return, reminding her that the actions of the past few days had not been a disturbing dream after all.

Today she'd be a bride. Fear and excitement battled in her belly. She wondered what her da would think of her marrying English. And not just any English. A Luttrell!

She threw back the covers, scooted off the bed, then knelt down to pray.

"Dear Lord, please help me through this day and don't damn me to an unhappy marriage with this Englishman." Then she added, "And please, if you see my father, tell him this is for the best. For Fyvie." She sucked in a shaky breath when a knock on the chamber door shattered her silence.

Heart slamming in her chest, she rushed back to the bed and covered herself just as quickly. If it had been Ursula, the healer would be at her side already, chiding her for sleeping in. Curious though over who'd be calling, she gave the visitor permission to enter.

The curly head of the bishop popped into view. "*Scusami. I heard a prayer coming from this room*," the holy man said. "May I come in for a moment?"

The bishop heard my prayer? Rosalyn's mouth fell open. She didn't respond, still shocked at the idea he'd heard her words.

"I would not have come unchaperoned on your wedding day," he said apologetically. She wasn't surprised when Ursula followed him in.

Stunning was the only word that could describe how beautiful her friend looked in her close-fitting, antique-gold gown, like an otherworldly fairy preparing for an enchanted ceremony.

Not only was Ursula breathtaking, but she'd gone as far as tying tiny sprigs of herbs throughout her hair, making Rosalyn wonder if Mother Nature wouldn't claim Ursula as her own.

The healer gave her a nod and a knowing smile as she walked towards the bed. She was grateful they'd settled their differences the night before. What had surprised Rosalyn the most, after she'd given her kinswoman the details of the court hearing, was Ursula's final approval.

It had taken the healer a few hours of stomping around the chamber, tossing herbs, and cursing at everything in sight before she agreed Rosalyn's arranged marriage was the best judgment the king could have decreed. A device in the end to give Rosalyn what she wanted.

As she replayed the conversation in her mind, she was

well aware that the wedding was permitted only after she promised Ursula she would consider an annulment later in the year. The healer had pointed out to her that once Rosalyn was able to re-establish the lairdship under the Macpherson name, she could cut the Englishman loose.

When the bishop clapped his hands together, Rosalyn swept her scattered thoughts away to focus on why he'd come. "You said you are responding to a prayer. Not everyone has a bishop who answers. Why am I so lucky?"

He paused to consider the humor in her words. "*Si*, it is not often one's prayers are answered by a knock on the door." He chuckled. "But in all sincerity, I would assume such on an important day as this." He paused and studied her. "At least a prayer for a happy marriage. After all, I am your officiant. I'm here to see if you have any questions or special requests."

"Special requests," she asked, cocking her head to one side.

"As in the ceremony," he clarified, then cleared his throat as if he wanted to avoid her request of an unconsummated marriage.

"Handfasting," she said, almost shouting the word. "'Tis tradition in most Scottish weddings." She wasn't certain what an Italian marriage ceremony would be like and she appreciated that the holy man wanted to make the process neutral, but if the bonds of marriage weren't presented in the Scottish tradition, even with a man of God officiating and under the roof of the King of Scots, she'd never feel legally married. And as odd as that sounded, it was important to her.

He nodded and grinned. "Then you will have a handfasting. I will talk with the king's clergy to prepare. I assure you, Rosalyn, you will have a wedding to remember."

She smiled at Bishop Passarelli. Over the days they'd spent together, she'd become quite fond of him, and he'd treated her like a daughter. It was as if her prayer was being answered and her father had given his permission. He would be there in spirit.

Rosalyn had never favored any of the men her da had selected for her and she thanked the Lord every day that he never forced her into marriage. And even if she was marrying English, she had to admit, Lachlan had some good qualities. She was grateful she was going to have a grand ceremony on the grounds of Edinburgh Castle, with a holy man second to the Catholic Pope officiating. And with the gift of her Fyvie in return. Yes, she would have a wedding to remember.

It wasn't until she heard the sound of the chamber door opening again and the soft chatter between Ursula and the bishop's men, that she was drawn away from the group to the full-length mirror. Something or someone was calling to her softly.

As Rosalyn reached the mirror and gazed into it, she took a shocked step backward. Instead of her own reflection, she saw her father's. When Rosalyn rubbed her eyes, then opened them again, he was still there. Her head spun a little, and the drone of conversation at the door faded away when she spoke to him. "Da, what are you doing here?"

"I wouldnae miss my darling girl's wedding day. Even as a spirit, I have some privileges."

Rosalyn sucked in a sharp breath, wanting to run into the mirror and hug him. "Da, I miss you so much," she whispered, emotion choking her. "Why haven you nae come to see me before today?" she asked, walking closer to his reflection.

"You didnae needed me afore now, my darling Rose. Simple as that."

That made her pause. As much as it made her proud, it also made her angry. For now, she was determined to hold back the tears, the fear, the uncertainty, hoping the answer to her next question would be the one she wanted.

"Even though I donna hear you, can you hear me?"

He let out a gut-busting roar, one she hadn't heard in four years past. "There are rules in the spirit world, and I cannae tell you much without penalty, but I can assure you, when you speak to me in prayer, I can hear you, darling Rose."

Her eyes teared up. "There's something I must tell you."

"I know you plan to marry English." He said it so plainly and without malice that her frown lifted.

"Y-You heard that part?" she asked. "Are you here to punish me, then?"

He laughed some more, holding his gut before answering. "Nay, darling girl. I came to give you my blessing."

Her mouth opened, then stayed that way as she wondered how he'd come to terms with that. As much as she wanted to argue the point, she was stumped by his words.

His blessing?

While she stared at him in disbelief, he grinned at her. "You are a clever and resourceful girl, Rose. I've never questioned your judgment. If you are marrying English, I am sure you have a damn good reason."

"Who are you talking to?"

The question startled Rosalyn. She looked at the mirror and then to where the voice had come from.

"What?"

Ursula came into view, meeting her at the mirror. "I said, 'Who are you talking to?'"

Rosalyn pointed to the mirror. But when Ursula peered into the mirror. Her da was gone.

She spun to face her friend. "You scared him away!"

Ursula's friendly countenance turned dark. "I scared who away?" she asked hotly, putting her hands on her hips.

For a moment, Rosalyn considered telling Ursula she'd

seen her father in the mirror, but the idea was so absurd, it made Rosalyn giggle uncontrollably instead. Her eyes clouded up with happy tears.

"I'm just emotional. 'Tis my wedding day," she offered, hoping the excuse of marriage day hysterics would allow Ursula to forgive her for anything out of character she'd do or say. "I was talking to da. Asking for his blessing. That's all. If he were here, he'd be giving me away."

Ursula's face relaxed into a smile again.

"Well, that's why the bishop's men were at the door. You see, the King of Scots himself will be giving you away."

At those words, Rosalyn swooned for a moment. She reached her arm behind her, hoping the edge of the bed was close enough to settle her knocking knees. She was even more nervous than before.

"He was fond of your father, and he said it was as if old Dengas had come to him in his sleep and asked him." Ursula started making her way to the door while she continued to talk, leaving her alone at the mirror again. "According to the bishop's aid, His Majesty woke this morn and sent out the decree for everyone in the castle to be ready at half-past five for the glorious ceremony."

"Well, if the king is giving me away, there's no going back now," Rosalyn said more to herself than Ursula.

"No going back," her friend echoed. "Only going forward." The healer paused and appeared to take stock of Rosalyn's pledge. "Then you must be ready for the day to begin?"

Rosalyn sucked in a shaky breath. "I promise, I willnae run away."

Ursula tossed her a warm smile and silently let herself out the door.

When Rosalyn's gaze returned to the mirror, she'd hoped to see her da staring back at her again. Who knew what kind of rules spirits had to follow. She wished she'd had more time to explain why she was marrying English. Her da probably wouldn't have cared if she loved Lachlan or not. And more likely, he would be happy it was all for Fyvie. For no one had loved the land and castle more than her da.

As she reach out to touch the cold glass where her father's reflection had been, she took in the weight of Ursula's words. *"No going back. Only going forward."*

CHAPTER 19

$\mathscr{L}$achlan stood at his chamber washbowl splashing water on his face, grateful it was cold. Ruminating about his circumstances, he cupped another handful and tossed on more, slapping his cheeks.

Five days ago, life was simple. Today, it was damn complicated. He stared into the tinted mirror above the bowl while the water dripped down his face. Shaking his head like a horse, he blinked through the dripping water.

"Feeling more like an arse than a horse today, Lachlan?" he asked, then grinned at his reflection.

Marriage. He'd always thought of it like a sentence to the gallows. But not today. Had he finally found his match? Someone who didn't swoon at his every advance? A woman who did not agree with him?

Ever?

But as he was getting comfortable with the idea, he was reminded why this wasn't right either.

The bride didn't want him. He was marrying a woman who hated the English, and worst of all, a woman who did not want to consummate the marriage. If that didn't make this Sunday black, he was suspected of stealing Fyvie Castle and the Golden Rose from the Scots.

As he reached for a rag to wipe the rest of the water from his face, he thought back to what the bishop had said to him in his chamber. *"I will deliver you from evil."*

No doubt, considering the evil nature of both his brother and father, Bishop Passarelli's words were more gospel than gossip.

Yet, the chance to free himself of the Luttrell name was worth almost any sacrifice, for it would be legal and his documents would be signed by a king. The idea of hiding away with a fiery redhead in the Highlands of Scotland become more appealing as he thought more upon it.

Whack! Whack! Whack! A fist pounded on the door. When Lachlan spun around, the unexpected guest had already burst into the chamber, like a charging runaway bull.

"There you are. Is it true?"

"Get out," Lachlan replied calmly, turning toward the mirror, still able to keep an eye on his unwelcome guest in its reflection.

"Well if it's true, then I'm staying for the wedding. You need a witness, do you not?"

"If I kill you now, there will be no witness to your death."

"Kill your own flesh and blood?"

"Only one of us would have the honor. I'd rather it be me."

His brother's laugh followed. It was a sound that pained Lachlan like his cheek being slapped by the hand of a haughty courtier wearing one of those oversized jeweled rings.

"Not welcome at my own brother's betrothal? What would father say?"

"I don't give a Devil's damnation what father would say. Frankly, I'm getting rid of the lot of you."

"Rid of us? Your family? Pray tell, has the idea of marriage made you mad?"

"Actually, quite sane." He squared his shoulders in the mirror.

"Brother, sanity can't be measured by the one claiming it, you understand?"

"Nor can a family bond be honored by the one breaking it," Lachlan declared, turning to face his twin.

"But family is about blood, not bond. Heraldry, not heart. Legacy, not love," Ethan said.

Lachlan flung the wet rag toward his brother, but the bastard ducked just before it would have stung his face.

"I would expect a friendly gesture like that from a wench," Ethan said, holding out his hand and taunting him with a flick of his fingers as an invitation to take him on. "Is that your best shot, Brother? Or has the impending wedding made you soft?"

Ethan should have seen it coming, but his face still wore a shocked expression long after Lachlan slammed him down on the chamber floor and the two began to wrestle on the king's fine rug, Ethan taking wild swings at Lachlan's head, but missing every time.

Lachlan laughed at Ethan's feeble attempts. "Would you be giving your brother a bloody nose before his betrothal?"

Ethan growled after he pinned Lachlan on his back, reminding him of the days when they were bairns, before Mother died. She'd have separated the two by now.

"A black eye would be even better," Ethan grunted out as his right fist swung close to Lachlan's cheek. But Lachlan arched his back at the right time and ducked away from Ethan's flailing arm.

"Fitting, from the Luttrell twin with a black heart," Lachlan retaliated. And in an instant, he managed to roll Ethan to his back. Straddling his brother's chest gave him control now, but Ethan didn't let up and swung his fists, punching at Lachlan's stomach.

Finally, Lachlan caught his brother's right wrist after an awkward swing, then flipped him onto his stomach, pinning him to the fancy flooring.

A little winded, but pleased with himself, Lachlan was grinning over the small victory when a knock came at the door.

In less than a heartbeat, the bishop strode into the room, taking a shocked step back after discovering the melee on the king's floor.

"The guards heard some unusual noises coming from here. They suggested a fight. But I waved them off and told them they were wrong."

The bishop stared at their awkward positions and after a long pause asked, "Were they wrong?"

Lachlan gave the bishop a sheepish grin as he released his brother and climbed to standing. He extended his hand to help Ethan up, but the idiot slapped his hand away and rolled up to sitting.

"What do you think, Father?" Ethan asked, groaning as he climbed to his feet on his own.

"A man of God never judges, he leaves that to the Almighty," the bishop answered, his eyes twinkling. If there was anything Lachlan could count on in the days since he left Berwick-upon-Tweed, it was the almost perfect nature of Bishop Passarelli.

"Let us pray," the bishop suggested, tenting his hands and closing his eyes.

Lachlan complied with an inward sigh, wishing he'd had a chance to cause his brother some physical pain. Instead, he hung his head and closed his eyes, anticipating the bishop's efforts to try to make them a functioning family.

"Dear Lord, I have before me identical twin brothers,

Ethan and Lachlan. Even though I have not known them long, I know them well. Both proud, ambitious young men, competitive to a fault, but brothers in the eyes of their countrymen and in the house of God."

As the bishop continued with good intentions, one moment Lachlan was struggling to focus on the prayer and the next he was biting his tongue to keep from screaming out loud while his black-hearted brother ground the heel of his boot into the top of Lachlan's bare foot.

Now, with eyes wide open and a heart filled with fury, Lachlan shoved his brother hard. Laughing when Ethan landed with a thud back on the floor. But the bishop did not falter. With a serene expression and eyes still closed, he soldiered on.

"And Lord. Even though they struggle with mutual respect, and don't show any outward signs of affection toward each other, I know you can help them regain their family loyalty and honor."

When the bishop opened his eyes, Lachlan plastered a serene and compliant expression on his face. After glancing sideways at Ethan, he wondered what his brother would do now that he'd regained his footing.

Relief filled him when he was greeted by a similar sideways calm expression from his brother. As if rehearsed, they both tipped forward in a bow, with their hands clasped together in prayer.

Lachlan spoke first. "Thank you, Bishop, for your blessings and prayers."

"Yes," Ethan chimed in, "if any day we should put our differences aside, it should be on my brother's wedding day."

The bishop appeared pleased as if he'd ended one of England greatest battles, clasping his hands in joyous celebration, his eyes bright. "Then my work is done here and God will continue to watch over you both." The holy man turned to leave. "Next I see you, Lachlan, will be in the chapel. God be with you."

"And also with you," both men replied in unison.

When the door closed softly behind him, Lachlan spun to face his brother. "Truce for today then," he said, extending his hand toward Ethan.

Not that he expected an embrace with a handshake, but Ethan turned away from him and walked toward the open window instead.

"Give you a leg up," Lachlan offered without jest, "right out that window."

"Do not act hastily, Brother, for I am not of that mind right now."

"Are you out of your mind, then?" Lachlan strode half way across the room, then stopped, trying to control his rage. "You most certainly should be, for showing up on my wedding day expecting to be welcomed, especially after your actions at Berwick with Ursula."

His brother tossed his head back with a haughty laugh. "Oh, you mean when I pretended to be you in Ursula's bed? Your ego cannot be that fragile, Brother. I was aiming to win a wager."

"At all costs?"

"Life should be lived at all costs, that's what father would say."

"And that's another reason why we differ on just about everything." Lachlan walked closer to Ethan. "What do you gain, Brother, by waiting around?"

"To see that Fyvie is finally in our family's holdings once more."

"With this marriage it will be. Don't you think I'll go through with it?"

"It's not you I'm worried about."

Lachlan grunted. "I will send you a missive with a copy of

the deed." He narrowed his eyes on his brother. "I thought you left yesterday. Your horse was missing."

"Do you track all my moments?"

"When you are suspected of stealing something. The Golden Rose is missing."

Ethan appeared unaffected by his words and shrugged. "I'm suspected of many things."

"That you are," Lachlan said before curling his mouth into a wicked smile when he realized he had a solution to Ethan's insistence on attending the wedding.

Later that afternoon, Lachlan found the perfect opportunity to get back at his brother after he agreed to meet him at the stables. He needed to be sure his brother would not interrupt the ceremony.

Now he had him where he wanted him as he wound the rope one more time around Ethan's wrists, finishing with a double knot.

"I cannot believe you are going through with this," Ethan grumbled.

"The wedding?"

"No, tying me up in here."

"Because of the company?" Lachlan laughed, but then his smugness disappeared. "I have my reasons," Lachlan admitted, "and one of them is trust. I'm sure you aren't surprised."

"Do you think I'll put an arrow in Rosalyn's heart at the service?"

"I wouldn't put it past you to put one in mine," Lachlan snapped back, then frowned and gave his brother a deadly glare. "But you poisoned the only other woman I ever loved."

"You know that was an accident, I—wait, you're in love?"

"You blamed it on me," Lachlan said, losing patience and ignoring his brother's question.

There was an awkward silence until Lachlan responded. "Ethan, you've always blamed your bad deeds on your good brother. With this marriage, I plan to start a new life, free of the Luttrells."

His twin's jaw clenched before he spoke. "I promised father I'd see this through," he grumbled. "If marrying the lass wins the castle, I need only witness the ceremony before the King of Scots."

He checked the knots around Ethan's feet and hands.

"You'll just have to trust that I won't get cold feet," Lachlan said with a tinge of amusement. Then he closed the gate to the pigsty and laughed when the sound of snorting mixed with Ethan's cries for help.

CHAPTER 20

*R*osalyn leaned forward, and Ursula whispered in her ear, "Nay, I've never seen a bride more beautiful than you."

When Rosalyn raised a brow, the healer narrowed her eyes, but she still smiled before she whispered, "Why would I lie? I have no reason to."

After Rosalyn gave Ursula a sideways glance, the healer *tsk*ed and grabbed her hand. "I'll let your groom do the convincing then," she promised, leading her to the back of the procession.

Rosalyn drew in a shaky breath and held it for a moment hoping the action might settle her frayed nerves. She was grateful the white lace veil hid most of her face, and she managed to eke out a trembling smile but bit her lip to steady it.

No turning back, she told herself. And if her da was right by it, so was she.

Rosalyn imagined her father looking down on her now as she stood at the end of a long chain of Scottish royalty, hoping he was proud as the parade of sorts began to move toward Edinburgh Abbey. The king had insisted she be married in the grand church, saying his chapel would never be big enough for all the nobility he'd invited.

Rosalyn craned her neck to see around the person in front of her while the Garter knights started the procession up the steps, moving through the abbey doorway. The ripple of movement made its way finally to Ursula, who stood by her side looking as nervous as Rosalyn felt.

The healer must have sensed her fear, because she gave her hand a reassuring squeeze. "Here we go," she whispered.

"No turning back," Rosalyn said as she walked more briskly now.

When she finally reached the abbey's grand entrance and entered the holy nave, her heart thundered in her chest. But before her fears totally consumed her, the vision of her betrothed standing next to the bishop gave her the courage she needed to proceed.

Rosalyn barely noticed the little girls giggling behind her while they readied her gown, for standing at the end of a long white runner dusted with red rose petals was the most handsome man she'd ever seen.

She filled her lungs with one deep inhale, then released the air slowly as she closed her eyes, holding an image of Lachlan that made her soul sing.

Wanting to confirm she hadn't gone mad, she popped open her eyes again. As she gazed at her betrothed, his steady, charming smile made her believe, at least for now, he was willing to marry her.

Lachlan was dressed in the finest red and gold brocade the Scottish kingdom could provide. His dark beard and mustache were trimmed to architectural perfection. His broad, muscled shoulders framed his masculine waist. Partly veiled by the embroidered gold and red cape he wore, his bare, tanned arms teased her.

Had the King adopted him as his own? For Lachlan appeared more royal than His Majesty.

When the King finally reached her side, his eyes crinkled with a smile, and Ursula hooked Rosalyn's arm on his.

Gasps of adulation rose from the pews as they walked slowly down the aisle. Rosalyn kept her gaze locked with Lachlan's, as if he was providing the compass to keep her straight on the narrow runner. Once they reached the altar, Rosalyn's hands were placed into Lachlan's. Then the bishop wound a silky, golden-tasseled cord around their wrists. Around and around the cord went until it couldn't go another time.

For a moment, it reminded her of when they were first bound together in the dungeon. She shivered, happy that this union was different, one she hoped would grant all her wishes.

After the handfasting knot was secure, the bishop came in front of them and tossed her a wink. Then he placed his hands on top of theirs before speaking.

"This cord represents the marital bond. It is strong enough to hold you together during times of struggle, yet flexible to allow for you each to grow. As your hands are now bound together, so shall your lives be bound as one. These are the hands of your best friend, holding yours on your wedding day as you promised to love each other today, tomorrow and forever."

The bishop paused for a moment, and Rosalyn considered the weight of his words. *Forever.* She was thinking perhaps a year. Could she make a promise before God to bind herself to Lachlan forever? She had been gazing into his eyes at the same time the bishop was speaking and now she closed them for a fleeting moment. But while her conscience was making noise, the bishop's voice drown it out with his words.

"These are the hands that will work alongside yours as you build your future together. These are the hands that will passionately love you and cherish you through the years, and with the slightest touch, comfort you like no other. These are the hands that will hold you when fear and grief fill your mind. These are the hands that will countless times wipe the tears from your eyes, tears of sorrow and tears of joy. These are the hands that will tenderly hold your children, the hands that will join your family as one."

Children with Lachlan? No, she'd already had his promise of a celibate marriage. They wouldn't have children.

Her gaze moved to Lachlan. He was watching her with such tenderness it took her breath away.

As the bishop began to untie the ropes, he said, "And lastly, these are the hands that even when wrinkled and aged, will still be reaching for yours, still giving you the same unspoken tenderness with just a touch. Let us pray."

Rosalyn bowed her head and started her own prayer with God, asking for His forgiveness if she made promises today she couldn't keep.

When they both finished, the bishop gestured to Rosalyn that it was her turn to speak. He'd helped her pen the vows she would now pledge to Lachlan.

She cleared her throat and gazed directly into his eyes. "You cannot possess me, for I belong to myself. But while we both wish it, I give you my name, Macpherson, which is mine to give.

"You cannot command me, for I am a free person, but I shall serve you in those ways you require. That is my wedding vow to you." When she finished, she nodded to Lachlan.

He squeezed her hands when he began. "I pledge to you the first bite from my meat, and the first drink from my cup. I pledge to you my living and dying, equally in your care. To tell no strangers our grievances and take your name, Macpherson, and carry it with honor." His eyes held hers as he finished the last verse. "This is my wedding vow to you."

Bishop Passarelli moved to stand between them, taking each of their hands and he held them high.

"A person standing alone can be attacked and defeated, but the two who can stand back to back, will conquer." Then he turned to Lachlan and released their hands. "You may now kiss your bride."

When Lachlan lifted her veil, she couldn't help but beam with happiness. Somehow, at least at this moment, her fears vanished. They were replaced by a sense of promise his pledge and loving attention could bring to their marriage. He raised her chin, and her damp eyes locked with his.

"You are beautiful, Wife," he whispered before claiming her lips with a gentle kiss. Not one she'd recognize from any of the other times he'd kissed her.

Applause broke out through the abbey and cheers of *huzzah* rose about them. Lachlan's arm circled her waist and he drew her even tighter. To the amusement of the crowd, the kiss continued while the bishop said his final words.

"May you know nothing but happiness from this day forward. May the road rise to meet you, and may the wind be always at your back. May the warm rays of the sun fall upon your home. And may the hands of a friend always be near. And finally, may the heart that loves you be true."

May the heart that loves you be true? Rosalyn pondered the meaning of that promise as Lachlan finally released her and the bishop spun her around to face the congregation and Lachlan followed.

As she stood in front of those who'd witnessed her vows before God, she started to fret. Would she be punished by the Lord if she wasn't true to her heart?

Before she could dwell upon it further, Lachlan took her

hand and led her down the steps from the altar and along the ivory runner still filled with red rose petals. Well-wishers crowded its sides from the pews. "Come, Wife, we've many to greet," he urged, waving at the adoring courtiers.

Rosalyn was not surprised at the grand reception they received. The Scots loved their weddings, English groom or not.

One man at the back of the church caught her attention before they reached the door. She turned to her new husband when she recognized him. "I dinnae know your brother was coming to the wedding."

"Neither did I," Lachlan said dryly.

CHAPTER 21

*L*achlan was grumbling something as he started down the path outside the abbey. He still held her hand, but his pace was faster than Rosalyn's legs wanted to pump.

"What are you running from?" she asked, panting, tugging on his hand to stop.

Turning, he gave her an apologetic shrug.

Still winded, she held her side and her ground. "Or should I ask from whom?"

That made Lachlan gaze above her head and toward the guests who were filing out of the abbey. After staring blankly over her for a few moments, letting her catch her breath, he returned his attention and gave her hand a gentle tug. "Come, Wife, we have a proper reception to ready for."

"And at this pace, I may beg for you to carry me, Lachlan."

"Lachlan? You should call me, Husband," he insisted, picking up speed.

Husband? Oh, my. Rosalyn hadn't even gotten used to calling him Lockie yet. "What about, sire?" she suggested.

Lachlan slowed to laugh. "Sire? As in Your Majesty?"

He paused for a moment and gazed into her eyes.

Then before she had a chance to protest, Lachlan gathered her up into his arms and began to race across the courtyard toward the keep's entrance. In a matter of moments, while she took deep calming breaths, he carried her across the entire lower bailey.

Once inside the king's grand castle, Lachlan strode briskly down the sconce-lined hallway. But instead of entering the great hall, he veered to the right down a corridor foreign to her.

"Where are you taking me La—Husband?" she asked, trying not to let the panic she felt show in her voice.

"To bed, Wife. Where else would we go?"

Rosalyn's heart started to beat wildly. "To bed?" she screeched, not worrying whether anyone else was privy to their conversation. "You promised we would not consummate the marriage."

"I did?" he asked innocently, his mischievous grin so close to her lips that he could have begun a seduction right there in the king's hall.

"You did, Lachlan. Set me down at once," she insisted, arching her back and squirming to put distance between their lips.

He laughed at her resistance and to show her he was in command, tossed her over his shoulder like a bag of lumpy potatoes, then swatted her arse hard.

She began to kick her legs in protest, thinking he'd give up the domineering way he was treating her and set her back on her feet, but instead, her resistance fueled the need for him to swat her bottom a few more times as he continued unrelentingly down the corridor.

"You will regret this, Lachlan," she said in a muffled voice with her lips pressed against his back.

A deep chuckle was the only response he gave. It rumbled

through her, making her more aware than ever that he could force himself upon her. He had the legal right now.

A loud thwacking sound brought Rosalyn out of her dread quickly when she realized Lachlan was kicking the chamber door open with his hands full of her squirming arse.

"Put me down, Lachlan. Put me down. This is not the way you want to start our marriage," she demanded, struggling even more violently after he'd kicked the door shut. "If you arenae careful it will end before it's begun."

And in an instant Rosalyn found herself face down on a fur coverlet.

"Before what's begun, Wife?"

Furious that she'd been tossed onto the bed as if discarded, she lifted her head so she could speak. "Am I no longer Rosalyn to you?" she asked, trying to hold back tears. "Only property?"

"If I call you 'Wife', I am not referring to you as a hog or parcel of land," he assured her, chuckling.

She couldn't see what he was doing from her position, but a loud thud echoed behind her that sounded like a boot dropping to the floor. Before she could take in another shaky breath, a second thud confirmed her suspicion.

"La—Husband," she began, but before she got the rest of her thoughts out, a bare-chested Lachlan leaped onto the mattress beside her.

"Oh, no! Off, off, get off this bed," she shouted, taking her hands and shoving against his muscular chest. The instant she touched his skin, a jolt of irresponsible passion surged through her body. No, she told herself, she had to fight it and him.

"I have nowhere else to go," he said with a husky voice, ignoring her pleas and staying put beside her.

She sighed and stopped her attempt to shove him off the bed. "Lachlan, why are we not in the great hall?"

"We will be, my love, after we've proven to the king that the marriage is consummated."

She wanted to start pounding his chest, but instead she bit her lip to keep from shouting out her protests again.

"Come," he said, swinging his legs over the edge of the bed and turning around on his stomach so he could reach for her.

Awkward in her long wedding dress, she tried to roll farther away from his grasp, but she kept her gaze on him as she moved. Half-expecting he would be angry with her for resisting, she was surprised when his dark eyes sparkled with mischief and his lips curled into a cocky grin.

While he began to strip off more of his clothes, she didn't stop, but rolled to the other side of the bed, getting to her feet as quickly and efficiently as she could.

Once she was steady, she eyed him up and down, relieved his breeches were still on as they stood at opposite ends of the massive marriage bed. Giving him a little nod, she raced for the door.

"You cannot escape, Rosalyn," he said softly and calmly. "The door is locked from the outside."

She ignored him and in moments was at the door, grasping the iron lever, pushing down with all her might. But the handle did not budge.

She let out an exasperated huff. "From the outside?" she gasped, spinning to face him, fists clenched at her side.

He nodded solemnly, but with that mischievous grin still on his face. "This is the marriage chamber. Did your mother not counsel you?"

Rosalyn took a step back and clung to the wooden door as if a cliff jutted out inches before her feet, wondering if other virgins had done the same.

She refused to be intimidated. "Of course, I've been counseled, but ours is a marriage of convenience. Do not fool yourself that 'tis anything otherwise," she said, finishing with a huff.

Dreading the outcome, she pressed her back to the door believing she had little recourse, as if she clung to the railing of a sinking ship. Rosalyn shuddered when she remembered what she'd been taught on coupling. Where the woman lay on her back and the man shoved his stiff cock between her legs, then pushed into her channel with a rocking motion until it hurt.

When Lachlan started a slow stroll toward her, Rosalyn began to move from the door, sliding against the wall away from him. Although there was no escape from the chamber, she wanted to give herself time to think.

"Those in the great hall need proof we have tied the knot, not only in ceremony, but with blood evidence."

Rosalyn's breathing became shallow and she closed her eyes, praying something or someone would come to her aid. Mayhap Bishop Passarelli with a kind word or prayer. But before she even began to believe that was possible, his lips were on hers in a moist ambush of passion. What little air she had left in her lungs was unable to make it to her head as she swooned slightly.

In response, Lachlan released her lips only to grab her arse and draw her into his chest. Without time to protest, he lifted her up into his arms again and carried her back to the marriage bed.

"Wife, you are not going to kick and scream again, are you now?" he asked, eyes glowing soft as he gazed upon her, his lips slightly reddened from his kissing.

She bit her tongue and shook her head. It would be in her best interest to play along until she figured out another way to stay a virgin.

He stopped short of the foot of the bed and set her gently

back on her feet. "That is better. I know you did not promise to obey me, but at least give me some cooperation."

Rosalyn nodded.

"Good. Now let's take a look at you," he said, gently tossing her veil aside and brushing her hair off her shoulders till it hung down her back. Then he reached forward as if to kiss her, but his grin moved past her lips to nip her earlobe. In slow, soft pecks he made his way down her neck, stopping at her shoulder, then his hands moved around her back and began unlacing her crisscross ties. When the bodice began to give way, her heart began to pound as if it wanted to be released from an iron cage.

Reaching the nape of her neck, Lachlan moved down to the swell of her breasts, propped high and proud. With his teeth, he tugged the ivory, silk fabric off one shoulder while she held her breath. And before his ministrations started up again, the bodice of her wedding dress drooped so low that her breasts spilled out.

Lachlan groaned and began sucking on one nipple that hardened like a traitor under his seduction. Her groin reacted with tiny spasms and her throat went dry. This was not in the counsel her mother had given.

"Wife, you are more enchanting than I could have ever dreamed," Lachlan admitted, as if surprised, gazing up at her after releasing her nipple, but continuing the seduction as he rubbed his thumb there.

What was Lachlan up to? Why was he toying with her like a wench? For if his aim was to take her virginity, should he dally with all of Scotland waiting?

But just as she was about to protest, his gaze met hers, revealing the passion trapped inside begging to be released. With his other hand, he shoved the remaining silk strap off her shoulder and let the wedding gown fall to her feet. She was totally exposed to her new husband's whims. Nothing covered her but her own passion.

"You are so beautiful," he gushed like a lad with a new shiny object. "I would savor you like a feast, but the guests and the king await." As he held her gaze, he gathered her into his arms and gently laid her back on the bed.

Even though he had every right to take her, and he'd ignited a passion storm inside her, she was not ready to give up her virginity just because a king wanted her to. So when Lachlan turned away from her and began to loosen his belt, Rosalyn swiftly and silently stole his dagger from its sheath.

Now, would she have the courage to use it?

CHAPTER 22

*L*achlan was relieved to find Rosalyn feisty, but not combative. Judging from the other moments they'd had together, she'd been like a wildcat hellion when she didn't get her way. No doubt the vows of marriage had challenged the boundaries she'd set, for tasting her now was more exhilarating than he'd ever imagined.

Sliding his embroidered breeches off proved more difficult than he expected. His manhood was so ready, it made his wedding attire difficult to remove. This amused him despite his frustration.

When he was finally free, Lachlan turned and took a wide stance with his hand on his hips, knowing it would make an impression.

And as he expected, Rosalyn's gaze shifted to his groin and her eyes widened. In just a few heart beats, a pink flush covered her, inciting his passion even more.

She was perfect in so many ways, and if he treated her like a queen, perhaps she would let him be her king and he'd conquer any doubts she had about his intention to make their arrangement beneficial for the both of them. For now, his shaft was commanding the room and both their attention.

As he approached her with a confident swagger, he watched the rapid rise and fall of her full breasts with their wicked tips beckoning him to touch her again. Yes, this was his wife, not a tavern wench, but he did not care which she was. He needed satisfaction. He needed to release his seed. He needed to be inside her.

Almost leaping onto the bed, he straddled her on his hands and knees, his shaft licking her belly. She groaned when he began to rub it against her soft stomach. And as if to tame him, she grabbed it hard like the handle of a whip and cupped his ballocks with the other.

"Aye, Wife, this is how a marriage should start." He looked down on her approvingly. "Holding your husband by the balls."

She giggled too, relaxing her face and her body.

He leaned down to nip her ear, then whispered, "This shall hurt just a little. Ere we've done it once, 'twill be easier and easier the second and third," he said soothingly.

She gazed up at him, but her expression changed after those words. "Nay, Lachlan, you do make my passion burn, but I shan't give you my virginity. I don't love you and I must have that." Her voice trailed off as she said the words and she looked away.

"You will lead me this far, my vixen, and then leave me?" he growled, his voice revealing his disappointment.

But his words brought her gaze back to him. "Nay, Husband, I will not leave you." She reached up and stroked his cheek. "You may hate me before the day is done, but I will always be compassionate. If I can relieve you of any pain, let me do it now."

He grinned. Yes, he thought, she was a healer, and if he

was in pain or sick, she would be by his side or at least answer his needs.

"Aye, Wife. Stroke me as you've done before," he insisted, then rolled over to his back beside her and closed his eyes. "If you do not need pleasure, I will not deny it of myself, especially when it pains me." He popped open one eye to gauge her reaction. "Perhaps after you see the passion it brings me, you'll reconsider."

She'd turned to her side, taking most of the coverlet with her and hiding all of her gorgeous curves. Not that they would stop him from reaching underneath. Feeling was better than looking.

"Come, Rosalyn, take me in both hands," he coaxed.

She let out a shaky breath and instead of staying cocooned beneath the covers, she threw them aside and in one graceful bound, straddled him. Taking his manhood in both hands, she gazed at it as if it were a prize, making his cock swell and heart pound.

With the skill she always approached her healing, she put the same effort into pleasing him. Asking him how he felt, if she was holding him the right way to give him the most pleasure, involved in all ways of wanting to satisfy him except for the act that would the most.

While he was reaching his climax, Lachlan gazed up at her tight bouncing breasts, wondering how she could give and not receive. And then he remembered something one of the mature ladies of the court had told him. She'd said just as men did not need to be inside a woman to rise to full passion, neither did a woman.

And with that in mind, even though he was almost in pain from his throbbing shaft, Lachlan decided not to take his release yet and gently reached inside Rosalyn's channel and began to swirl his two fingers there.

Her once-serene face transformed into a hellion on fire. She cried his name and pounded his chest with her fists.

"What is this, Husband?" she asked, gasping and straightening up, fisting her hair as if would alleviate the fire burning inside her.

When her hands splayed across his chest again, the red fiery tresses were in total disarray, shooting in all directions. And instead of pounding his chest again, she clawed her nails through the curls.

"Husband, you have bewitched me," she accused. "You must have covered yourself with an herb that would make me react this way. This is not natural," she said, shaking her head.

If he wasn't so ready to come, he'd have laughed. But it was no longer time for play, it was time to finish it for the both of them.

"Come, Wife, do what feels right," he choked out, his throat so tight with passion.

With no more than that instruction, she placed her mouth on his shaft and did what most women would never do. She brought his to climax with her sweet, seductive tongue. And at the same time, he did not abandon her. No, he slid his two fingers into her channel, this time from behind her tight little arse, and circled them around rhythmically while she brought him out of his need.

With a complete squeal of delight, she collapsed beside him.

"What was that, Husband?"

"Marriage benefits. But now there's the business of answering to the king."

She smiled at him. And then out of nowhere a dagger rose over her head. His immediate instinct was to knock if from her hand, but in his satiated state, he had little coordination or speed and before he knew what had happened, there was blood on the sheet between them.

"What? Wife?" he said, inspecting his arms and limbs. No, he was not bleeding. Then his gaze traveled to the lovely, but disheveled creature across from him. As he scanned her quickly, he was relieved to find only a narrow cut on her thigh.

"'Tis my dagger," he said, not realizing his voice was shaking until the words were out.

"Aye, Husband. You must watch your back at all times around me." She leveled her gaze.

"Little minx. You could have killed me."

"Aye, Husband, I had the opportunity, but I chose not to," she said with a wicked, sly smile, her eyes sparkling like a sorcerous.

"Mayhap 'twas you who bewitched me, Rose."

She bristled at the namesake.

"For now, I'll allow you to call me, Wife," she said, tossing her disheveled hair behind her back.

"Well, I'm grateful you did not become both a bride and a widow on the same day and your cleverness or lack of commitment has solved the problem for the king," he said with a hit of sarcasm.

He *tsked* and touched her thigh, pleased though the cut had dried already. "If I had thought of this, it would have been my blood," he said sincerely.

"Do not doubt the resources of a king. I am sure he has a healer or advisor who can easily tell the difference between a man's blood and a woman's. I can."

He snorted at that, but gave her a grateful smile. "Well, then, ready yourself for the great hall." He nodded to the tall wardrobe in the corner. "'Tis filled with dresses and everything you'll need to become a lady once more. I can help you with lacing your dresses, but you'll need a lady's maid to do something with that hair."

Naked, Rosalyn strolled over to the tall oval looking glass in the corner and burst out laughing. "Aye, Lockie, I may need a whole team of ladies' maids to right this."

Although he didn't want to leave her now, he was certain one of the servants would be knocking at the door shortly for the evidence, so he quickly dressed back in his wedding attire as Rosalyn attended to her wound. After she'd wrapped it in a clean cloth, she turned to him. It was just a brief moment before he was across the room, gathering her into his arms again.

"I know you do not love me, Wife," he said with such sincerity that it was comical enough to make Rosalyn burst out laughing.

"Aye, I do not love you, but you have not said that you love me either." She waited for a response and when nothing came from him, she snorted. "I assumed as much."

"Well, I promised to be truthful."

"At least we agree we are starting our lives together in a loveless marriage."

"I cannot wait to see what happens next, Wife."

CHAPTER 23

It wasn't long after Lachlan had left her with a passionate kiss so intense Rosalyn was almost willing to reconsider her protected virginity, when one of the king's maids came into the chamber with a short curtsy, then stripped the bed of its sheets and promptly marched out.

At first Rosalyn thought her new husband's story was designed to coerce her into consummating the marriage, but the actions of the king's maid proved he'd been truthful all along. About everything. Even though she'd almost changed her mind that morning, expecting the king and the bishop to understand her reasoning. Yet, something in Rosalyn's heart kept telling her this was right.

After another parade of maids had come and gone with mathematic precision, Rosalyn proceeded to the great hall with one of the Garter knights. He was a giant in size and stature, as well as quiet and stoic when they walked down the corridor. Her curiosity couldn't be contained so she started a conversation.

"My name is Rosalyn. What do they call you, great knight?"

The imposing figure next to her coughed. "Well, my lady, I can assure you my fellow champions do not call me, great knight. You may call me Red."

"Pardon my direct nature, but I'm curious if you have any word on the missing Golden Rose."

"My lady, you needn't trouble yourself with the logistics of our search. 'Tis your wedding day. I know firsthand the kitchen has been hard at work fixing pheasant, mutton stew, swan, and more, for I was shooed out near moments before I came to your door."

It was Rosalyn's turn to laugh. "But of course, you may find it odd, but I have a vested interest in its prompt return. You see my new husband is suspected of having a hand in its disappearance, and you can understand my reasons for wanting his name to be cleared."

They had reached the great hall entrance and the knight stopped and turned, gesturing she take his arm for escort. As she did, he bowed.

"My lady, if I may let you in on a confidence, it is not your husband, but his brother that is more the suspect. That is all I can share for now," he confided. Then as if a sorcerer cast a spell, Red transformed into a ridged, fierce protector when he guided her to the dais. Once at the head table, he helped to her settle properly onto the ornate chair between her husband and the king.

Then the King of Scotland shot her the smallest sideways grin and stood with his chalice high in the air.

Rosalyn's attention shifted to take in the massive gathering room filled with knights, lords, ladies, royal servants, and entertainers. She drew in a full breath as if to fill her lungs with courage. She had to pinch herself to make sure she wasn't dreaming. It was beyond her imagination to even consider one, if not all, of the goings on today as improbable: being married in a royal abbey, given away by the King of Scots, in a ceremony led by an Italian bishop. And the most outrageous part, to an Englishman.

But the spirit of her da had given his approval and because he'd been a favored landholder and loyal to King James, she'd had been treated like royalty herself.

"A toast," the King commanded, and all those seated at the dais and those about the great hall rose. He turned to Rosalyn and Lachlan, seated on his right.

"To Rosalyn, who will be like a daughter to me." He tipped his chalice. "And to Lachlan, her newly betrothed. Although English at birth, he has taken his wife's surname. And news has reached him today that his father is dead, clearing the way for him to embrace his new family and clan."

The room burst into cheers of *huzzah*. Rosalyn immediately sought her husband's gaze for confirmation. It had been no secret that he'd hated his father. But now that the family patriarch was gone, did he really need to be married to her? Without his father's greed and hunger for her land and her castle, would he forgo the quest and leave her? If she'd asked herself those questions a week ago, she would have prayed for a resounding, *yes*. Now, she was not so sure. Lachlan's reassuring gaze and smile fed an already complex connection. One she had trouble sorting out, but she could easily tell that the news had pleased him. But what of his brother? She furrowed her brow, knowing Ethan was as much a thorn in her husband's side as his father.

Rosalyn scanned the high table and did not find him there. She searched the rest of the royal throng, but still could not spot a face like her husband's while the bishop proceeded with a formal toast.

"May there always be work to do. And your purse to hold many coins for you. May the sun always shine on your window pane. May a rainbow be certain to follow the rain. May the hand of a friend always be near. And may God's love and grace always be there."

The King raised his wine to toast Rosalyn. Then his chalice clinked with hers, followed by Lachlan's.

More loud cheers of *huzzah* followed as she turned to toast her husband, but instead of joining cups, his lips toasted hers in a ravenous show of affection.

Before Rosalyn could gently break Lachlan's hold, the King's snorting rung in her ears and rowdy guests began to cheer them on with encouragement.

Finally, Rosalyn pushed him away and took in a deep breath, her cheeks burning with heat and embarrassment. She'd talk to her husband later about his affectionate advances.

After that kiss and a few more stolen ones, she was soon giddy from mead and music. And as the evening progressed, her new husband became more and more enchanting. He treated her like a queen, his charm melting her heart.

When the minstrel's final ballad ended, Rosalyn rose to her feet, teetering on her toes, woozy from the wine and the hour. Luckily, her husband scooped her in his arms before she lost her balance and the remaining guests cheered as if he'd won a contest.

She couldn't help but finally allow Lachlan his displays of affection. His charm seemed to always to win her over, even when her anger toward him sparked a flame.

The laughter and stomping of feet and cheers faded while Lachlan carried her toward the marriage chamber they'd shared earlier that afternoon.

Flames flashed bright on the walls of the corridor from the sconces lighting the way. Most of the castle dwellers were either still imbibing in the great hall or to bed. Now she was eager to talk to her husband, free from the King and his guests.

"Husband, are we to share a chamber tonight?" Rosalyn asked with some trepidation, unsure whether or not he'd have the courtesy to let her have the room to herself. There had been no time before their betrothal to discuss were he would sleep tonight, or even what the next day held.

If there'd had been a normal courtship, even an arranged marriage for the advancement of heritage, Rosalyn would have shared her hopes and dreams, her inner self. Now, she wasn't sure what a future with Lachlan would hold, and she wanted some control.

"Would you have me sleep with the King's farm animals?" Lachlan responded, chuckling. "Have I made such an arse of myself? Is that where I belong?"

Despite her tense demeanor, Lachlan's self-deprecating humor cut through her defenses and made her laugh, too.

"No, husband, 'tis, well, you see—"

"I have promised to protect you and I cannot think of a better place for me to do that than at your side, even when you sleep." He slowed to glance down at her with that look that always made her melt.

When she gave him a shy grin in return, he groaned. "Wife, do not look at me like that until I have you in my bed again," he confessed, his head jerking up to watch where he was going.

As he strode quickly down the long corridor, Lachlan's face drifted in and out of shadows, the flickering flame highlighting his handsome face, and Rosalyn began to relax. Although she'd been uneasy about this union from the start, Lachlan's concern for her seemed genuine. Even if his loins guided him.

This time when they reached the chamber door, he was more civil about opening it. He stood sideways and with a slight stoop, he reached the lever and opened the door with ease. In a few quick strides, he was at the bed's edge, laying her on the soft coverlet, a warm glow in his eyes and a face full of chagrin.

"Wife, do not move from that spot," Lachlan instructed in a tone that was neither intimidating nor demanding. When he gazed down at her from the bedside, Lachlan appeared less beast and more beau. "A feather is a necessity for our next exploration. I will return shortly and trust you will not need to steal my dagger again."

A flash of his charming smile assured her that there was nothing to fear as she watched his muscular arse walk out the chamber door.

Rosalyn sighed and her gaze drifted to the ceiling. She stared at the painted cherubs above her.

Odd. Rosalyn did not recall noticing them earlier in the day, but she'd been either starting at Lachlan, or pinching her eyes shut. And as much as she enjoyed gazing at the playful, pudgy purveyors of love, she closed her eyes and slowed her breathing.

The wedding day had brought a mixture of emotions. Like an experimental potion full of reliable ingredients, calculated risk-taking, and ancient wisdom, the outcome of its power remained uncertain. Only time would tell if their marital remedy would produce the results they both sought. Lachlan's father was dead. Lachlan had shown no remorse. There was no love for his brother. Perhaps that was why his taking the Macpherson name was a good idea after all.

How surprised her mother and sister will be, she imagined, when she returned to Aberdeen with a new husband to reclaim Fyvie.

Noises from merry courtiers outside her door were loud enough to bring Rosalyn's thoughts back to the present, making her wonder what was keeping her husband. A man who wanted to bed his new wife should have returned by now.

A feather? Wasn't that what Lachlan had said he was going to bring back? She was so ticklish, something she'd hoped to hide from him. If not, he would get the best of her. Perhaps she'd be the one doing the tickling. She could only hope. No, she'd insist.

But as much as she wanted to admit she was less terrified than before about being alone with Lachlan, she wasn't sure she wanted a feather in the bed, no matter who did the tickling.

Perhaps a sleeping herb could deter him. A drowsy wife would not make for much sport. And she was in luck, for she had such a potion at hand.

After rolling over to the edge of the bed, Rosalyn rummaged around in her travel satchel until she found the miniature vial and popped the top off. A few sips, would do the trick she thought.

After downing the sweet concoction and returning the potion, she closed her eyes and took in a few deep breaths. *It won't take long.* Just as her lids were feeling heavy, the chamber door opened and shut.

"Why you are still dressed atop the bed?" the muffled voice asked.

But before she could answer, she was flipped on her stomach, arms pinned to her side, and her skirts yanked over her head.

When a hand reached between her thighs, Rosalyn became wide-awake.

CHAPTER 24

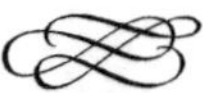

"What is this, Husband?" Rosalyn shrieked. Lachlan's hands were violating her. "You promised I would not be treated like property. Stop this at once or I will scream," she threatened, slamming her thighs shut on his hand.

Lachlan grumbled something and finally took his hand away.

Rosalyn lay there on her stomach, with her face turned away from his body, taking deep breaths, grateful to be freed from the suffocating pillow and his domination. What happened to the gentle man who'd wooed her hours ago?

"Do not think you can keep me from my marital rights, woman," Lachlan said, breaking the silence and her brief respite.

Rosalyn refused to answer him. Instead, she rolled off the bed, then backed away.

When she reached the hearth, she lowered to her knees facing the bed. Boiling inside with anger, the flames licked her back and fueled the fire inside her belly.

Shaking with anger, she addressed him from the safe distance. "I made it clear, this is a marriage of convenience and there would be no consummation. If you refuse, I'll go to the King and the bishop at this hour. I will wake them and demand an annulment. Do you understand?"

The bulky shape that dominated the bed did not move or speak for the longest time. Rosalyn couldn't imagine that he'd fallen asleep, so she stayed perched on her knees in front of the fire like an animal ready to run. Ready to sprint to the door if he came too close.

Just then Lachlan leaped from the bed to his feet, startling her out of her thoughts. The lapping flames of the fire quickly revealed he was sporting only his manhood and nothing else.

As he approached her, his chiseled abdomen muscles rippled. She wanted to keep her eyes on his face, but it was clouded in darkness. The glow of the fire illuminated his lower half, drawing her attention there instead.

He stopped in front of her. "Woman, I do not wish to bring all of Edinburgh Castle to our door at this hour, so I will accept your refusal. And if that is your condition of marriage, so be it, but you must agree to my condition as well."

She didn't move or speak for a few moments and refused to look up at him as she contemplated her options. This time she didn't care if he'd experience pain from being full with need.

Let him suffer.

When she continued her silence, he broke it for her. "Your lack of words speak for you. And now that you've had a good long look at what you could have had, I'll leave you. But I will be back in the morn. Be ready to travel. To Fyvie."

To Fyvie? A spark of hope flickered in her heart. Was he

drunk? Perhaps that's why he was acting like a demon possessed.

"Aye, I see the delight in your expression. To Fyvie we shall travel, but your condition of this marriage is to make me laird of Fyvie and chieftain of the clan. Of all Aberdeen. I must have your full backing and support."

His condition is what he meant. What of her rules? But if he was drunk, this was not the time to argue with him.

His demands crushed her spirit and she was reminded of the day they'd first met, when they were tied together in the dungeon of Berwick Castle. When she found out he wanted Fyvie. Of course, it wasn't just Fyvie he wanted. He wanted the lairdship all along. A new surname and a new start.

At her expense.

These were her choices? Give up her bed or give up her claim to her clan?

After a short little prayer for guidance, Rosalyn knew what to say. "I accept your condition so mine can be honored as well." She sucked in a deep breath. "Now that we both understand each other, get out," she demanded.

Turning away from her, he snatched his trews and boots from the floor and quickly dressed in silence while her cheeks and body cooled off. Grateful, at least for now, that she would keep Lachlan's out of her bed.

Without even a nod or a goodnight, he stomped out the door as if he hadn't won. What did he expect? To have it all? Her love and Fyvie?

While she was settling back in bed, deciding to sleep with her clothes on just to be safe, the key turned in the lock. Rosalyn sighed. Lack of trust would be a hallmark of their marriage if it started this way on day one. Just as she'd been shackled to her him on the day they'd met, the first day of the marriage held the same promise.

As the sleeping herb finally began to take effect, Rosalyn

was grateful she'd been awake enough to fend him off. Why had he tried to force himself on her moments ago, when evidence was required earlier in the day?

With the little clarity she had left, Rosalyn realized she'd been a fool and was determined not to be fooled again.

CHAPTER 25

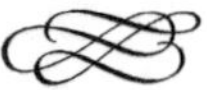

*E*ven though her traveling bags were packed and ready by the door, Rosalyn refused to be undermined by her new husband again. If Lachlan said she should be ready to travel to Fyvie in the morning, she would comply, but she was determined not to hand over the family's lairdship once they arrived. He'd deceived her into granting the transfer of her surname, but she would not allow him to strip her of her rightful inheritance.

Walking over to the lead-glass window, Rosalyn stood gazing at the sky, the dawn about to break in the distance. Kitchen maids scurried about below, drawing water from the deep well in the lower bailey. While Rosalyn envied the women's freedom, she did not relish the work. Even though she was a prisoner in marriage, she'd promised herself last night before falling asleep, that she'd find a way to have Fyvie and the lairdship. Yes, she could lead the clan. Surely, she'd have much to prove, but she was ready. Ready for any battle. She had her da's fighting spirit.

As expected, it wasn't long before the lock in the door

turned noisily, letting Rosalyn know someone had come to claim her.

A petite, hooded figure dressed in black materialized on the other side of the door as if aided by witchcraft, making Rosalyn reach for her dirk.

When the mysterious visitor drew back her hood, she grinned at Rosalyn and asked, "Who were you expecting, the King himself?"

Rosalyn relaxed and returned her dagger to boot, grateful she knew this witch. She rushed forward and wrapped Ursula into a big sisterly hug. "I'm so glad 'tis you," Rosalyn gushed, not hiding her enthusiasm. "What are you doing here?"

"Escorting you to Aberdeen, of course. You need a lady's maid and I have volunteered," she said, stepping back.

"You, a lady's maid?"

"What? You doubt my skills and sincerity?" Ursula asked as if she'd been wounded.

That made Rosalyn laugh. "Well, I've not yet seen you braid hair or change a bed, but I can at least vouch for your healing skills."

That made Ursula crack a smile again. But just as quickly, her expression turned serious. "Lachlan was in the kitchen early. As I was I looking for some rosemary to aid an ailing stomach, I overhead his plans to travel to Fyvie with you this morn before the rest of the castle was up and about."

Rosalyn sucked in a shaky breath. "Aye, my husband's actions are no secret to me. I was given two choices, either consummate the marriage or give him the lairdship of Fyvie, complete with the chieftain status."

Ursula's brows drew together with concern.

Rosalyn gave her friend a reassuring touch on her arm. "I've remained a virgin so far." Rosalyn teared up, but did not want her eyes red when Lachlan did come for her, so she held them back.

Ursula's gaze softened and kindness glowed behind the concern. "I know you well, Rosalyn. You've given up control of Fyvie now to protect yourself, but I'm sure that will change once you've made it back to Aberdeen."

Rosalyn gave her friend a big squeeze. "Are you sure you want to make this journey?"

"I need a home, too, and I wasnae going to beg, but I hoped you would take me in. And Joshua too." She hesitated, but then said, "Once we are married. He is on good terms with your clan, and I believe he'll take my surname as Lachlan did yours." She winced. "Though I have nae castle or riches to offer him."

"Nor does he need them because he loves you." Rosalyn smiled at her friend and squeezed her hand. "Aye, come, be part of my family. I know my mother would welcome another healer and will be happy to invite you to be a sister of mine," Rosalyn promised, giving Ursula a hug. "And please send another missive asking Joshua to meet you near Fyvie," she urged. "Perhaps this one will reach him."

They broke their embrace when the door opened and Lachlan entered. He glanced about the room taking note of her packed bags by the entrance. "Good day, Wife. I trust you slept well?" He came to her side and gave her a gentle hug and a peck on the top of her head.

Rosalyn glanced up, ready to give Lachlan an earful, but before she could a Garter knight filled the doorway.

"My lady, are you ready?" the knight asked politely, taking her bags in hand.

Rosalyn nodded. "My maid is joining us and—"

"My things are already on horseback, my lady," Ursula interrupted with a curtsy, followed by a wink only Rosalyn could see.

The knight bowed slightly. "Well, then, I shall escort you both to the horses," he offered. "I am certain Sir Lachlan has much to prepare." He gave her husband a nod and stepped back from the door.

The knight led them first to the great hall, allowing them to pack foodstuffs for the journey, then he followed them down the corridor while Rosalyn exchanged cheese and bread with her friend.

As they walked to their horses and readied their satchels, Rosalyn expressed her confusion to Ursula over Lachlan's actions. "This morning, he'd appeared as if nothing unusual had transpired the night afore."

When her confidante shrugged her shoulders without offering a rational explanation, Rosalyn decided to shake off her concerns for now, because love swelled in her heart for the new Highland sister she'd be bringing back to Aberdeen. Then relief surged through her as they mounted their horses and readied for the road ahead.

Rosalyn glanced about the group Lachlan had assembled. Four Garter knights, four squires, and two cooks. She was grateful for the protection the King would provide and the charity he'd bestowed on her. However, she was troubled by the hasty departure, unable to say her formal goodbyes to those who had been so kind to her. But before she dug her heels into the palfrey, Rosalyn noticed a white-robed, curly-headed figure rushing across the bailey.

In an instant, she recognized Bishop Passarelli, delighted he must have received word of their early departure. But even as the holy man hustled across the courtyard, Rosalyn couldn't help but be uneasy about their abrupt escape and inappropriate manners. What guest left before thanking their host?

"Lady Rosalyn," the bishop called to her as his curls tossed in the brisk breeze. "I must speak to you," he shouted to her, slightly out of breath.

She was apprehensive as he approached. The bishop had become like an adoptive father to her since they'd met and she was embarrassed that it appeared she was rushing off without a final word.

She leaned low when he approached. He gave her an awkward hug as she sat upon her horse. "Bishop," she said in her own breathless voice, "I'm so pleased you came to say goodbye."

"Yes, my dear," he said, keeping his voice low so only she could hear. "Goodbye with a warning." His face clouded and his brows drew together in a hard line. "The Golden Rose is still missing, and the King believes either Ethan or Lachlan have stolen it. Perhaps they worked together?"

Rosalyn glanced at her husband, relieved to find him busy talking to the Garter knights. "Bishop, what can I do?" she asked, wanting to tell him what had happened with Lachlan, wishing she could prove her husband had the Rose and to ask the King to lock him up. That would solve all her problems, but of course she couldn't.

The bishop put his hands together. "I will pray for you, for your path is not easy," he said with compassion in his eyes, as if he knew everything she had been through. "But I cannot return to Italy until the Rose is in the hands of its rightful owner. The King has invited me to stay as an assigned group of knights investigates the Rose's disappearance. Although His Majesty insists that the pope's Christian honor does not require a gift such as the Golden Rose, I'm certain the pope would not hear of it, nor would I want to abandon my duty."

Then his face grew serious. "The King wants you to spy on your husband. And he will compensate you handsomely if you find the Rose."

Wanting to solve both their problems with one solution she said, "Bishop, I promise I will be vigilant in my observations as I travel with my husband to Fyvie Castle. Ethan attended the wedding, but I've yet to see him since. As far as I know, his brother came only to report on his father's death, and happened upon our wedding day. I imagine Ethan has returned to Somerset to handle his father's affairs."

But just as it appeared the bishop was about to say goodbye, an odd question popped into her head. "When the culprit is caught and proven guilty of the crime, what is the punishment?"

The bishop studied her for a few moments before he answered. "The crime has already been committed in the eyes of God, so for me, the guilty party asks for His forgiveness."

"Yes, Father, of course, but what of the legal punishment?" she asked as her eyebrow twitched involuntarily making her reach and scratch it to hide her reaction.

"That would be the King's decision of course, but I understand those who are found guilty of a high Scottish crime are hanged."

"Hanged?" she said louder than she meant to and clapped her hand over her mouth.

"I hear beheadings happen over much less," he said grimly. Then his gaze softened when he must have realized her concern for her husband.

"Now, as the ambassador to the Golden Rose, I'm certain the King will allow me to have a say in the matter." He patted her hand. "Do not worry. The return of the Rose is more important than punishing the guilty party, I assure you." Then he brightened. "And there will be a reward for anyone who aids in its return."

Rosalyn had to admit that initially she had wondered if her husband had stolen the Rose and ratting him out could be beneficial to her in so many ways. But at the same time, she did not want to be responsible for his death, nor his brother's. Still, a reward from the King was another matter.

"A reward, Bishop?" she asked, then realized she had asked out loud.

The bishop clapped his hands together. "You've heard the phrase, a king's ransom?"

Rosalyn couldn't help but smile as Lachlan called then for the group to roll out.

CHAPTER 26

While Lachlan paced in the maid's cubbyhole, his mood matched the darkness. His stomach told him it was well past breakfast and he was not only starving for food, he was hungry for his wife. Patience had progressed to provoked anger. How could it be that not a single maid had come to retrieve the fresh linens and threshes for the morning duties?

Lachlan was about to pound on the door once more, when it was thrust open instead. Fortunately, he stopped or he would have punched the frightened woman on the other side. That did not seem to matter, for she started screaming like a banshee and the soiled bedding flew up and out of her arms.

He tried to make apologies, but it didn't matter. The maid wouldn't stay for pleasantries, nor did she collect items she'd come for. Instead, she ran past the dirty pile of linens without another word.

Lachlan wasn't concerned about any of this at the moment. He raced down the empty castle passageway toward the wedding chamber. Bursting through the door like a barbarian, he came to a screeching halt just inside the door, startling yet another maid into a screaming frenzy.

"Now, now," Lachlan said in his best soothing voice. "I'm Lord Macpherson, and this is my chamber."

The frightened woman didn't look any more assured that he wasn't there to murder her. He could imagine how he appeared, with straw threshes sticking to his normally meticulous beard and hair.

As he began tossing off the straw, he tried to keep his voice soft and his demeanor calm. "Have you seen Lady Macpherson?"

The maid shook her head and gripped the linens in her hands like a protective shield against her chest.

"Well, then," Lachlan said as he backed out of the room. "Carry on." He spun on his heel and headed to the great hall. Surely, someone there would be able to direct him to Rosalyn.

When he entered the gathering room, he found a few courtiers at the trestle tables. Because it was late morning, only a couple unassigned knights and squires were there, too.

As he took a seat at the empty dais table, a serving maid approached with a trencher of hard-boiled eggs, ham, fresh bread, and a goblet of ale. "Bless you, woman," he said after she set the foodstuffs in front of him. She gave him an odd look, making him think he could still be wearing a stray straw or two, but he didn't care at the moment.

After a few bites of the food, followed by a good wash of ale, Lachlan sensed someone approaching from behind and stiffened. A friendly pat on the back assured him there was no threat.

"What are you doing back at Edinburgh, my lord?" asked a familiar voice from behind him. "Were you not off for Fyvie this morn with your new bride?"

Lachlan spun from his chair to his feet, knocking it over as he turned to find a startled Bishop Passarelli.

"My bride off to Fyvie?" Lachlan asked, almost choking on the morsel of bread he'd been chewing. "What say you, Bishop? I do not understand."

The bishop's calm demeanor returned, along with his complementary placid smile. "My Son," he said in a steady voice, placing a hand on Lachlan's arm to steer him back to his seat, "let's discuss this civilly and I promise I will help you."

Lachlan drew in a deep breath, then reluctantly righted the overturned chair and returned to his seat. As the holy man took up one beside him, Lachlan downed the remaining contents of his goblet, then waved the server over to refill it.

"Start from the beginning, Bishop," Lachlan said, trying to keep his voice calm. "When I searched for my wife this morn, after being locked in the servant's closet all night, thanks to my brother, she was not there, and you say she left with *me* this morn for Fyvie?"

Damnation. Lachlan felt the tension in the air grow. Ethan was pretending to be *him* and he had already deceived everyone, including Rosalyn. Although he didn't expect she was in any immediate danger, he was ready to saddle up and chase after them when the bishop put his hand back on Lachlan's arm.

"*Si*, your wife is with your brother, but she is also traveling with the healer, four Garter knights, and their squires. She is not alone with him."

Lachlan yanked away from the bishop and pounded his fists on the head table. His chair knocked backward for the second time as he stood. "Bishop, I don't want my brother anywhere near my wife. He killed my mother, the only other woman I've loved, and I'll not let him do it again."

The bishop nodded grimly. "I gave Rosalyn my blessing

and God's. That should provide some protection. Even if you are not a deeply religious man, Lachlan, you must take some comfort in that." He gestured for him to sit and the holy man closed his eyes. "Let us pray," he said in a firm voice.

"Dear Father, Lachlan is distressed over a deceptive act by his brother, Ethan, against his new wife, Rosalyn. Please keep her safe from harm until Lachlan is able to come to her aid. And Lord, please protect Lachlan from his brother. Amen"

"Amen," Lachlan echoed, opening his eyes. "Thank you, Bishop. I will make haste, but cautiously and with God's guidance. Now, I bid you *arrivederci.*"

Lachlan began to rise, but the bishop's hand remained firmly on his arm. "Not so fast, young man, I'm going with you."

Lachlan wasn't about to yank his arm away from the bishop, but his renewed calm was starting to fray. The last thing he wanted was an elderly bishop and his entourage of holy men holding him back on the trail.

"With all due respect, I must refuse your assistance. You understand a posse of priests would slow my progress."

The bishop grinned and his eyes danced with merriment. "No, my Son, not a posse of priests, just me and more of the English knights. Remember, I'm an accomplished horseman and a trained swordsman. Besides, I have vowed to return to the King the missing Golden Rose of Scotland and I believe I can accomplish your goal and mine at the same time."

Lachlan had forgotten he'd lost the challenge to the bishop on the trip to Edinburgh and weighed his offer. Perhaps the holy man would be a good negotiator when he joined his brother, but what was this about the Golden Rose?

"All right, you may join me and I thank you for your generosity, but please, pray tell, what news do you have of the Rose?"

"My spies have it under good authority that it is your

brother who has taken the Rose. Someone who fits his description is suspect."

That made Lachlan pause. "Someone who looks just like me, you mean?"

"I'm inclined to think, based on what I know about you, Lachlan, that it is your brother who may be the guilty one."

"But many know, including the King, that I was the last to see the Rose."

"True, but an innocent man would never volunteer that information," the bishop said with knowing nod.

Lachlan was grateful for the holy man's belief in his innocence. The bishop was proving more conniving than Lachlan had given him credit for.

And he had spies.

* * *

EDINBURGH TO ABERDEEN was a five-day journey. Rosalyn knew it well, having traveled it many times alongside her da. With only girls in the family, her father did not hesitate to help them learn the wool trade and she'd built up a tolerance for life on the trail.

Ursula, on the other hand, was struggling with the rigors of hours in the saddle. Her saving grace was her vast resources of herbs at the ready to help with everything from saddle sores to bee stings.

Luckily for Rosalyn, the first two days of travel had passed pleasantly enough. She had bunked with Ursula and avoided any intimate contact with Lachlan. She was grateful she'd hardly even spoken to her new husband.

And with Ursula at her side, the friendship grew as they had much to debate when it came to the foliage at their daily stops and campsites. Coming from different clans, each woman had her own secrets and antidotes for many of the same common herbs and everyday plants.

At first, Rosalyn had questioned the trail Lachlan had chosen, knowing it wasn't the most popular with the merchants, but he'd insisted, although more rugged, it was more direct and would cut the normal travel time in half, allowing them to reach Fyvie before nightfall.

Now that she was within miles of the castle, the fringe of Aberdeen's territory, she began to worry about being accepted back into the clan after having married English. Having married a Luttrell.

It had been four long years working the wool trade with her Uncle Angus out of a tidy manor in the hamlet of Black-dog, not far from Fyvie's gates, biding her time 'til this month, when she'd come of age.

Not that Rosalyn was any wiser now than she'd been at seven and ten, but the law was the law. For even though her da had bequeathed the castle and lairdship to Rosalyn at his death, Nicholas Luttrell had kept her away.

And that's why after her twenty-first birthday and Nicholas's sudden disappearance from Aberdeen, she'd risked everything with a stolen king's seal and papers forged at Berwick. What judge would take the word of a lass even when she'd come of age?

Now with Nicholas dead and his sons, Lachlan and Ethan, warring over castle and the clan, was there even a Luttrell on guard?

Wild warrior-like cries startled Rosalyn out of her worries.

The clan?

She screamed as a band of kilted Highlanders with mud-smeared faces charged them, hand axes high and swords drawn.

When three of the attackers came toward her, she

screamed even louder, hoping to startle them. Steering her horse with her knees, she freed her hands to ready her bow, arming it with an arrow from her quiver.

As she held her aim, the three Highland warriors stopped immediately and lowered their weapons.

That made Rosalyn grin with pride until the noise of horses behind her made her glance over her shoulder. To her chagrin, it was more than just her threatening arrow that had slowed the attackers. Four knights had formed a line behind her with their longswords dawn and shields held high.

No doubt the Highlanders expected a surprise attack to be in their favor and had underestimated the strength of the party, for almost all but one man drew up short before making contact with the English knights.

That one brave warrior ran head-on with his sword to parlay, stroke for stroke, with the Garter knight called Red.

It wasn't long, though, before the aggressor was laid to the ground by Red's sword and Lachlan dismounted to join them.

"Donna let me bleed to death, English," the injured Highlander shouted. "Put me to death and be quick about it."

Red hesitated. "What say you, Lachlan?" The knight was under oath to follow the orders of his leader, and in this case it was her husband's decision.

Rosalyn looked about the group and then a shrill scream came from behind her.

"No! No! Do not kill Joshua."

Shocked by the outburst, Rosalyn spun in her saddle to find Ursula shoving her way between the horses to reach the fallen Highlander.

"Spare him, he means no harm to clan Macpherson or to our group."

When Lachlan hesitated, Rosalyn spoke up. She recognized the colors of these men. "'Tis true. This man and his companions are from Clan Fraser, friends of the Macphersons who rule these lands. I am Rosalyn Macpherson, daughter of Dengas Macpherson. These men should be spared. No doubt they thought the English were invading their neighboring lands and rushed into protect what belongs to my family."

When Lachlan stayed silent, the Garter knights followed her lead, reaching down to help the fallen man to his feet. By that time, Rosalyn had dismounted and joined Ursula, who provided a blanket from her saddle. Then the healer led the three of them to a small clearing.

Rosalyn didn't linger long. Once she was certain the injured clan member was tended to by Ursula with the proper care, she turned to address the two groups.

The Highlanders were gathered on the far side of the trail talking in whispers, while the knights, squires, and Lachlan sat mounted waiting for direction.

For Rosalyn, it was a defining moment. One that gave her courage and the confirmation that she could lead men.

"Highlanders, knights, squires, and those of noble of birth, we prevented loss of life over a misunderstanding of alliances. Thanks to the quick reactions from both sides, we can be grateful that potential foes can become friends. Ursula and Joshua intended to meet in Aberdeen, not over his wounds, but in the woods. Who would like to accompany our party to Fyvie Castle, the home of my clan?"

The huddled Highlanders gave one quick glance at their injured friend, then spread out into a long line. With weapons overhead, they cheered. Then the leader stepped forward, "We all follow you, Lady Rosalyn."

With her heart full and her confidence soaring, Rosalyn searched her group for Lachlan, but he was busy digging into his satchel for something. Fair enough, if he didn't question her leadership, she would snatch it from his grasp.

"Welcome, men. Let's build a transport for Joshua and we'll be on our way. If we work quickly, we can make it to the gates of Fyvie by nightfall."

And quickly they worked. It wasn't long before the knights and Highlanders had created a strong bed of sorts that could be dragged along the back of a horse like a sled.

As the band of men fell into a caravan, she followed behind Lachlan. He appeared uninterested in the goings on of the group, or her, for that matter. While she decided it wasn't worth her worry, her gaze was drawn to his oversized deerskin satchel. Big enough to pack a weeks' worth of clothing, perhaps a thick blanket, or even the stolen Golden Rose of Scotland?

As the bag bounced against the horse's rump, Rosalyn studied its movements. There was definitely something heavy and bulky inside. Now she'd have to find a way to snag it before it disappeared.

Settling into her saddle and squaring her shoulders, she sat taller than before. Surely, her marriage was one of convenience and a gamble with her future, but she'd never been one to make safe decisions.

The more she thought on it, the more she was able to distance the emotional entanglement she'd had with Lachlan. Even though he'd kept his distance the past two days and hadn't tried to take her as he'd done on their wedding night, she wasn't certain his actions toward her were sincere. For in the days since their marriage, he'd spoke mostly of the lairdship and not once of their future.

The future was on her mind through the rest of the ride and as nightfall crept in over the rolling hills of Aberdeen. Rosalyn heaved a sigh when Fyvie Castle finally came into view. Her heart began to beat faster. What type of welcome would she receive?

Approaching the massive entrance with their winding

caravan, Rosalyn scanned the familiar parapets, filled with at least a dozen guards. When they started to cross the draw-bridge, the main gate opened and a group of four knights started toward them.

Lachlan held up his hand and called out to halt the horses. The other party stopped, too. One knight from each group dismounted and met in the middle of the drawbridge. To Rosalyn's relief, happy recognition replaced guarded scrutiny. No doubt these were some of the original Garter knights they'd expected in Berwick-upon-Tweed. Their leader addressed Rosalyn's group.

"Lords and Ladies, I am Sir James Luttrell, future Duke of Somerset, a Garter knight, and guardian of this castle."

A Luttrell? Her happiness faded. Had another Luttrell already laid claim to the lairdship?

While she fretted, Sir James continued to address their group, introducing the other knights in his party. When she found Lachlan unexpectedly at her side, he leaned over slightly so only she could hear his words.

"Say nothing, Wife, you may regret."

CHAPTER 27

Lachlan silently cursed. They'd been on the trail to Edinburgh for two days and there had been no sight of Ethan's retinue. And according to the bishop, Ethan's group had only a half day lead. But no matter how hard Lachlan's team of eight rode, with fewer stops and short respites, they hadn't caught up with Ethan yet.

Lachlan was beginning to wonder if his brother's group was traveling to Fyvie at all. His twin could have told the bishop of his plans, then convinced his party to travel to another part Scotland. Or to Somerset, for that matter, to hide Rosalyn. There was no telling, because the Garter knights would follow Ethan's orders. They wouldn't suspect his twin was doing anything wrong. And if Ethan had the Golden Rose of Scotland, it would be easier to sell if he were traveling through England.

Bishop Passarelli must have sensed his uncertainty. He turned his horse around and met Lachlan at the edge of the trail where they'd stopped.

"Lachlan, have faith," the bishop said, holding both his

reins and his hands in prayer. "Although they elude us now, God's will is strong."

"We are at a disadvantage, Bishop. Between an Italian priest, an English Lord, and six English knights, none of us are very familiar with this countryside."

"*Si*, Lachlan, 'tis clear we are taking the most-traveled path, and I sense your discouragement every time we encounter a traveler going the opposite direction with no news of Ethan's party. If we don't meet up with them on the road, we will in Aberdeen."

Lachlan hoped what the bishop said was true. He was anxious about the safety of Rosalyn, but he would be more at ease if he knew she was already at Fyvie, where she had some support.

He hoped, too, that her people would welcome the real Lachlan Macpherson. But he needed to arrive in time to confront his brother, before Ethan was sworn in as laird and chieftain.

If he was too late, would there be a way to reverse the award? He had to expect that with the bishop's trust in God's will, all would be right soon.

* * *

ONCE INSIDE FYVIE'S castle walls, Rosalyn scanned the group of servants who'd lined up to greet them. As they dismounted in the lower bailey by the stables, it was not long before one of them came rushing toward her.

"Lady Rosalyn, you are home," the young girl gushed. "My prayers have been answered."

Rosalyn remembered her well. "Sweet Catherine. Aye, your lady has arrived home." She smiled at the young girl, but before she had a chance to ask Catherine how she was doing, the rest of the staff queued up behind her.

Ursula stood by Rosalyn while some of the men got busy putting away the horses. It was only Sir James and Lachlan who stayed behind.

At the moment, Rosalyn did not care what her traveling companions thought of her welcome. She was going to relish every moment of it. These people had served her for years and were like family. She was happy to greet each one of them personally.

After the last servant woman came forward with a little bow, she took both of Rosalyn's hands in hers.

"Greta!" Rosalyn immediately recognized her childhood nursemaid. Then Rosalyn threw tradition aside, drawing Greta into her arms. She gave her a hug with squeal of delight. "I've missed you so," she confessed softly in the care-taker's ear.

Greta held on and Rosalyn did the same, not wanting to let her nursemaid go as the memories came flooding back.

"Lady Rose," Greta whispered in that familiar, loving voice, "your mother and sister are prisoners somewhere in Aberdeen." The servant released her and bowed.

"So good to see you too, my lady," Greta said in a formal tone. The maid's eyes met hers and gave her a knowing look. "Good to have you home, my lady." She curtsied. "I shall wait 'til yer ready and escort ye to yer room."

While Rosalyn plastered a smile on her face for appear-ances and waved the staff back to work, her mind began to whirl. Her mother and sisters were prisoners? Somewhere in Aberdeen? She wished Greta could have given her more information.

But Rosalyn was determined to keep her combined anger and panic in check. Boundaries, allies, and castle ownership needed to be established with a cool head and a strong constitution.

Rosalyn turned to James and Lachlan with the same plastered smile she'd used to see the staff off. Both men, a few yards from her, stood in similar stances, arms crossing the body and legs spread wide as if their boots were roots reaching into the earth.

Does James know he's related to Lachlan? Perhaps *that's* what Lachlan wanted to keep secret when he'd threatened her at the gate.

She mimicked their stance and grew serious. "Men, I am home. This is my birthplace and where generations of my family have led Clan Macpherson." Secretly, she prayed that the two would hear her out. "My da, Dengas Macpherson, gave me the title of laird on his deathbed four years ago, but before he was buried and his body cold, Nicholas Luttrell stole Fyvie Castle from the Macphersons. Aye, he forced me, my mother, and my sister out." Rosalyn stood on her tiptoes wanting to appear taller. "I want it back."

Sir James and her husband both stared at her for a moment, neither speaking. She wondered if they'd consorted while she'd greeted the servants.

Could the two be brothers? Or were they distant cousins? Both men had tall, muscular frames, but that was where the similarities ended. Lachlan's sleek, black, and meticulously groomed hair and beard were a stark contrast to his brother's. James looked like a wild Norse God, his golden hair tossed wildly about his shoulders in the brisk evening breeze.

Finally, Sir James came forward, taking her hand and turning to Lachlan. "I welcome you both to Fyvie Castle," he said in a formal but warm tone. "Greta will show you to your chambers. Later, we will all meet in the great hall. If you are here to claim Fyvie, we have much to discuss."

Rosalyn wanted to talk now, but she was determined to keep up the appearance of a calm clan leader. No doubt, she'd have to be patient and let Sir James explain the process.

She felt less anxious, though, when Greta hooked her

arm. Striking a childhood chord, she wanted to skip across the lower bailey as they'd done when she was little, but Rosalyn held herself in check for Lachlan fell in step with James behind them.

The walk across the familiar lawn seemed both pleasant and torturous. Of course, being reunited with a loved one, even if wasn't her mother or sister, made Rosalyn want to weep with joy.

On the other hand, she was anxious, too, because Lachlan and James would have private time together. Even though they were married and he carried her name, they were still both vying for Fyvie.

When Greta and Rosalyn reached Fyvie's keep, she stopped and turned to watch the two men deep in conversation. They had cut to the right and were going into the main entrance.

"Greta, you trust me, don't you," she asked in a hushed whisper even though they were alone. When Greta nodded, she continued with a request. "I need you to follow me, but don't ask any questions." When Greta nodded again, Rosalyn started across the bailey, walking quickly with her nursemaid at her heels. If it wouldn't have drawn the attention of the guards on the parapets, she would have broken into a run.

Once they'd reached the horse stables, Rosalyn took a sharp turn at the corner and headed toward the entrance. Pushing Greta ahead of her, the servant followed her pantomimed directions until they entered the well-appointed horse barn.

Once inside, Rosalyn pressed a finger to nursemaid's lips, then led her by the hand through the back of the stables. Rosalyn needed to search Lachlan's satchel before anyone else did. She'd watched the groomsmen lead the warhorse away with the bag attached to the saddle. Surely, his destrier would be feeding by now.

After winding around a few rows of empty stalls, Rosalyn found success. The massive bay was chomping on some fresh straw and looked to be in good spirits, giving her a whinny when she approached his stall.

Rubbing his snout cautiously, she noticed his bucket was empty. Good, she thought, he should be approachable.

Motioning to Greta stay on guard, Rosalyn quietly entered the stall and began searching for Lachlan's bulky satchel, hoping a stable hand hadn't already taken it first.

Kicking straw with her boots, she scanned the stall in the dim, late-afternoon light. She noticed right away that the saddle had been removed and placed on a rack. Her stomach sank first with disappointment, then did flip-flops when Greta coughed.

"Hello, good sir," she said brightly to someone outside as Rosalyn dove for the floor and covered herself in straw.

CHAPTER 28

The straw was scratchy, stifling, and made Rosalyn want to sneeze. She grabbed her nose and pinched it between her thumb and middle finger trying to keep it under control.

Greta was talking to someone outside, and it was important for her to stay buried, but now that she was under the straw, she couldn't hear a thing. As much as she wanted to hold her breath, she knew that wouldn't work and did her best to stay still, hoping Greta could manage. Luckily for Rosalyn, just when another sneeze threatened, Greta called her name loudly enough for her to hear.

Tossing the straw off in all directions, Rosalyn inhaled a deep breath and rose to her feet just as Greta poked her head over the gate. The nursemaid grinned broadly, then reassured her, "He's gone. Yer safe."

"*Achoo!*" Rosalyn wrinkled her nose. "Greta, you helped me hide from Rowen when I was little. Nothing's changed, has it?"

Although she was still smiling, Greta's eyes clouded with concern. "My lady, nothing's changed in my heart, but much has changed here at Fyvie. Although it may be gossip, the servants who travel about Aberdeen say Mary and Rowen have been jailed."

Rosalyn sobered. "Oh, Greta, I hold no power here. How will I find my mother and sister?"

"My lady, no one is certain when they were last seen at Fyvie, but I know it was before Sir James arrived. Although he appears to be a rigid leader of men and merciless knight, he's quite the contrary."

Greta's confession made Rosalyn wonder how James could be a son of Nicholas Luttrell's if he were not consumed by land ownership.

"Greta, I'm pleased to know Sir James is as noble as the Garter knights are fabled to be, and thankful it was not he who is responsible for their disappearance. As I get my bearings, he may be someone I can trust, but until then, I have many who I cannot."

Her nursemaid gave her a sympathetic smile. "Yet, there are many ye can trust, my lady. Like that stable boy who stopped here moments ago."

"You can trust him?"

"Thaddeus said he was sent to fetch the satchel for ye husband." She grinned again. "I lied and told him another had taken it, but then straight away, I asked for God's forgiveness."

The satchel. "If that's why he'd come, then it must still be here." Rosalyn spun around in her spot. Her eyes finally adjusting to the dim light as she scanned the stall again. Then she spotted it. She'd walked right by the bulky thing.

With the warhorse content in the other corner, she rushed to the bag and yanked the flap up revealing a soft dark green blanket inside. Excited about the prospect of what she'd find, Rosalyn dropped to her knees and set the satchel down so she could reach both hands inside. Gingerly she removed the mysterious bundle.

Greta poked her head over at that moment. "What is it, Rose?"

She smiled up to the only person other than her da who dared call her Rose. Greta was like her father in many ways, strong, bold, with no tolerance for injustice.

"I'm about to find out. Keep watch a bit longer," Rosalyn pleaded, her hands shaking while she began to unwrap the blanket.

Once she had the green blanket unfolded, she discovered a purple, velvet cloak beneath. After she worked with the cloak, a bulky shape began to emerge.

Rosalyn's heart beat faster as she gently unrolled what she hoped was the Rose from the last piece of fabric.

Aah. Even though she'd seen it before, the gift from the pope was breathtaking. The gems gleamed despite the low glow of light.

She gave the Golden Rose a quick assessment and was happy to find all the roses, stems, and jewels in place. It was only the oil that had seeped out of the top in transport. Otherwise, it was in as good condition as the day the bishop had proudly paraded it before the nobles at Berwick Castle.

Rosalyn breathed a sigh of relief as she quickly rolled the object back in the cloak, then rewrapped the blanket, swaddling the rose and gently pushing the bundle back into the satchel.

After closing the stable door behind her, she gave Greta a huge hug.

"You were the best of your da's girls," Greta said whistfully after Rosalyn released her.

Rosalyn smiled. "Come, I am in need of a hiding place for this," she said, patting the bundle.

Greta's eyes crinkled when she grinned at Rosalyn. The

nurse was in her elder years, with graying hair, but she moved with the grace of a dancer despite her age. The maid waved her to follow. "I have the perfect spot."

Greta led them out of the stables the way they'd entered, then continued along the castle's south wall. Luckily for Rosalyn, the Rose wasn't heavy and she was able to walk naturally with it hidden under her cloak, following Greta around the perimeter and into the armory.

After producing a sizable iron key from deep within her apron pocket, Greta turned it, unlocking the massive armory door, and the two slid silently inside.

The cavernous room was one of Rosalyn's favorite hiding places and she hadn't been surprised when Greta decided to take her here.

Her nursemaid handed Rosalyn the key. "You have the twin to this," she reminded her.

"Aye, my skeleton key." She paused, remembering. "Mine unlocks all the important doors in the castle from the outside or inside." She had fond memories of how this key had helped her escape many scrapes as a child.

Rosalyn placed her hand against her thigh, happy to find her pouch full of precious items lay safe beneath her skirts. She needed the key to access the final hiding place. With all the traveling by horseback and a change of clothes, she'd forgotten to see if it was still securely tied around her leg until now.

Flipping up her skirt to gain access, she loosened the furry bag from its hiding place, opened the pouch and drew out the key.

Walking past the new lances, maces, and shields, Rosalyn made her way to the farthest corner where the oldest weapons were stored.

There it sat, just as her she'd remembered it: the Viking treasure chest.

"Do you recall the fables you used to tell?" Rosalyn asked, motioning to the maid to join her as she knelt down before the old chest. She opened it with her skeleton key and carefully placed the entire satchel inside.

"That your da had been captured by a great Viking raider named Strykar and had barely escaped with his head, yet alone the Norseman's wool?" Greta asked, giving her a no-nonsense expression. "Those werenae fables," the nursemaid said in a flat tone.

"Well then, tell me again how da came to have this chest," Rosalyn said, raising a suspicious brow.

"Just because you are all grown up doesnae mean you are any smarter," Greta replied with a smirk and a nod.

Rosalyn scrunched up her face and pursed her lips. That was the face she'd given Greta when she hadn't believed the nurse's tales.

Greta laughed. "Come sit by me like old times, before the men start looking for us."

Rosalyn let out a tiny squeal and almost climbed into Greta's lap.

Once she was settled, Greta brushed the stray stands from Rosalyn's brow. "Your da was quite the explorer in the early days of building his wool trade. Before he was your da and before he was laird of Aberdeen."

Rosalyn's heart filled with pride as she was reminded how adventurous, enterprising, and brave her father had been.

"'Twas on his second trip by boat to Norway that your father and his soldiers landed on the southern coast in a port city known as Oslo."

Most of the Macpherson's family wool was brought back to the Highlands from France, but now she remembered in the early days, it wasn't.

"When yer father first started, he traded with the Vikings of Norway and one in particular, a Norseman named

Strykar. He was a giant. Taller than any man your father had ever met. Your da described him as a barbarian, eating raw fish and killing men with his bare hands.

"Strykar was a suspicious man and he didnae believe your father had come to barter for the wool, but to steal it. When you da gave him deer skins in exchange for the sheep's wool, the Viking spat on them, saying they were inferior.

"Not long after, your father and his men were locked in a prison and marked for death. Fortunately for your da, a Frenchman he knew was in Oslo and heard about your da's plight. He traded with your da, giving him superior furs for the deer skins, allowing the Viking to get a fair trade and the Frenchman to aid in your father's release.

"But over the years, Strykar and your da became friends. When winters came, the Vikings brought the wool. They had no qualms about sailing the frigid seas or walking our frozen winter lands. But after they delivered the wool and your da invited them to visit the last time, the giant and his men wiped out all his stores of mead, not to mention fought and killed his own on Fyvie's land. After a few weeks of this behavior, your da was ready for them to leave. But he knew he couldnae just order them away, so he concocted a plan."

Rosalyn found herself entranced by Greta's tale, just as she had been as a young lass, hanging on to every word. She really didn't care if the story was real or imagined, it was about her da.

"Do you remember your cousin Rebecca?"

Rosalyn nodded. She was her da's sister's only daughter. Although Rosalyn never liked speaking ill of anyone, she had to admit that a union with Rebecca would be a sentence to damnation.

"Your da told Strykar one night in the great hall at dinner that he would honor the Viking giant with an engagement to Rebecca and introduced them. Your da insisted the Norseman's reputation would be damaged and his God, Odin, would wreak havoc on every one of his family members in Norway if he didn't agree to the proposal."

Rosalyn covered her mouth with both hands.

"You must remember the woman had a shrill voice that sounded like a screeching goat with a face to match."

Rosalyn burst out laughing.

"Well, the threat worked. Strykar and his men were gone before the sun rose the next day and either they left their chest of treasures in haste, or as payment for their freedom.

Your da didn't care, for he was happy to be rid of them," Greta finished, dusting her hands off as if to rid herself of something disgusting.

Whether truth or no, Rosalyn's heart was full of happiness to be back at Fyvie, even with so much uncertainty swirling around her. She gave Greta another generous hug, then turned her skeleton key in the oversized chest, locking the Golden Rose of Scotland safely away.

In moments, her key was stashed in the safety of her skirts again and she was making her way with Greta to her childhood room, anxious to find out if it looked anything like it had when she'd been forced out by Nicholas Luttrell.

Bishop Passarelli had kept Lachlan's spirits high along the last of the trail that led to Fyvie Castle, but he was hanging on to his last strand of patience when Rosalyn's home finally came into view.

Approaching the gate, Lachlan gripped the reins of his destrier, anxious to make inquiries. Were his brother and Rosalyn behind these walls?

While the gate ground nosily and the jagged bottom of the iron portcullis raised like sharp teeth, a group of mounted knights galloped forward and met them halfway on the bridge.

The bishop held his rein-wrapped hands in prayer before his chest as he spoke. "Good Garter Knights, we have been sent by King James to find a missing wife and his Golden Rose. Our sources tell us they both are within your fortress."

Lachlan reined his horse beside the bishop's and studied the mounted men before them. *Hostile or hospitable?* As much as he wanted to tell the knights he was the new laird of Fyvie and chieftain of the Aberdeen clan, he was uncertain what awaited them.

One of the Garter knights moved forward. "Who requests this entrance?"

"I am Bishop Passarelli, a missionary of the pope." He turned and gestured to his group. "And this is my escort. Will you welcome and assist us?"

These could not have been the same men who'd left Berwick-upon-Tweed with Rosalyn just four days ago.

"I am Sir James Luttrell, custodian of castle Fyvie and a Knight of the Garter. We welcome friends of King James and the pope," he said and steered his horse to the side as did the rest, allowing their group to enter.

Once inside, Lachlan studied Sir James as the men dismounted and Fyvie's squires rushed to attend to their horses.

A Luttrell? He'd never heard his father speak of a Sir James. Perhaps a distant cousin?

Sir James clapped his hands and the servants lined up ready to serve. "See these men to their quarters," James said crisply, like a man used to commanding, and the servants scurried forward, waving them to follow.

The bishop took at a slight bow. "Thank you for your welcome, but before we take advantage of your hospitality, I do have a few questions if you will entertain walking with us."

The knight did not appear to be put off by the request and fell in step with Lachlan and the bishop. The holy man had a way about him that put everyone at ease, and this included Sir James.

Walking with purpose and hands in prayer, the short-legged bishop kept stride for stride with the hulking knight. "You said you are custodian of this castle." He took a little pause, then turned to look up at the knight looming tall above. "May I ask what that means?"

Lachlan wasn't surprised the bishop was so direct, but he was taken aback at Sir James's deep laughter.

"Good Bishop, you may ask me anything you like. I am bound by the Garter pledge to be honest and forthright in all things as I serve my English king. I've been instructed to keep particular information to only a privy few and will let you know if I cannot answer your questions."

Lachlan believed Sir James to be forthright and so far, he had no reason to think he would be anything but honest.

"However, if you want privacy, and it appears you are in earnest to seek answers before we meet again in the very public great hall, then follow me."

The knight steered them down a corridor that veered off to the right and he then led them down a winding staircase to a secluded room that appeared to be a place where the knights of the castle would meet and plan attacks. The walls of the room were completely lined with weapons of all kinds. Six massive trestle tables, crowded by long benches, occupied the middle of the retreat.

"I can assure you we will not be overheard in this chamber," James promised, closing the heavy, latticed wood and iron door behind them.

After the Garter knight gestured for them to take a seat at one of the tables, the bishop cleared his throat and began again.

"Thank you, good sir, for this privacy. If not for the weapons, it reminds me of some of my prayer sanctuaries back in Rome," he said wistfully, as if longing for home and the comfort of a quiet and celibate life.

Lachlan relaxed his jaw. A Luttrell family member could be a help or a hindrance. Because he'd not been formally introduced yet, Lachlan hoped he'd have time to determine which surname, Luttrell or Macpherson, would serve him best before he'd have to commit.

"Now, then," the knight began, "you asked about my custodianship."

The bishop's tight gray curls bounced when he nodded, making Sir James smile with amusement. As always, the holy man was unassuming for his high position and childlike in his enthusiasm.

"'Tis a long story, but the short of it is my father is dead and this was his property," the knight admitted.

Lachlan smothered his surprise. Sir James was more than a relation, he was his half-brother.

The bishop placed a hand on James's arm. "My Son, I am sorry for your loss."

James paused for a moment as if wanting to choose his words carefully. After blinking hard, he finally said, "He was not a good man, and he will not be missed."

"I will pray for his soul," the bishop promised and said a silent prayer. When he opened his eyes he and leaned forward, as if to gossip. "Then you are here to establish order?"

James nodded. "Since I arrived shortly after my father's death a week ago, there have been claims made and demands raised. I had at least a half-dozen yesterday, one today, demanding the castle," James admitted as if frustrated by the obligation.

The bishop nodded in a sympathetic way and patted the knight's arm. "No doubt a burden you wish to unsaddle. How will you go about reviewing the claims?"

James's weary expression drew a little darker. "In the great hall on the morrow, I will preside over a hearing of all petitions. Those who are daring to claim the lairdship must prove they are worthy."

Then the knight's expression lightened. "But you are not here to make a claim. Tell me more about the missing wife and the Golden Rose you speak of. Why do you believe they are here?"

The bishop continued to keep James engaged in the conversation and after the most pertinent information about the journey to Fyvie was shared, James waited patiently for the bishop to explain the rest.

"My story too, is long." The bishop sighed. "But like you said, I'll get to the short end of it. A gift of great significance, priceless some would say, is missing and we believe a guest of yours may have it in hiding."

James crossed his arms and looked back and forth between the bishop and Lachlan.

The bishop leaned forward, clasping his hands together. "*Si*, this gift was intended for the King of Scots, a gift from Pope Innocent VIII, called the Golden Rose," the bishop told James, his tightly gripped hands shaking. "I will not be able to return to Italy, to my home, until it is delivered to its rightful owner."

James seemed moved by the bishop's plea. The more he observed his half-brother, the less he appeared to be like his other sibling. Lachlan was grateful that James appeared genuinely interested in the bishops concerns when he asked, "Do you know why this priceless Rose would be here at Fyvie?"

"I suspect it may be with a man who claims to be laird of this castle. He's traveling with a woman," the bishop said.

James eyes narrowed. "We've had so many guests arrive in a fortnight, most who claim to be the new laird. But there was one who traveled here with a woman today." He cast his gaze to the ceiling. "From Edinburgh, I believe," he finished, then looked over at Lachlan.

When James finished speaking, Lachlan tried to keep his expression from changing, but inside his heart leapt.

Could she be here?

"A beauty with fire-red hair. For certain you would have noticed this lady," the bishop offered.

Lachlan expected James to move his attention back to the bishop when he spoke of Rosalyn, but he continued to watch Lachlan.

"Is this lady your wife?" James asked Lachlan directly.

The bishop turned slightly red.

"*Scusami*, where are my manners?" the bishop said. "This is Sir Lachlan, and his new wife is the other missing Rose."

"Her name is Rosalyn," Lachlan stated flatly. "She may allow the bishop to call her Rose, but reserves it for a select few." He glanced at the bishop and offered an apologetic smile, then he turned to James with concern in his voice. "I suspect she was taken here."

James kept his eyes on Lachlan. "Against her will?"

"Or she's run away," Lachlan suggested awkwardly. He hadn't considered that a possibility until now. "She has family in Aberdeen," Lachlan offered.

"The castle grounds are vast. We have hundreds and hundreds under roof," James said, "but you are welcome to seek both missing Roses." He looked directly at the bishop. "I trust you will protect the privacy of others in your search."

The bishop's graying curls bounced in agreement.

Then James's attention turned back to Lachlan. "And you, Brother, we have much to talk about."

"B-Brother?" Lachlan replied.

"I've met your twin and your wife," James said stoically, then paused and stared at Lachlan. "How is it that our father, Nicholas, named you both Lachlan?" Then he cocked his head. "Perhaps because like me, no one could tell the two of you apart?"

CHAPTER 30

Rosalyn spun in a circle with her arms outstretched as if she were ten years old again. Her chamber. She was finally back in her chamber. She turned and turned until she collapsed into a tangled pile of dress and giggles on the tapestried floor while Greta watched her from a seat by the hearth, just like she had when she was little.

Rosalyn gazed about her childhood room full of beauty and whimsy. Unicorns galloped across the walls, painted by one of Aberdeen's most acclaimed artisans. Her white-canopied bed sported bright-red velvet drapes, where she'd spent hours hiding and playing games.

"Aye, Rose, the other servants and I fought to keep it the same as when ye left," Greta said proudly.

Rosalyn glanced over at her former nursemaid just as she was swiping a tear from her cheek.

"We prayed you would be back as rightful heiress, and here ye be," Greta gushed.

Rightful heiress? Yes, that's what she would like to believe as she rushed to the hearth and sat at the feet of the woman who'd been like a mother to her. "Do I dare to dream the people of Aberdeen, our clan, and the servants at Fyvie, will welcome me back?" She gazed up at Greta. "To allow me to lead?"

With a loving gesture, Greta brushed the stray hair from her brow. "Darling Rose, I cannae speak for the clan, nor the people of Aberdeen, but I can tell you with all the confidence in my soul, the servants of Fyvie love you and will follow you anywhere you lead us, just like your da."

The words warmed her heart and had her beaming inside with pride. If only she could rid herself of Lachlan and gain the trust of the clan and the people of Aberdeen, then she would find a man, a righteous, brave Highlander to join her in the wool trade. Perhaps they'd even venture to Norway together to barter for some of the finest wools of all the kingdoms.

As Greta stroked her hair, Rosalyn's dreams lifted her spirits. Her nursemaid had shared the news, that the Garter Knight Sir James, current custodian of Fyvie, would hold court on the morrow and make judgement on all the claims for her castle.

How dare others come forward to seek what is rightly mine?

"Why are you frowning, child?" Greta asked, bringing her out of her musings.

"Oh, Greta, I must find a way to win Fyvie. I have to convince Sir James that the castle should be mine."

Greta gazed down at her with that loving wisdom that can't be forced or faked. "Darling, Rose, do not trouble your pretty head over those details." She grinned widely. "Leave it to me. I will show you, and Sir James, who should be rightful heiress of Fyvie. Will you trust me?" Greta asked, her gray hair shining bright from the flaming light behind her.

Rosalyn nodded.

"Good," she said. "'Tis settled, now no more fretting." She

*tsk*ed. "You pretty yourself up, and I shall see you in the great hall for the evening meal."

Rosalyn sighed, but nodded in acceptance. Sometimes it felt good to be bossed about by someone who loved her. She still missed her mother, and the news that she could be in prison somewhere in Aberdeen with her sister worried her terribly, but for now, she had to focus on gaining control and then she could rescue her family.

After Greta let herself out, Rosalyn was surprised to find a number of newly sown gowns in her wardrobe. What Greta had said was true, they'd been planning her return.

Now, what to do about Lachlan and the hearing in the morning? She felt so conflicted. Before the marriage, Lachlan had been charming, attentive, even doting at times, making her hate the English less. But then on the way to Aberdeen, he'd been cold, insulting, and distant. When they'd been close, he'd been demanding. She was grateful to have remained a virgin, but threating him with public humiliation had kept him away.

Now that she looked back upon the events leading up to their union, Rosalyn was certain Lachlan had only pretended to be smitten with her. Acting, to convince her that the idea of marriage would set things right. For they truly were not.

But if Greta was certain the servants and those beyond the castle walls would support her leadership, then she wouldn't need Lachlan and she could follow through with an annulment after all.

A light rapping sound on her chamber door shattered her solitude. And before she had a chance to make an inquiry, Ursula seemed to magically appear.

"Oh, my, are you a witch?" Rosalyn asked with breathless surprise. "I could swear you materialized out of the air."

Ursula gave her a smug smile. "Witch or healer, which am I? Perhaps both," she said, her eyes gleaming mysteriously.

Rosalyn rushed to her friend and grabbed her hands. "How is Joshua faring? I've been so wrapped up in my own needs, I had not looked into how your Highlander was doing."

Ursula squeezed her hands. "Do not worry, he's been in my good care and is improving enough for me to seek you out and share some information with you."

"Information? Like spy information?" Rosalyn asked, rubbing her hands together.

Ursula took her one hand and let it swing between them. "Aye, like spy information. Come." She led her to Rosalyn's bed. The two climbed up and settled in the middle of the whimsical flower-covered comforter. Still in her linen sheath, Rosalyn shivered more out of excitement than from a chill.

"Tell me, spy, what have you uncovered?"

"Ethan is here with Bishop Passarelli," she whispered excitedly, as if there were spies listening in from the outer passage or outside the window.

Rosalyn capped her hand over her mouth. If Ethan was here, he might challenge her claim to Fyvie. He was Nicholas Luttrell's son, too.

"Why do you think he's here, and why do you think the bishop is with him?"

"Good questions, but I donna have those answers. I wanted to warn you that trouble was brewing."

"Do you think the bishop believes Lachlan has the Golden Rose? Perhaps Ethan made the bishop believe that he has it and they've followed us here with a plan to defame Lachlan and take everything from him." She paused and swallowed hard. "From me."

Ursula must have picked up on the fear in her voice for her friend put an arm about her shoulder. "Now, I didnae come here to worry you, but to warn you of what you could be facing. When the bishop and Ethan arrived, the Garter knight who is the custodian, took them to a special meeting room. The two did not even take water or rest before they walked with the knight to speak."

Even though Ursula was trying to assure her that what she was saying was helpful, it complicated the situation even more. Rosalyn shivered again, but now because of the dire circumstances.

Ursula must have noticed, for she gave her a sisterly hug, making Rosalyn grateful for the support. But with her da gone and her husband estranged, Rosalyn's only hope for male support was Bishop Passarelli.

"I must speak to the bishop," Rosalyn said finally.

"Aye, he's the only one you can trust," Ursula agreed.

But then Rosalyn began to think the worst. "If Lachlan, James, and Ethan are blood brothers, who's to say they couldnae all three band against me and take back the castle that their father had stolen from my da in the first place."

With a sober nod, Ursula gave her another hug. "Come, let me dress you to be the heiress you shall become."

* * *

ETHAN'S PLAN TO have the Golden Rose and Fyvie was unraveling. With the news that his brother and Bishop Passarelli had arrived, he was going to have to resort to the kind of deviant behavior that would make his father proud. Walking briskly, he reached the chamber door the servants said belonged to Rosalyn.

Without knocking, he burst into the room and startled the two women inside.

Ursula stopped lacing the corset that bound Rosalyn into an emerald-colored gown that hugged all her curves in the right places.

For a moment, Ethan was speechless and so were the women. It was Ursula who responded first, returning to her work and finishing the last tie. Then she gave Rosalyn's rump a quick pat.

"There ye are, love. You are ready." The maid turned to face him and delivered an ugly sneer. "It appears your husband wants a word with you."

She gave Rosalyn a hug, and when the healer walked by him on her way out, she watched Ethan through wary eyes. If he had been the cowardly type, he would have sworn Ursula gave him the evil eye. But he shook it off after she passed and she left the chamber quietly.

"Why must you enter my room so abruptly?" Rosalyn asked. "You promised me you wouldnae treat me like property."

She put her hands on her hips and glared at him. The angrier she was, the more beautiful. Actually, if he had his way and worked his plan, she'd be angry all the time.

But Ethan had no time for love or the soft pleasantries of keeping a wife happy. Ignoring her plea, he walked toward her now, circled her waist and with one quick movement, slapped her hard across the face.

CHAPTER 31

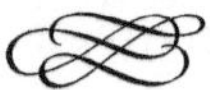

Rosalyn staggered back. Stars circled before her eyes. She went limp in Lachlan's arms, her legs buckled, and she gingerly touched the spot on her face where he'd struck her. The pain in her jaw was excruciating, and she tried to move it a little to make sure it wasn't broken. Closing her eyes in reaction to the pain, she dared not open them. She hung limp against him, hoping he'd think she'd passed out.

Through the fog of her pain, and fighting a rising nausea, she could not imagine what she'd done to prompt his anger. Had he found out it was she who had stolen his satchel?

Lachlan said nothing now as he lifted her into his arms. But instead of walking toward the bed, where she had imagined he would rape her, he walked toward the chamber door instead.

"Say a word or voice an objection, and I'll break your neck," Lachlan said in a harsh whisper.

Although she was only half-conscious, she understood his threat and kept still, her head lay across his forearm.

Through tiny slits in her eyelids, she watched the ceiling

of her chamber pass by as they entered the corridor. Lachlan strode quickly while she squinted through her lashes, recognizing every turn he took. But as much as she hoped they'd encounter someone, anyone, no one crossed their path.

But her panic began to rise when he started down the stairs to the dungeons. Even if she wasn't dazed from the slap to her face, she couldn't do much to fight him, and there was nothing to prevent him from hitting her again.

As her mind spun in the pain and agony of her current state, a tiny cloud of reason began to emerge. Of course, she thought, he wanted her out of the way for the hearing in the morning. It would be Lachlan standing before Sir James as either Macpherson or Luttrell, whatever surname gave him best advantage. And he would consort with his brothers for the sole right to Fyvie.

As much as she believed a woman could walk in a man's path, she needed to accept that no titled man would support her claim to be laird.

Rosalyn fought back tears, still wanting Lachlan to believe she'd passed out from his blow, while he fumbled with a key in the cell door until it clicked.

Somehow, he managed to kick the ancient door open, and it groaned as if speaking for her pain.

Rosalyn was grateful that he didn't just drop her on the floor once they were in inside. Instead, he lay her down on the cool stone floor which provided some relief to her damaged cheek.

She almost held her breath, but she remembered she wasn't playing dead, just helpless, while she listened.

Finally, she let out her breath when the key turned in the lock and his footsteps faded away.

The tears began to fall as she sat up and hugged her knees. Tucked tightly into a ball, she opened her eyes and assessed her surroundings. Even though she wasn't happy about where she was, Rosalyn was grateful she'd only been slapped, not a beaten or raped.

To her relief, the dungeon was not as bad as she'd imagined. A sconce burned in the outer hallway, confirming that Lachlan had planned this all along.

But when Rosalyn turned to inspect the cell behind her, she almost screamed. There, in the corner, lay two women huddled together, unmoving.

Surely, if they were sleeping, they would have been disturbed when Lachlan had entered the cell, but she hadn't noticed any sound or movement coming from the corner.

Moving slowly as not to threaten or startle the women, she rose to her feet and began to inch toward them.

Once she was closer, her heart leapt and she fell to her knees before the pile of humanity. A weak hand reached toward her. "Do not trouble yourself, good princess. We have been prisoners here for as long as we can remember."

* * *

As Ethan walked up the circular stone stairs from the dungeon, he was pleased at how easy it had been to lock Rosalyn away. At least the first part of his plan was complete.

Next, Lachlan.

After that, there was the business of finding the Rose. That idiot stable boy he sent to retrieve his satchel never returned. The lad was so nondescript, Ethan couldn't even find him to levy punishment.

Fortunately for Ethan, he'd befriended a young squire at Edinburgh who'd agreed to be his apprentice. Like him in spirit, the boy had already helped procure Fyvie's dungeon key. Then he'd spied on the bishop and Lachlan for him. Now he was certain he could count on his loyalty to help with his brother, as he made his way toward Lachlan's chamber.

When his spies told him Lachlan and bishop had arrived today, Ethan had to assume Lachlan had followed him here to find Rosalyn. With time ticking away, and very little of it left to accomplish his plan, Ethan must now restort to extreme measures to keep Rosalyn and Lachlan from the hearing tomorrow.

He had just rounded the corner of the corridor that would bring him to Lachlan's door when he came within inches of colliding with Bishop Passarelli.

They both took a step back. The bishop seemed startled. "There you are, Lachlan," the holy man said, taking his arm, "I was hoping to talk to you before dinner."

Ethan had to think quickly before they arrived at Lachlan's chamber. "Good Bishop." Ethan spoke to mimic Lachlan as he had with Rosalyn. "I was looking for you as well, but my chamber is being cleaned." He shrugged helplessly. "It is full of servants."

Ethan steered them around in the corridor and nodded to his squire as they rounded about to head the other direction.

With the subtleness of a spy, the squire nodded back, then took off toward Lachlan's chamber.

"*Si*, Lachlan. We can talk here as long as there's no one to listen in," the holy man said, lowering his voice and glancing over his shoulder where the squire had been.

When he looked the other way and all was clear, the bishop leaned in toward him. "Lachlan, as I promised earlier, I will find Rosalyn and tell her what has happened. Surely, she must think Ethan is you and may take a pledge before Sir James tomorrow for Fyvie Castle. Once that happens, it will be difficult to reverse the judgment." He paused and swept his gaze up and down the corridor again.

When he was certain they were still alone, the bishop

continued. "You said yourself, you wouldn't put it past Ethan to do something irrational if he found out you were here. I thought you had agreed to stay in hiding . . ." he said with concern, peering up at him.

Ethan nodded. "Yes, Bishop, I will have my evening meal in my chambers like we discussed. But you don't know the extent of the wagging tongues of the servant maids. As soon as they are finished, I'll be back in hiding." Ethan shrugged again and the bishop patted his back.

"*Scusami* for my overprotectiveness. I understand how much your brother's deviant ways disturb you and I will continue to keep my vow to do everything in my power to help you, as you've promised to help me find the missing Golden Rose."

Just then, a group of servants came around the corner. Bawdy laugher bounced down the once quiet hall. Shortly after spotting Ethan and the bishop, the rowdy servant's hushed whispers replaced their bad manners.

Then the holy man turned to Ethan and said, "God be with you." And without further circumstance, the bishop followed the servants around the corner. Ethan spun on his heel and headed back to Lachlan's chamber.

Cracking the door slightly, Ethan set his eye to the tiny opening and peered in. As he'd hoped, the squire sat on watch in a chair while Lachlan appeared to be asleep in the chamber bed.

Ethan eased himself inside, then closed and bolted the door behind him.

"Did it work?" Ethan asked Benjamin.

"Aye, sir, the work is done," the boy answered, pointing to the tray on the chest across the room. A good portion of the food had been eaten, but not all.

"Does he have a fever?" Ethan asked, walking closer to the

bed to peer down on his brother, whose face was clammy and pale.

The boy shrugged. "He has been moaning while I have been at his side."

For a moment, Ethan found himself wracked with a terrible sense of dread, as if staring at his mother, burning with fever from the berries he'd given her before she died.

He tried to shake the memory, but it hung on like a witch to her wicked spell. Ethan had few regrets. Killing his mother was one of them.

Yes, he'd tried to lie and place the blame on his twin brother. Ethan had been destroyed by her death. All he wanted was the pain to go away and it to be someone else's fault. That time he'd been innocent.

Lachlan's groan shook the nightmares from his thoughts, reminding him that was another time and place.

Focusing on what he had to do, Ethan reached out to his brother's brow and found it burning with fever. Satisfied with the poison's work so far, he began stripping off his tunic.

"We can move him now. But first, you'll need to dress him in my clothes." He tugged off one boot while he continued the plan in his mind. "Have you found a discreet path to the dungeon?"

"I located a tunnel the servants use to drop bedding to the lower level. The opening is down the hall."

The boy had promise.

CHAPTER 32

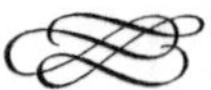

"Mother, 'tis me, Rosalyn," she whispered. Both the women were rail thin and it appeared they had not bathed in weeks.

"Nay, you cannae be my Rosalyn," her mother said softly. "She is in Berwick-upon-Tweed with my brother, Angus, securing Fyvie Castle for us."

Rosalyn wanted to weep for the dream of coming back to Fyvie in full glory that had been dashed because she'd married an Englishman. A man she had hoped would learn to love her and she him. Now, that would never come to be, for she hated him with all her heart, like an enemy.

Rosalyn hung her head and sobbed before them. How could she claim to be family when she'd let them down? She would not blame them if they wanted to disown her and demand she take the Luttrell name.

Rosalyn continued to cry, unsure if they were coherent enough to communicate with her. She wished there was something she could have done to change the course of events.

A gentle touch on her forehead made her pause for a

moment. The feeble fingers weren't firm, but the gentle gesture of sweeping her bangs off her brow was genuine enough for her eyes to open.

There, gazing at her, was her mother's sweet face, full of recognition and love.

Rosalyn grinned through her tears and glanced over to her sister, Rowen, who threw her arms around Rosalyn.

Her mother put her arms around them both. Being reunited with her family made her heart soar and her disappointment disappear.

After a few moments of sheer happiness, Rosalyn drew back and took a closer look at the two women.

"How are you? Have you been here since I left for England?"

Her sister and mother looked at each other as if uncertain where to begin.

"You tell her, Mother," Rowen instructed.

Rosalyn let out a grateful sigh. Even though she'd barely recognized her mother and sister at first, now that they were sitting side by side, the two appeared more tired than traumatized.

Her sister grabbed her hands and squeezed them tightly. "Wasnae long after you left for Berwick-upon-Tweed that we came back to Fyvie thinking it was safe again. But a sennight later, Nicholas Luttrell had returned. Our original instincts were to leave as soon as we could, but then we reconsidered, believing we could hide until he left again.

"He was distracted by a Knight of the Garter. Wasnae interested in finding us at the moment, but getting revenge against this knight."

Rowen threw a cautionary glance toward their mother. "But then I was too bold and snuck into my chamber to sleep one night rather than in the servants' quarters, and he caught me in the hallway."

Her mother put her both hands across her heart. "I donna blame Rowen for the two of us being thrown in the dungeon. First, he put her down here, but I was caught trying to help her escape," her mother explained. "But we havnae see him in weeks. I am not sure what has happened, but the servants donna know we are here. British sentries, with ugly dispositions, are sent twice a day with bad food. When this new one entered with you, we just wanted to be invisible here in the corner."

Even though they were all prisoners at the moment, Rosalyn was happy. Her mother reached over to brush the bangs way from her face again like she had when she was little.

With the corners of her eyes crinkling into soft lines, her mother cocked her head to the side. "Now, darling Rosalyn, how is it that you have fallen into the same fate? What of my brother, Angus?"

Rosalyn let out a long sigh. "Well, we arenae leaving here anytime soon, so I have plenty of time to tell my tale. While you were dealing with one Luttrell, I was dealing with another."

The time passed quickly and after a few more tears, Rosalyn had explained how Angus had gotten sick en route to Berwickshire and she'd left him in a monastery to recover. And most importantly, how and why she'd agreed to be married to an Englishman.

"So you see why I despise the Luttrells even more than before?" Rosalyn asked, her story finished. And none too soon, for footsteps echoed down the corridor, and fear grabbed at her heart again.

"Shh," her mother warned.

Rosalyn pointed toward the darkest corner of the cell. Her mother and sister moved quickly and silently to huddled in the shadows, as Rosalyn return to the spot on the cell floor where Lachlan had left her. She hoped he was checking to see if she was still unconscious, or better yet, it was the sentry with food.

As she lay on her side, the cool, hard surface of the floor eased the last of the burning pain in her cheek, but Rosalyn was not prepared for the sound of more than one pair of boots.

As she lay facing away from the cell door, the way she'd been left by Lachlan, Rosalyn fought the urge to turn and follow what was happening in the corridor. Her common sense—no, fear—won over. Instead, she lay as still as possible, straining to hear more of what was going on outside the cell.

The echoing footsteps grew louder and closer. Then the cadence turned to scuffling just a few feet from where she lay. The cell door opened across from hers.

"This one here. I have the key," a voice mumbled in a hushed tone. More shuffling followed, then the cell door opened and shut. A loud groan surprised her. Clearly, this was not a sentry with food.

Another groan sounded from across the dungeon. That ignited a second round of swearing. Then silence.

"What's going on?" a groggy male voice questioned.

The only response was a loud *thwack*. It sounded more serious than the slap she'd received. Could it be Lachlan with another victim? Bishop Passarelli? Then the footsteps retreated.

Silence ensued, and she wanted desperately to know what was happening. Were there two, three, or more involved in the punishment of another Fyvie guest?

Without wasting another moment, she risked her safety and rolled quietly across her back to her other side.

Lachlan? He lay curled in a ball on the ground facing her in the opposite cell. She almost jumped up to protest her treatment and that of her family until she realized he was unconscious. For a moment, her stomach turned sour and she remembered the time in the bishop's wagon when he'd fallen ill and she'd done everything in her power to save him.

Why was Lachlan here? Could he and his brother James have had a falling out over Fyvie, and this is how Ethan and his Garter knight brother planned to take the castle from the new Macpherson bride and groom?

Yes, Lachlan was still alive, for his chest rose and fell. Instead of thinking how much she hated him, she wanted to rush over to help him.

He groaned again and clutched his gut, like he'd eaten something vile. As she studied him more closely, she noticed he had an ugly red ring around his right eye on its way to black.

Rosalyn flinched when she was tapped on the shoulder. So consumed by what was going on across the corridor, she'd forgotten about her mother and sister in the corner behind her. They'd both gotten brave and joined her on the floor.

"Do you know the bloke, Rosalyn?" her mother asked with a quiver in her voice. No doubt after weeks in this hell, she'd gotten sensitive to anything happening in the dungeon.

"Aye, Mother, that prisoner *is* my English husband."

CHAPTER 33

$\mathcal{L}$achlan moaned as he drifted in and out of a strange dream. As much as he wanted to remember the events of the day, he could not quite keep them in order.

One of the images that seemed so out of place was the one before him now. The more he tried to focus, the harder it became to do so. And when he did have a moment of clarity, it was Rosalyn's face he saw on three different women. They stared at him as if he were dead.

The eerie feeling was nothing compared to the rest of what was going on inside him. Until he'd accepted the platter of food in his chamber and downed a big portion of it, he'd been fine. Although he'd eaten his fair share of undercooked meat and near-raw vegetables, he'd never been this ill afterward. He'd been so miserable he'd contemplated ignoring Bishop Passarelli's warning to stay in his chamber and scour Fyvie for Rosalyn.

Yes, he really needed her attention right now, and that partially explained why he was having visions of her. Three different versions of her. One with fiery-red hair, one with dark-brown hair, and one with gray-white hair.

Even though it hurt to move, he was close enough to find out if they were real or an illusion.

Reaching out, he was surprised when his fingers touched cold iron. At the same time he touched the bar, a united gasp came from the three Rosalyns.

How human they appeared. Not ghostly or ethereal as he'd imagined an illusion to appear. Nor did he expect to have the imaginary figures speak or interact with him. But he'd never had encountered anything like this before, even when he'd been too drunk to get out of his chamber bed.

"Lachlan?" one of the Rosalyns called out.

He wanted to answer, but his lips would not cooperate. He felt as if a warhorse had trampled him. He could not even part his lips to give a response. All he could manage was a nod.

"What happened to you?" the same Rosalyn asked, the one with the red hair. The woman he'd married. The healer he'd been searching for. The one he needed now.

Whispering among the Rosalyns began when he could not respond. They huddled together like a tribe and it occurred to him if there weren't three women behind the bars, he would not see them so distinctly. They continued to focus on him in an agitated way. Couldn't these women see he meant them no harm?

While he was working to gain the strength to answer, all that came out was a loud, agonizing groan. It sounded to him as if his heart was trying to speak to his wife through this torment. He hoped in some way she would understand and give him some encouragement. He waited, drifting in and out of the horrible pain that consumed him.

"Well, I must thank whoever is responsible, because you are no honorable man. I hope they hang you for what you've done," was the last thing he heard from Rosalyn before he passed out.

* * *

As he readied for the great hall, Ethan stared into the mirror. Smiling at his reflection, he tallied up the score. Both Lachlan and Rosalyn were out of contention and he expected them to stay that way. Gloating, Ethan turned from the mirror and strode to the door. Once in the hallway, he found his faithful squire waiting and ready for orders.

"What can you tell me?" Ethan asked in a whisper.

"'Twas only moments ago I arrived at your door from my visit to the dungeons. Both the woman and the man were unmoving. You can rest assured they will be in that state for some time," the lad finished with a confident nod.

"Good. Then guard the door here and do not let anyone in. Tell them Lachlan's asked not to be disturbed."

The boy nodded.

"Good, lad, you will be rewarded handsomely for your loyalty. Now keep your post and I will return to you after I have supped in the great hall."

With that promise, Ethan spun on his heel and in a short time was striding into the great hall anxious to find his half-brother James. His hope was to make a direct appeal at dinner and have his brother agree tonight to his award of Fyvie, and ultimately, making it unnecessary for a hearing in the morning. After the castle was secured, he'd figure out what to do with the prisoners in the dungeon.

Ethan thumbed his beard thoughtfully. As new laird and clan leader he could let his brother rot in the dungeon. Then after Lachlan's death, his grieving widow would have to finally agree to his demands. That would suit him.

Walking toward the dais now, Ethan spotted James

climbing the steps. His half-brother took his place behind a chair in the center of the head table.

A number of other wealthy lords began to gather on the dais. One big brute of a man wearing a kilt, no doubt a Macpherson or near-enough cousin, took a seat before James took his, ignoring customary courtesies.

Finally, Ethan reached the dais just as another kilted, red-faced Scot approached James. But Ethan managed to maneuver around the Scot to embrace James first. "Good to see you, Brother. Thank you for holding my place by your side."

Following the current decorum and not waiting for a response, Ethan slammed his arse into the wooden high-backed chair just as the snubbed Highlander let out a defensive growl.

"Now, sir," James addressed the ruffled Highlander, "there are plenty of seats here for distinguished guests." He pointed to the two empty chairs next to Ethan, although there were five men standing on the podium.

When that didn't appear to placate the man, Ethan tried another tactic. "Here, you may have my wine tonight. I am abstaining." Then he lifted his full goblet from the high table and offered it to the brute hoping to diffuse his anger.

The man assessed Ethan as if he'd gone mad, but snatched the pewter cup without hesitation, spilling some of the golden mead in his haste. The offer of double the alcohol must have helped the Highlander get over his initial displeasure, for he then headed to where James had pointed. But just as one scuffle was resolved, another problem surfaced. Ethan bit back a groan when he spotted the bishop climbing the dais steps. The holy man excused his way past the others to take the final empty spot. At least there was another man between them.

As James raised his goblet, the other disgruntled guest stomped off toward another trestle table nearby.

Highlanders were an unruly lot. Ethan had learned much about the Scottish clans in the four years his father had ruled over Aberdeen and his family had occupied the castle.

James waited with his goblet raised until all were seated. "Nobles, knights, ladies, and distinguished guests, welcome to Fyvie Castle. As the reigning heir to the Luttrell holdings, I invite you to dine with me tonight on the last evening of my custodianship." He raised his mead higher. "For tomorrow, Fyvie will have a new laird and ruler."

While hushed whispers mixed with rowdy cries of *huzzah*, James waited for the room to stop buzzing, then continued. "Many of you have come to make a claim. Whether of Highland birth, Aberdeen clan leader, or British royalty, the most worthy will be chosen." A loud cheer arose from the crowd, but as Ethan's gaze roamed the room, he noticed many did not join in the revelry.

"To the new laird of Fyvie," James shouted.

"*Huzzah!*" rallied the enthusiastic guests in the great hall as James took his seat between Ethan and the giant Highlander. His brother gave a nod to those at his table and the trenchers, laden with venison, pork, lamb, and turkey, began moving among the guests. Servants streamed into the great hall the filling the guests' cups with mead. No doubt many were unaccustomed to the spread before them.

The Highlander to Ethan's right, the one who had accepted his goblet, did not seem embarrassed in the least that he was two-fisting the king's mead—perhaps celebrating a victory Ethan would never allow.

Once the other men began to eat and engage in conversation, James turned to speak to him.

"I assume you'll be among those at the hearing tomorrow?"

Ethan nodded.

Then his brother gave him an eerie stare, as if looking straight through him when he said, "I killed our father. He deserved to die, Ethan. I shall never regret my actions."

Ethan did not know how to respond. His ruse was up and as was his ire.

CHAPTER 34

osalyn regretted her words. They should have burned her tongue and scorched her lips. Perhaps her wish to have Lachlan hanged was a bit harsh, but she had little love left for her husband right now.

After the outburst, her mother and sister had wondered why she'd spoken so unkindly to her new husband, but she had to remind them it was because of him and his father that they were all in the dungeon and not in the great hall enjoying their reunion.

Now that Lachlan was unconscious across the corridor and his unexpected arrival had been discussed at length, the three women huddled together trying to stay warm in the drafty dungeon cell. As Rosalyn finally felt a sense of family again, she wanted to find something to uplift them while they passed the time locked away. Rosalyn decided they should share what they loved most about Fyvie.

"No matter whether I'm here in the dungeon or far away on a trail, this castle is home for me," Rosalyn confessed. "Surely, if I were to be punished, I'd rather be locked in my chamber room than this isolated cell, but the roof above is still the same."

That made her mother chuckle. "Well, you were locked in your chamber room more often than you werenae, darling girl," she said to Rosalyn, but then she looked at her sister. "Both of you, I swear, may have minded me more if I have locked you down here instead."

Even though the raw truth was ugly, the thought of her mother locking them in the dungeon was absurd and she burst out laughing.

"I know that laugh. That sweet beautiful sound, a melody for my heart," said a weak voice that could be no one's but Lachlan's.

She frowned. How could Lachlan slap her senseless one minute, then speak so fondly of her the next? No doubt her mother and sister were thinking the same. She struggled with the dichotomy of it all.

"Rose, the missing Rose. I've lost you forever, haven't I?"

Lachlan's incoherent mumblings spoke volumes.

Her mother searched her eyes. "What does he mean when he says he's lost you forever? Were you missing?"

Rosalyn tried to hold it back, but the sigh escaped and carried with it all of the frustrations she'd been holding inside since she left Fyvie. Although it could have been easy to break into tears again, Rosalyn had been tested more in the past few weeks than she'd ever been in her one and twenty years. She refused to digress, even if her mother was willing to listen.

"Nay, the prisoner does not speak of me. He is mumbling about the Golden Rose of Scotland and its disappearance." Then she lowered her voice. "Many believe Lachlan stole it before it was to be delivered to King James as a gift of peace and great honor from the pope."

"Oh, Rosalyn. You've married a monster," her mother

exclaimed. "Not only has he beaten you and treated you poorly, but he's attempted to steal a prize of honor for our king." She grabbed Rosalyn's shoulders and gave her a shake. "You must get an annulment at once."

Rosalyn drew in a frustrated breath. Whether she stayed married to Lachlan for a few more hours or a few more days, she agreed with her mother, but first she had to be sure Fyvie was not sacrificed by her actions.

"Aye, I will rid myself of this man," she promised shrugging off her mother's hold, "but I must be cautious. I suspect his twin brother, Ethan, is working against him or he's joined up with his half-brother, Sir James Luttrell, the Garter knight who is custodian of this castle."

Both her mother and her sister gasped.

"Sir James is a son of Nicholas Luttrell and brother to Lachlan?" her mother asked, mouth agape.

"Aye, fair lady, that is a fair assessment," came Lachlan's weak voice from across the way.

When Lachlan answered for her, she turned toward him as did her mother and sister.

Although he hadn't moved, his eyes were open to slits and he held his gut gingerly. Even though he was in pain, there was something about him. Something was different.

Rosalyn shook her head. No, it was her healer heart that was speaking, not her rational mind. She had to remind herself how evil he'd been to her since they'd been married.

Her mother let out a sigh, resigning her anger. "How can this be?"

Rosalyn wrung her hands. "Garter Knight, Sir James, is a son of the tyrant that ran our family off this land and stole our rightful claim to the clan. When he arrived o'er a week ago, he established order and set about to find the rightful heir to this clan and castle. But—" She stopped mid-sentence, not sure how to proceed, who to believe, which men were consorting against her, and which were with her.

Lachlan groaned again and their attention swung in his direction once more. What they hadn't expected was to find him sitting up and leaning against the bars peering over at them.

"Good ladies, and my lovely wife," he said in an agony-filled voice, "please hear me before I pass out again." Wincing once more, it was obvious he was dealing with a lot of pain. One thing Rosalyn had learned about him in the short time she'd been in his company was that he did not give in to pain easily. And because he was so proud, he tried to hide it from her.

As she studied him through the bars, it was easy to see with his clenched fists and anguished expression, he was doing that again.

"Listen to me now," he insisted. "You may not believe me, but hear me out," he pleaded with genuine angst. "Ethan. 'Twas Ethan who stole you from me and took you here."

Rosalyn gasped, and she covered her mouth as he groaned and shifted his position.

"You know how he can modify his voice and copy my mannerisms. Even our parents had trouble telling us apart."

Rosalyn ran to the cell bars. She reached her hand out, wanting to help Lachlan. Of course, why hadn't that occurred to her? She'd been so wrapped up in Fyvie and how she could get to what she wanted through him, she was guilty of being insensitive to everything around her. She'd been a muttonhead, consumed with what she wanted. The two men were identical. Neither Ursula nor the bishop had been able to tell them apart even when they were together.

"Oh, Lachlan, will you forgive me?" she begged. "How could have I have doubted you?"

He gazed at her with a painful smile plastered on his lips.

"There's too much to tell, but I'll be quick about it, I'm dying, Rosalyn. I'm sure if it." He gulped in air as if he couldn't get enough of it. "Ethan's poisoned me." Lachlan spoke so softly she wasn't sure she heard him correctly. "James killed my father. I'm not sure if Ethan and James are working together. I can trust only you."

Emotion caught in her throat. "He poisoned you? Are you sure?"

Lachlan's eyes bore into hers as if he was trying to tell her something his lips could not. He nodded as his body began to slide against the bars and he passed out cold on the floor.

She spun around to meet the bewildered looks of her mother and sister. "What?"

"You love him," her mother said plainly.

She shivered, not from the cold, but from the realization that she might lose him. And right now, there was nothing she could do locked up in the cell. She pounded on the bars in frustration, grabbing one in each hand and yanking them as if they'd give way. After a few moments of irrational behavior she sighed, then bowed her head and started a silent prayer.

Dear God, if I am the chosen one, chosen to deliver the Golden Rose to the King of Scots, You must help me. I have the Rose, but I must have my husband by my side to make this happen. Please give me the resources to save him.

As she stood there by the wall of bars separating her from Lachlan, her sister and mother came behind her and each rested a hand on her shoulders.

When she sighed, Rosalyn released the bars and her hands fell to her sides. But one hand struck something familiar.

A glimmer of hope rose to the surface of her gloomy thoughts. She spun around, freeing herself from their thoughtful hold to face them. A slow smile emerged when she rolled up the hem of her skirt and yanked free her precious fur pouch.

"The key. I have the key."

"Your da's key?" her mother asked, surprised. "I thought it was stolen."

Rosalyn tried to hide her guilt. "It was stolen," she admitted sheepishly with her head bowed. Then she glanced up at her mother, "But I've used it for good," she promised, taking her ma's hand and placing the furry pouch in the center of it. "Hold this," she instructed, while she reached for the ties and pulled the bag open, then dug around in the precious cargo.

Her face lit up with satisfaction when she found what she sought and drew it out as like a prize.

Rushing to the bars as she'd done before, this time with excitement, she pushed the key into the lock and held her breath. With some sticky resistance, the key wobbled around in the hole until Rosalyn jiggled it in a little deeper. Once the key slid into the locking chamber, she took both hands and turned the head to the left.

When the catch released and the cell door swung open, she finally let out her breath.

CHAPTER 35

*E*than blinked rapidly after James's declaration. Fortunately, the loud-mouth Highlander distracted James before Ethan had to lie.

He wasn't surprised his father had been killed at the hands of someone he knew, even less so that it was carried out by James, a noble Knight of the Garter. No doubt James had personal reasons for killing their father. But Ethan would seek retribution nevertheless. He only needed James as an ally until Fyvie was awarded, then he'd settle the score. For even if his father's death had been at the hands of his English king, he could not let it go unavenged.

Nicholas's cunning was a testament to his longevity. Besides James, there were no doubt other Luttrell family members, his ex-wives, his castle staff, who wanted him dead.

Fortunately for Nicholas, he'd been on good terms with the Tudors. At his cousin Henry VII's crowning, his father was reinstated as earl and regained Dunster Castle in the southern shire, the crown jewel of the Luttrell holdings.

Then Fyvie had been reconfirmed by King Henry VII, although it had been his former father-in-law who had originally gifted the property to Nicholas.

Why the Macphersons continued to claim ownership was still a mystery to him, but with his newly formed plan, he'd be able to squelch their interests for good.

Ethan had remained quiet after James's initial declaration, and his half-brother had not given him any attention as the meal progressed. Clearly, the obnoxious Highlander was expressing his interest in Fyvie and that had dominated James's attention.

Yet, it was clear that James had met Lachlan. How much had his twin revealed? What had he claimed? If his ploy had been fully exposed, wouldn't James have demanded some answers?

With servants continuing to refill goblets at the high table as if the mead were merely water, it was not long before the two-cupped brute at Ethan's side was drunk and surly.

The clansman sneered at Ethan. "What does an Englishman want with a Scottish rose?" the Highlander asked with a distinct slur in his brogue.

Rose? Does this fool know some of my secrets?

Ethan decided not to be ruffled by this idiot and tapped the goblet closest to the Scot, ignoring the man's direct question by asking one of his own. "Had your fill, Brother?"

"I arenae your brother, my name is Osgar," the bloke declared, kicking his chair back as he leapt up. The heavy, ornate seat toppled over, and the conversation at the dais stopped. After the head table went silent, a wave of broken conversations traversed from table to table throughout the great hall. Even servants froze in their tracks.

All eyes were on the red-faced Highlander who was weaving back and forth as he stared down at Ethan.

"Get up," Osgar ordered.

Before Ethan blinked, a chair screeched loudly and he could feel the air rush behind him, certain James had climbed to his feet.

The brute looked to James and said, "I didnae mean you."

Ethan stood, holding Osgar's gaze as he fingered his hilt. "This is how you repay my generosity?"

"I donna need a sword to get my point across," the man said, winding up his right arm and curling his fingers into a fist.

Ethan waited for the arm to come around and the bloke to take a swing. With his sluggish reflexes, the man was more embarrassment than threat and Ethan ducked out of the way in plenty of time. But when he heard a *thwack*, he sprung around to find Osgar's fist had connected. He'd struck James in the chin instead.

Ethan wanted to laugh, but held back, waiting to see what James would do. As he watched for his half-brother's reaction, it was clear James was in control. He raised his hand high in the air and within moments, four knights crowded the table where the drunken Highlander swayed.

While the man spewed oaths, the knights secured his arms behind his back and walked him off the platform. And even though Osgar was drunk, he should have sensed he was outnumbered. But no, the man struggled against his hold and shouted at the top of his lungs until he was finally escorted out of the great hall.

The ruckus echoed down the corridor until finally the heavy wooden door to the keep slammed and silence followed.

James hooted with laughter. It was so infectious that everyone at the head table joined him, followed by those in the front tables, and it rippled through the rest of the guests. James was still on his feet and raised his goblet.

"A toast to those who continue to drink and can hold

their liquor, best of luck to you on the morrow for now there is one less contender for Fyvie."

"*Huzzah!*" was the response from the guests.

While Ethan waited for James to take his seat, the sound of the empty chair moving beside him piqued his interest.

Even before he turned to satisfy his curiosity, a familiar voice asked, "What are you doing here, Ethan?"

The bishop's direct question caught him off guard as he spun around to greet him. As much as he was comfortable lying, he wasn't with a man of God. Then, it was if his dead father's ghost gave him a push, he tipped forward and said , "Good Bishop, how nice it is to see you."

The bishop leaned forward, too. "Let me ask you more directly. Two Roses are missing, and I believe you have both of them."

Ethan returned the bishop's condemning gaze with a no-nonsense glare. "What do you mean by two roses?"

The bishop's eyes narrowed. "The Golden Rose and your brother's wife, Rosalyn. Both went missing when you left Edinburgh. Coincidence?"

"Perhaps you were not privy to this information, but I am my father's executor. When I found out just before I arrived at Edinburgh that he was dead, I informed my brother Lachlan and King James, then took off immediately for Fyvie. This is why I traveled to the home of King James to begin with. Lachlan, up until this very moment, has been unable to secure that castle, one of our family's holdings recently reinstated by King Henry."

Ethan glanced over his shoulder to confirm James was still engaged in a conversation before he lowered his voice and continued. "Cleaning up after Lachlan's failures occupies much of my leisure time. What he's done with his wife, I cannot say."

Ethan sat back and crossed his arms, satisfied that he'd been truthful after all.

The bishop's normal child-like expression turned dark. For a moment it appeared he would question him further, but finally he said, "I'll pray for your soul." Then the holy man stood up and walked off the dais.

Ethan relaxed his tense muscles and clenched jaw. As he scanned the room, he realized that in the short time he'd been with the bishop, most of the great hall had cleared except for James who was quietly finishing the meal that had been interrupted by too many Highlanders. Now was his chance.

* * *

ROSALYN WIPED Lachlan's brow with the hem of her skirt. He was feverish and shaking. If he'd been poisoned, as she suspected, there would be a few things she would need immediately.

Dashing quickly back across the dungeon corridor, she entered the unlocked cell where her mother and sister waited. "Saving Lachlan isnae going to be easy, yet I must do everything in my power to help him now that I know the terrible treatment I suffered was at his brother's hands, not his own."

Her mother and sister nodded their approval. "We donna mind putting ourselves in danger to help. What can we do?"

What can they do? Rosalyn pondered that for a moment while the two waited anxiously before her. Surely, she was more in danger if she ventured from the dungeon to the upper chambers of the keep. She needed to reach Ursula, but neither her mother nor her sister would know her by sight. Ursula would have the herbs Rosalyn needed.

Rosalyn snapped her fingers. "I have it. You two take the servants' stairs and find Greta. She'll shield you both and will know how to find the Highland healer, Ursula, who is my ally. I'll need her herbs for treating Lachlan's poisoning," she said, rushing through the instructions. "Promise me neither one of you will do anything but this. I want you safe."

Rosalyn was relieved when they both nodded and pleased she could envision a brighter future. She'd reunited with her family, the chance of stopping Ethan was more plausible now, and thankfully, she'd found Lachlan was not the monster she thought she'd married.

But there were a number of logistical challenges that still lay ahead. First, they'd have to wait out the next guard visit. Her mother had mentioned the daily food drop by was just before sunset.

As if they were all thinking the same thing, the three turned to the loophole window. They were fortunate the day had been sunny and it was easy tell the sun was setting. If that wasn't enough, Rosalyn's stomach was protesting the lack of food.

"I regret having to do this," she said as she fished her skeleton key out of her pocket, "but I must lock us all back in the cell until after the food is delivered."

Rosalyn hurried to Lachlan. After checking his fever and giving him a passionate kiss on the lips, she locked his cell door.

Just as she was removing the key, the scuffling of heavy boots sounded on the stairs beyond the turn in the corridor. She rushed to her mother and sister, and quickly locked them inside. Silently, she laid back on the spot where Ethan had left her, while her mother and sister huddled in the darkened corner.

As the footsteps grew closer, Rosalyn shivered, hoping it

was food that was on its way to them and nothing worse. When the heavy footfall stopped, she kept her eyes closed. Even though her back was to the gated cell door, she cringed.

"Still asleep, I see. Even my brother. Well, then, there's no need for food after all."

CHAPTER 36

Keeping as still as possible, Rosalyn listened intently to the sounds of the dungeon.

As much as she wanted to flip over, even partway with a pretend groan, she did not want to risk Ethan's interest in her. She also prayed silently that he'd leave Lachlan alone too.

But a groan from her husband's cell had her heart racing. And the shuffling footsteps made her panic.

"You bastard," one of the Luttrell brothers uttered in a soft pitch.

Rosalyn held her breath. Were the words weak enough to have been Lachlan's, or were they were spoken by Ethan so only his brother could hear?

She waited. Her breathing shallow, her heart pounding.

"What did you call me?"

Goosebumps ran up Rosalyn's arms. Unless Lachlan had a miraculous recovery, it was Ethan who spoke last for the voice was loud and commanding.

"You heard me easily enough, and you know how fond I

am of that name for you," Lachlan replied. Although low in volume, his voice was high in venom.

"Well, call me names all you want, for you know you are dead to me."

Dead was a word Rosalyn did not want to associate with Lachlan.

"At least I am grateful for that, or else you would have a conscience about what you've done to Rosalyn," Lachlan shot back in a shaky voice. "Leave me here, but release her. She's done nothing to you."

Ethan gave a wicked laugh. And now she understood why he hadn't laughed when he was pretending to be her husband. It was very different from Lachlan's jovial one. Laughter was hard to fake.

Since the two of them had been talking, even though Lachlan's voice was weak, they were different and she should have suspected something was wrong. Never should have believed Lachlan could have been so mean to her.

"You do not know what I've done to her, do you?" Ethan asked.

"You'll soon be a dead man," Lachlan lashed out. "And you are a coward if you do not step inside this cell now."

Rosalyn weighed her options. If she said something to support Ethan, perhaps she could stop Lachlan's brother from entering his cell and killing him outright. Her husband had no strength.

The sound of a key turning in the lock made her heart slam against her bodice. Never had she felt so helpless. About to go mad with fear and frustration, Rosalyn could no longer hold her tongue.

"Ethan, if you touch your brother, you shall never touch me again. I swear it," she said, rising from the cold floor to stand tall in the cell, prepared to fight on behalf of her husband with her wit and her passion.

He spun around at her words. With a long, seductive gaze he ogled her from head to toe. "You threaten me?" he asked, chuckling. "Both of you." He glanced back and forth between them. "Behind bars, beaten by my hand, yet you both try to intimidate me when I have the upper one?"

"Ethan, I donna threaten you," Rosalyn said, "I'm merely laying down my rules. Now that I know you are not my husband, you will not have access to my chambers unless I give you permission."

He crossed his arms over his chest and contemplated what she'd said. Surely, he'd forgotten that she'd only been obeying his wishes because she thought he was Lachlan. Let him believe he might have a chance with her if it would buy both she and her husband the time they needed.

"Rosalyn, I forbid you to give him permission to anything, do you hear me?" No doubt Lachlan was trying to shout, but his words were barely above a whisper. She understood he was trying to protect her, even if it was in a domineering way.

"Lockie," she said sweetly, "my love, you are on death's door." It would break his heart for her to say what was coming next, but she hoped after she said it, he would understand why. "I must think of my future and that of this castle. I donna wish to be a dungeon dweller, but to support the clan leader who will rule this castle for the ages. I—" Her voice cracked. "I love you, but know I must do what is best for me." She wanted to weep after she said those words, but she forced herself to be strong.

"Well, Lachlan," Ethan said as he turned the key back the other way, then faced Rosalyn, "it appears I can have all my heart desires, your death, your wife, and your castle. I will let the work be done without me having to force it to a close."

There was a glazed but predatory look in Ethan's eyes as he acknowledged her through the cell bars.

Her gut lurched, but because it was empty, she had nothing to fear but the man who ogled her again. She silently thanked the Lord that she was separated from him by iron bars and that they were not secured in a darkened chamber with no one to hear her screams. The thought of any contact with Lachlan's evil brother made her promise that if he did not die on her husband's blade, he would die on hers.

So she kept mum, worried her body or her voice or her emotions would betray her now. She even tried not to blink, but kept her gaze steady despite her loathing the man whose eyes were locked with hers.

Silence enveloped the dungeon for what seemed to be the length of a midday meal. Lachlan had either passed out or was so angry with her response, he was repulsed. Her mother and sister had remained silent as well, and with Ethan the only one free to leave the place, Rosalyn wondered why he lingered. Perhaps he was still assessing her. Deciding what his next move would be, or even waiting out Lachlan's death.

Lachlan? Her heart lurched for a moment, but she kept her gaze cool and steady. The longer Ethan stayed in the keep's lower recesses, the more precious time ticked away.

Finally, she decided to break the silence. "I await your return and to hear the final judgement on the castle."

Perhaps that was all he'd been waiting for, because he turned on his heel and started back toward the stairs, but he gave her one last glance after he'd taken his first step, as if he'd catch her making a face at him, or her rushing to the bars to fuss over Lachlan.

Fortunately for her, she'd remained steady like a soldier ready for inspection. She may not have even blinked, congratulating herself on her newfound skill.

Apparently satisfied to leave husband and wife in separate cells once more with his malicious plan in place, Ethan snickered before he moved on and finally out of sight. When she did move toward the dirty dungeon bars, it was to push her face as close to them as she could stand to make sure he was truly leaving, listening for the echo of his steps ascending the stairs. When nothing stirred, she felt safe to move about freely and motioned her mother and sister from the corner.

In a rush against time, the three pressed forward to the cell door. Rosalyn fitted the skeleton key into the lock then released the mechanism that kept them prisoners.

"Quickly now," she said with an urgency she could taste, "go to Greta and have her send Ursula with a poison antidote for me. Understand?"

Both of them nodded. As malnourished as the two were, Rosalyn wasn't sure how good they would be at completing the task, but it was her only chance at saving Lachlan.

"Be careful and tell only Greta where you've been and what you've seen," she warned. "We cannae trust anyone else."

Once they left, the door shut behind her and Rosalyn hurried to Lachlan's cell. After she'd let herself in with the skeleton key, she dropped to her knees beside him. Glancing at the sun shining in from the high loophole window, Rosalyn promised herself to take matters into her own hands if the poison antidote did not arrive by dusk.

Lachlan groaned when she touch his forehead. The fever was still raging, and perspiration covered his pale, handsome face. She'd read about vampires in some of her childhood fables and she imagined they'd look like Lachlan did now.

His crisp widow's peak defined his brow line and his glossy black hair, growing from its point, swept back into a dramatic crescendo at the nape of his neck. Never had his skin been so vampire white.

Rosalyn sat staring at him for some time, wishing her first days as a married woman would have been spent with him and not his brother. She was relieved and angry at the same time.

Glancing up at the window, she realized that there was only little light left in the sky. Her gaze drifted back to Lachlan and she wiped his brow again with her skirt. He startled her when he grabbed her hand.

"Do you really love me?" Lachlan asked, his eyes fluttering open momentarily and then, as if they were too heavy to hold, they closed again, but a smile flickered across his face.

"What?" Rosalyn asked, dumbfounded that he was speaking and trying to open his eyes.

"You've forgotten already that you said you loved me?" he asked in a hurtful tone.

For a moment she banished her worries about his fever, her longing for Fyvie or where they were, and she leaned down and kissed him with all the passion her soul could muster.

Desire swelled in her heart when his arms circled her waist and he crushed her to his chest. Although it must have taken Herculean effort, he began kissing her back.

Instead of the hide and seek he often played with her tongue, this time his lips corralled hers as if she was a wild horse ready to buck him. She was so grateful to be with him again, to have his heart beat with hers. Realizing that just moments ago she was comparing him to a lifeless vampire.

But even if Lachlan was as nocturnal, he needed to maintain what strength he had. It might be hours before Ursula arrived. With only concern for him, Rosalyn loosened her hold and gave Lachlan a few last delicious pecks on his swollen lips.

But he pressed her for more, speaking awkwardly into her mouth. "I'd rather you show me, not tell me, you love me, any day."

CHAPTER 37

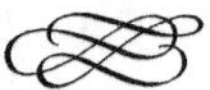

When Ethan entered the great hall the next morning, he was feeling confident. Cocky, even as he sized up his competition. In addition to the Luttrell coat of arms, Ethan wore a smug smile. He wanted his competition to know who they were dealing with.

Ethan was also pleased his conversation with James had been productive yester eve. James had listened to his arguments and had nodded agreeably throughout his plea.

Never once did Ethan lead on that his father wanted Lachlan to be the one to win the property back. Instead, he promised to be the more responsible twin.

Ethan also reminded James how Lachlan had relinquished the family name, and for that reason alone, his twin should be out of contention.

James even nodded favorably when Ethan had insisted Fyvie stay in the Luttrell family. And neither of them brought up Rosalyn's claims.

Ethan also told James, as a knight serving his king, he could keep his post. Otherwise, the Garter knight would require a leave of duty to preside over both an estate in Scotland and one in the south of England.

Ethan pledged to make the sacrifice. With the two working together, he promised the Luttrells could be an insurmountable force once again.

But as much as Ethan campaigned for the award, James refused to make a promise before the formal hearing.

Now, on the dais where they'd supped the night before, his half-brother sat with two Garter knight sentries standing on either side. A long trestle table before them, served as the court bench.

The room buzzed with conversation. Highlanders wearing matching clan plaids, stood in small groups. Families of fathers and sons consorted over their claims.

As the whispers among the Highlanders became more noticeable, Ethan shifted his gaze to the back of the hall for his own edification.

To his surprise, a sizable group of servants, led by a woman, moved straight to the front of the hall and stood before the makeshift court bench.

James nodded to the woman, then after clapping his hands together, the buzz in the hall stopped. "Take your seats," James ordered from his companding position. "Will those making a claim raise their hands?"

Immediately, the arm of a farmer shot up. He was sitting at one of the front tables. When Ethan let out a loud *harrumph*, the laborer turned around with his mouth agape making Ethan laughed at his reaction, as did many in the great hall.

James took a gavel from the table and rapped on it three times. "Welcome clansmen, nobles, and servants. Although I usually start with the proceedings in the order of attendance, I will break with that decorum and allow the lady to go first out of courtesy."

One of the Highlanders stood. "Donna waste all of our precious time, Sir James. You cannae be serious about hearing a servant woman's claim to Fyvie, can ye now?"

The servant woman walked forward and stood in front of James. After raising her hands and clapping them above her head, an army of servants filed in behind her. Cooks, stable boys, farmers, serving maids, more than fifty. When they couldn't stand directly behind her, they filed in around the rest of the front tables.

James stood to address the group. "Good people. This is quite unusual. As members of the serving class, you must be well aware you may not own land. What claim do you make this morn?"

By the time James finished addressing the servants, the rest in the great hall were on their feet and had moved toward the front to witness the claim. Ethan followed suit.

The leader of the group, the servant woman, stood before James at an angle and Ethan could see her face. She was tall in stature and wore a simple gray shift that matched her aging appearance. She wore her silver hair drawn back in a tight knot at the nape of her neck, and with no adornments. Even though she appeared to have little significance to those in the room, it was apparent she was empowered by someone. No servants were this bold on their own. James had already made the point. They could never be landholders.

While Ethan considered the servants who stood behind her, he was grateful they were unarmed. Otherwise, they would have been a formidable group, a potential tyranny in the making.

He'd expected the Highlanders to cause some ruckus, but assumed the clans to be more boastful than baleful. Now he was grateful all would abide by his brother's decision, for the Garter knights were revered and operated with the granted authority of the king of England.

Ethan studied his half-brother's face as the servants finished taking their places. His patience appeared to be running short. "Speak," he commanded.

The woman blinked quickly. She took a half-step back, but stood steady.

"Good sir," she began in a clear voice, surprising Ethan. "I am here to represent Rosalyn Macpherson, daughter of Dengas Macpherson, who was laird of this castle and whose family has held the only Scottish rule over Aberdeen since I've been alive. She's of age now and deserves her rightful place."

A low murmur of voices swept through the hall, but no one challenged her claim. When the modest disturbance settled, Ethan noticed the woman take the half-step forward she'd relinquished moments before.

Brimming with more confidence, she continued. "Unfortunately, neither my mistress nor her husband are available to appear here due to illness. The rest of her family has been in hiding."

The room erupted this time in a louder conversation among groups of family members, no doubt over speculation as to why so many of the Macphersons were absent.

James pounded the gavel on table and took command of the proceedings again.

"Good woman, if I understand you, there is no one from the former laird's family who can attend this hearing and you have been asked to make the claim on their behalf?" James asked with as much respect as Ethan imagined he could, but his half-brother did not keep the sound of disbelief from his voice.

When the servant woman hesitated, a man standing directly behind her stepped up to join her. "Good sir, my name is Simon Rothberg and I am the castle's steward. Greta is a woman of her word and we," he gestured to the impressive group of servants gathered, "are here to support her plea for Lady Rosalyn." He bowed slightly, then faced James again. "May I speak freely, my lord?"

James nodded but did not relax his stance nor could Ethan. He was pleased his plan had worked so far, but he hadn't expected advocates for the family to rally on their behalf.

Simon appeared to be close in age to the woman he stood next to, with graying hair at his temples and a slightly stooped stance, as if his years of working had taken a toll on his posture. The man shuffled a little forward and clasped his hands together in front of his heart.

"Sir James, I was born in this castle. So was my father and my father's father. As far back as our family can recall, we've served the Macphersons. The lairds of this clan have always been fair to their servants and have cultivated our loyalty. For that I am forever grateful." He paused for a moment as if collecting his thoughts, then he grinned broadly. "Lady Rosalyn. Have you met her?"

James nodded.

"Well, when I describe her, you may recall, my lord, she has a fighting spirt and reminds me more of a lad than lass sometimes."

With that admission, the group of servants began to chuckle and smile. It was clear she was loved by those who served her, making Ethan squirm. He was never comfortable with adoration or gestures of caring.

Simon's face grew serious. "And because we honor her and support her leadership, we are prepared to die fighting for her," he said as he raised his fist in the air and those behind him did, too.

James steepled his hands together in front of his chest. "I'm impressed with the loyalty you all share for your lady. No doubt that's what most leaders strive to achieve.

However, if given the need to defend this castle, Lady Rosalyn will need skilled soldiers and knights, not bakers and farmers."

Now it was the clan groups turn to snicker and smile, making the servants look about and shrink their ranks, shuffling closer together.

"Loyalty is important, but I cannot award this castle on the pleas of servants. The king would never support it, so I must table this hearing until after the midday meal."

Some disgruntled rumblings surfaced right away, but immediately subsided when James's attention went from the servants to the loudest offenders.

"Regardless of the displeasure of those who join me today, I will give the Macpherson family a few hours. Clearly, even if their contention is to rule over this castle, a family member must be found to come before us," James declared, then he snatched the gavel up and pounded on the wooden table. "Dismissed."

This time the room erupted into a loud ruckus. No longer needed to abide by decorum, the clan groups and smaller gatherings of servants began to talk about the unusual proceedings. Ethan turned his back on them all and began to make his way to the exit. He was disappointed that James had not just dismissed the servant's claims as bogus and award Fyvie to the Luttrells as he had expected.

With the great hall full of opposing interests, Ethan decided it was better to leave and revise his plan. For what he feared now, was word of James's appeal reaching any remaining Macpherson family members in Aberdeen.

Until this hearing, he'd been certain Rosalyn and Lachlan had plans to make the claim by themselves. Yet, to secure his future, he needed to stop the gray-haired old lady from letting details of the hearing leave the grounds of Fyvie.

Stepping back from the main corridor at the intersection

to the servant's hallway, Ethan waited for Rosalyn's supporters to disperse. Being servants, not nobles, no doubt they had chores to attend to and would need to return to their tasks.

Greta. She was his target now. As he zeroed in on his mark, he trailed her, unseen in the shadows. When she led him to the dungeon staircase, he was not surprised.

CHAPTER 38

The cell door swung shut, but Lachlan would not let go. For a dying man, that was quite extraordinary. But Rosalyn wouldn't give up, and she pushed against his chest. Finally, their lips parted.

"*Och!* You've cured him without my help," a familiar voice said.

Rosalyn straightened her skirts as she stood to greet Ursula at the cell door, grateful her grinning but sarcastic friend was finally here to help.

"I'm so relieved to see you." Rosalyn gave her friend a big squeeze and when she released her, both women's smiles faded. "We have work to do." She grabbed Ursula's hand and led her to Lachlan. "'Tis it night or day?"

"Day," Ursula said with a heavy sigh that spoke to her frustration. "Ethan assigned a sentry to guard the dungeon staircase. It was only moments ago that the watchman nodded off and I was able to slip by him."

Rosalyn shuddered. She was grateful that Ethan was busy with other matters and had sent someone less ambitious than himself to watch.

Ursula squeezed her hand. "Your mother and sister are safe, and I know some of what transpired here, but tell me of Lachlan," she said with a serious tone, dropping to her knees opposite Rosalyn.

Her lips moved to a slight smile. "As much as you think I've done nothing but kiss my husband, he's been pale and cold to the touch with short sessions of fever-like sweats." She gazed own at her now-sleeping husband. "His voice is weak, he's barely able to stand, and he said right after his midday meal, he'd fallen violently ill."

"Ye be right to call for my help. Poisoning is the likely cause of his symptoms," Ursula said, feeling about Lachlan's gut.

Ursula's head shot up. "The hearing?" Her friend's gaze met hers. "Have you lost Fyvie because of this man?" The deadly calm of her tone escalated Rosalyn's confusion.

She sighed and blinked back tears. "Honestly, I donna know," she admitted. She swallowed hard. "Greta offered to go on my behalf. But when Lachlan was locked up in the state he's in—well, I put my mother and sister in danger, sending them to the servants' quarters to bring you here for help. I trust Greta to protect my family, but I'm not sure she was able to carry out her plan."

Ursula gave her a look of dread. "You trusted a servant to ask for your rightful ownership of Fyvie and you stood beside a man you donna love?"

The corners of Rosalyn's lips took a down turn and she furrowed her brows. A *harrumph* came out before she could articulate her feelings.

"She loves me," came a weak, but boastful response from Lachlan. Although his eyes stayed closed, a slight smile danced across his pale lips.

Ursula's gaze darted from Lachlan to Rosalyn. "He donna lie!" she almost shouted.

"Shh, keep your voice down," Rosalyn said after giving the healer a sheepish grin.

Her friend let out a few soft *tsks*, shaking her head. "Love over land. Lachlan wins?"

"Life over land would be more appropriate," Rosalyn defended, not denying what her friend claimed was true or not. Clearly, her heart and head were conflicted.

With her lips pressed into a thin line and one brow arched, Ursula turned from her and began tossing herbs out of the satchel she had stashed under her skirt.

Rosalyn's eyes widened when the healer drew a pestle and mortar out of the hiding place too. When she turned back to Rosalyn, she froze. "What now?"

"I am astounded by your preparation," Rosalyn admitted with a smile. Then her heart warmed. Taking in a big sigh first, she eked out the words, "Thank you."

Her friend *tsked* again. "You are my sister of the heart. I would do anything for ye," she promised, then turned her attention to the herbs. In a few short moments, Ursula had turned leaves and flowers into an aromatic pomace.

Finally satisfied with her work, Ursula looked up to meet Rosalyn's gaze, but the healer appeared puzzled.

Now it was Rosalyn's turn to ask, "What now?"

"How do I feed this to him when he's, um, unconscious?"

Rosalyn grinned. "Give it to me." She tossed her hair behind both shoulders like a pony shaking its head. She scooped up a small portion of the paste on her middle finger and her gaze caught Ursula's. "I don't want to endanger you any longer. I have what I need."

Her friend laughed. "Nay, you want to entertain your husband and you donna want me to watch," her friend accused, tossing her a mischievous look.

Rosalyn felt her cheeks heat. "This tactic worked before."

She paused. "In the bishop's wagon when Lachlan had been poisoned by our potion."

Her friend cracked a smile. "At least it wasnae you who tried to poison him again."

At that moment, Lachlan raised his head slightly and turned toward Rosalyn. Although his eyes were still closed, his lips parted to speak. "You tried to poison me?" His words were filled with hurt.

It was Rosalyn's turn to chuckle. "My dear husband, it was Ursula who wanted to poison you." Her hardened gaze met her friend's. "Remember, you two didnae always get along," she reminded him.

He grunted. "No excuse to poison a man," he said grudgingly.

At that, Ursula rose silently.

"Aye, but this time she's come to save you. You must forgive her now," Rosalyn urged.

Lachlan was silent for a while and just when her panic began to rise, he grunted. "All right then, if I live, I'll forgive her." He paused dramatically. "But if I don't, I'll blame both of you and I hope you'll rot in hell."

Her head snapped up to gauge her friend's reaction and she found her only smiling. Then Ursula said, "I hope for your sake he lives. I already know I'm going to hell."

And with that, she let herself out the cell door and silently disappeared down the corridor.

Rosalyn released another sigh. Gazing back to her husband's handsome but still pale face, she hoped he would forget what he'd heard. As much as she hated to be in the dungeon with Lachlan, she knew this was where she belonged. For a fleeting moment, she'd wanted to leap up and chase after her friend. How complicated her life had become since her da's death.

But it was time to save Lachlan. With her right middle

finger full of antidotal herbal paste, she laid down by his side as she had in the wagon, days before their nuptials. Rolling over, she press herself to his body and began tracing his lips with her pinky finger, careful not to lose any of the precious paste from her middle finger. When Lachlan's lips parted and he let out a reactionary groan, she popped the finger full of paste into his mouth. Immediately, he began to suck on her finger. As he began the rhythmic motion, the paste dissolved and all that was left was his lips around her sensitive skin.

She wasn't surprised, but rather relieved, when her groin began to get moist and heat traveled through her. In the chill of the dungeon, a romantic heat wave was welcome. Her eyes closed and she relaxed into the sensation. As she relaxed, she began to realize how tired she was. So sleepy.

Wasn't this nature's antidote for fear and exhaustion? Being close to someone you love? A love that could end before it began. While she'd been chasing castles, he'd been chasing her. How had she been so blind? But then through her exhaustion, her rational mind reminded her he was English and conceited. But he was also caring, kind, and considerate. How could she resist?

While she lay thinking about all that was right, her finger fell away and she wrapped her arm across his chest and sighed. Lachlan was silent, but his breathing was steady. She reached her idle hand to his brow, but it was still feverish. Perhaps the herbs weren't working. Poison was a tricky thing, much more difficult to treat than a common ailment. And as he'd reminded them, he'd survived a previous poison attempt. She could only hope he was more impervious than most.

When the door to the cell swung open, she gasped and shot straight up to sitting to find Ethan standing in the opening with a disgusted expression on his face.

"This just warms my heart after I've bloodied my hands."

CHAPTER 39

*E*than opened the cell door without unlocking it. Shocked that the two remained in the dungeon when freedom beckoned, especially for Rosalyn, he let the cell door creak closed by itself behind him.

Lachlan hadn't moved, making Ethan wonder if his goal was complete and Rosalyn was just mourning her loss. Although her eyes were shooting daggers and her fiery hair looked like she'd ridden horseback through the wind with no hood for protection, his brother's wife appeared more ready for battle than in need of comfort.

"You are the Devil," she screamed, "with blood on your hands." Jumping to her feet, Rosalyn reached under her skirts and withdrew her dagger.

Ethan mentally cursed himself for not searching Rosalyn before he left her unconscious on the cell floor.

She circled in front of Lachlan as if to protect his body.

"Is he dead?"

"Aye, and you are responsible," she said with venom in her voice.

He let out a wicked laugh. "Oh, my, that's quite a compliment, m'dear. Most people call me irresponsible."

She gave him an evil look and spat in his direction. "Rosalyn, you are a widow now. But don't fret. I look and sound just like Lachlan," he said, walking closer to her and drawing out his own dagger.

"Donna flatter yourself. You are nothing like him."

"Oh, then I'm better looking," he said, taking another step toward her.

She took a measured step backward. "You disgust me."

He cut the distance between them. "Pray tell, why the toy knife?" he asked, trying to provoke her even more.

"I would love to end your life right now. Leave you dead next to your brother. Your lives began together, 'twould be fitting for you to die together," she suggested, releasing an evil laugh.

As he continued to stare, she began to slash the air in front of her with the dagger.

"I killed Greta," he confessed and held up his stained hands. "This is her blood," he lied, hoping to shock her. To break her. It was pig's blood. But his false claim produced the desired result. Rosalyn stopped slashing, and her arm dropped.

As he stared at her, Rosalyn's face took on an eerie, satanic expression. Her eyes grew frantic, like a woman who had lost all senses. Like a witch.

"You are going to hell," she denounced in a flat tone.

"I never wanted to go to heaven, and there's only one alternative. I've accepted that fate. Now you must accept yours."

She glared at him. "If you plan to kill me, the least I can do is give you some nasty scars before you take the last of my breath," she promised and began to slash the air again with her weapon.

No, he would not kill her. He required her assistance, even if she was going to give it unwillingly. So he needed another lie.

"Your mother and sister are being held hostage until Fyvie is awarded to us. I will pose as Lachlan, and as my betrothed, you will support this lie," he demanded.

Rosalyn eyed him up and down, no doubt noticing he wore Lachlan's clothes. Then her arm dropped and the dagger made a clanging sound when it hit the stone floor. Her shoulders slumped and her head bowed.

Ethan drew in a deep sigh of relief. James required a Macpherson at the hearing, and he needed assurance that he had the one Macpherson who could secure his fate with Fyvie. He was no longer confident his half-brother would award the castle in his favor without her.

When Ethan had left the great hall earlier, James had not even acknowledged his presence at the hearing. Once he'd hammered the gavel, James had turned his back on the proceedings and left the great hall through the owner's corridor without a glance or nod in his direction.

No, Ethan could not trust a Luttrell and that was the same reputation he'd earned from all those Luttrells before him. As with most families, it was one of your own blood who stood in the way.

Thankfully, James was a half-brother, not a full-blooded Luttrell. When they had spoken last night it was clear James cared little about land or castles, particularly Fyvie.

But that was not the case for Ethan. Fyvie was where he'd bonded with his father, where he learned how his father had coerced the clan to do his bidding.

Soft sobs moved Ethan out of his musings and reminded him there was work to do before the hearing. He needed her to be presentable for the great hall.

As her gaze rose, he was greeted by a dull stare. The fire inside her was gone. A lifeless haze covered her features. The light in the dungeon had not changed since he'd returned, but the glow of her eyes, the spark in her movements, the fire of her hair, all had dimmed as if water had doused the flame of her soul.

Ethan moved toward her, stooping low to scoop up her dirk. With a few efficient movements, he secured the weapon within the sheath of his own dagger.

When her eyes swung to the dungeon floor, he grabbed her chin and tilted it up so she had to look at him. "I need your word that you will join me at the hearing and pretend I am Lachlan Macpherson."

"What happened at the hearing this morn? Fyvie was not awarded?"

"You need not know the details." The last thing he wanted was for her to know the support she had. "You had unlocked the cell door. Why did you miss the hearing?"

When her gaze darted to Lachlan, he had his answer. "Love over land?"

"I prayed I could help him."

"And your prayers were not answered. Perhaps you are going to hell with me? Your own lies may be too vast for penance." He laughed when she threw him a disgusted look and he moved to embrace her, but she jumped backward and leveled a killer stare at him.

After that cold reception, he pointed her to the corridor. He walked with her back the way they'd come the night before. With the threat of her family's lives in the balance, she said nothing to the servants they passed in the corridor, although each one they encountered appeared to struggle with hiding their surprise at seeing her.

The fact that she'd been missing due to a supposed illness

helped disguise the fact that she did not look well at the moment. Ethan was grateful they'd walked through the lesser-traveled corridors without questions as they approached Rosalyn's chamber door.

Just as he was reaching for the handle to the entry, a voice called out, "Rosalyn, there you are."

Turning, Ethan spotted a dark-haired woman with her hands on her hips standing at the end of the corridor like a sentry.

He hadn't expected this kind of disruption, wanting now to disappear inside her chamber with Rosalyn and shut the dark-haired demon out.

"Stop right there," the woman threatened, rushing toward them.

"She's one of my handmaidens," Rosalyn said softly. "If you want me ready for the hearing, I will need her assistance."

Ethan hesitated. Then he recognized the dark-haired beauty, the one he'd tried to bed to win Lachlan's earldom. He had not planned for Rosalyn to speak to anyone before the hearing, and especially not Ursula, but when he looked down to assess Rosalyn again, it was clear she could not go to the great hall in her current state of dress.

He hesitated with one hand on the door lever and the other on Rosalyn's arm, deciding not to let on that he recognized the vixen.

Ursula softened her hard gaze and gave him a forced smile. "Aye, Rosalyn is in need of my services," the woman suggested, grabbing Rosalyn's other elbow. As if she expected him to release her, Ursula started off toward the chamber door, but Ethan held on.

Strung between the two of them pulling her, Rosalyn cried out.

"She stays here," Ethan growled.

The dark-haired beauty nodded and finally released her.

"Of course, my Lord," she said with compliance in her voice. "Let me see what's needed and then I can bring back the ladies in waiting. She will require at least three to set this right," Ursula said in a disparaging way, looking Rosalyn up and down.

Ethan grunted. "Very well, but I will be right out here," he promised.

* * *

ONCE SHE WAS inside the chamber and the heavy door was closed, Rosalyn collapsed into Ursula. Not wanting her sobs to reach the other side of the door, she sucked in her cries as best she could.

Ursula put her arm around her waist and walked her to the chamber bed. "Come, sister, sit with me for a moment. What has happened? Was that Ethan outside?"

"Aye," she said between gritted teeth.

Ursula's eyes narrowed at the news. "This does not bode well. What of Lachlan?"

"I'd given him the paste, but he was not getting better. When Ethan appeared in the dungeon, I told him his twin brother was dead."

She shook her head when Ursula's eyes filled with concern. "I wanted Ethan to think Lachlan was dead so he wouldn't be tempted to finish him then and there." She sucked in her sniffles.

Ursula brushed the hair from her eyes in a comforting way and said, "Word in the servants' quarters is that James made no award this morn. At least we can be certain he's not banded with Ethan. Sir James demanded a Macpherson be present even though the servants stood in your place, led by Greta."

"Greta's dead. I fear for my mother and sister. Ethan will spill blood to get what he wants," Rosalyn said through her tears.

Ursula appeared shocked by the news. "Greta was killed at the hands of Ethan?"

"I saw the blood on his hands myself. Now, he has my mother and sister. They could be next," she choked out, her voice thick with emotion.

"Your mother and sister are not in danger," Ursula said, looking straight into her eyes. "They are in my chamber. I just left them moments ago." She leaned in closer. "He's lying again," Ursula stated plainly.

Rosalyn collapsed with relief against her friend's shoulder. "Of course he's lying. That's the language he speaks," Rosalyn mumbled into the sleeve of Ursula's gown, grateful that the reason she'd left with Ethan was no longer valid. She straightened and began wiping her tears with the edge of her skirt.

"What about Fyvie and the hearing?"

"I donna give a damn about Fyvie. I must fight for my family, they are what matter most," Rosalyn said, her Macpherson spirit coming back. "Lachlan, first," she vowed while rummaging around in her skirt for her pouch.

A big grin marked her success. Then as fast as her trembling fingers would allow, she opened the pouch and withdrew the precious Philosopher's Stone.

"*Och!* You are willing to sacrifice it?" Ursula asked, shaking her head like it was a sin.

"Aye, Lachlan is worth the sacrifice," she replied with all the conviction she could muster. "Now you must help me. Use your power of persuasion on Ethan. Send back the ladies in waiting, but convince him you've been called by the bishop, or another lie. Somehow you must get to Lachlan."

Then she gave Ursula a quick hug and pushed the stone into her hand. "You know what to do with this?"

Ursula nodded, her friend's eyes gleaming like the gem in her hand. Then she held her fist high above the stone.

"Smash it," her friend said with earnest and the motion to match.

CHAPTER 40

The sound of the cell door creaking open reminded Lachlan of where his head rested, on the cold stone floor of the dungeon. He opened his eyes to a stream of light coming in from the loophole window above and squinted against the tiny but brilliant glow.

His eyes needed adjusting, so he closed them again, too tired to care about who had entered. The fever, chills and gut-wrenching pain had continued to plague him, but he had not always been awake. He actually hoped that someone had come to kill him now and put him out of this misery.

"No greeting for an old friend?" said a familiar woman's voice.

Ursula? No, she would not call him friend.

"You are not looking well, but I'm here to help," said the voice again in an all-too-chipper manner for Ursula.

Lachlan grunted. That was all he could muster from his throat. He couldn't speak, but he ventured to open his eyes again while he turned on his side to face the voice.

Ursula.

There she sat gathering items on the floor next to a

ceramic bowl as if she was sitting at the high table selecting food stuffs for her trencher.

She was focused, not even giving him a glance while she worked. He watched her select from tiny bottles and dry herbs. But when she unwrapped a red gem from a fine cloth, Lachlan was certain he'd seen it before.

Ursula must have finally noticed his gaze, because she gave him a sidewise glance. "'Tis the Philosopher's Stone," she said, answering part of the question his mind was working so hard to solve.

Lachlan's brows and nose crunched closer together.

"Belongs to your wife," she said while shaking a few liquid drops into the bowl. "'Tis more precious than any stone you will ever find." Adding a dash of this and a bit of that from the miniature bottles about her, the healer did not look up while she worked.

How he wished his voice was not evading him, for he wanted to know what she was doing and where his wife was, and why she was missing and why Ursula was here with him instead.

"Save your strength. What she gave you afore wasnae strong enough," she answered one of his unspoken questions. When Ursula dug into the satchel at her side, Lachlan's brows arched high and he blinked in disbelief after she pulled out a petite hammer and chisel.

"You are probably wondering what I'm doing," she finally said, looking up from her work for a moment.

If his eyes spoke, they must have pleaded for some truth, because she nodded as if she understood.

"Ne'er forget, some healers can read your mind," she warned with a slight smile, "so be careful of your thoughts when you are in the presence of one." Then she tossed him a wry grin.

Lachlan had forgotten. His wife never said she could read

his thoughts, but he was certain Ursula could. For now, he was grateful for that.

As if she'd forgotten him, she put the chisel on the stone's surface, then raised the hammer and let it hover high above.

Lachlan's heart lurched for a moment. Did she mean to destroy something so precious?

Without battling an eye, Ursula let the hammer fall hard on her mark and the stone shattered into a fine powder.

While Lachlan studied the broken pieces, he realized the stone had not been a gem after all, but a container made of glass to house the reddish powder that lay among the large shards of its faux housing on the golden silk cloth.

Watching Ursula work reminded him of a sorceress at an occult altar. If she'd come to make a final poison Rosalyn had commissioned so she could have Fyvie for herself and put the blame of his death on his brother, so be it. That would be at least a fitting end to his life and put him out of his misery.

"'Tis not poison, Lachlan," she said softly. "Despite your deranged thoughts, your wife loves you and is doing everything in her power to save you. But she's in danger now. That's why I'm here, so once I save you, you can save her." She took her attention from the powder before her and focused her intense gaze on Lachlan.

His heart began beating stronger. If saving himself meant saving Rose, then nothing would stop him from getting out of this dungeon with Ursula's help.

"Good, you understand now and your will to live is stronger. I can sense it in you and see it in your eyes." Ursula studied him closely. "You do love her," she said with conviction.

His eyes closed momentarily and he nodded with all the strength he had. When he opened them again, she was carefully adding the fine red powder to the bowl.

"Because I can sense you have no knowledge of the power

of this powder, I am going to tell you how your wife is making the most generous of sacrifices," she promised, starting to pummel the paste with the pestle.

"To some, the Philosopher's Stone is a myth, going back at least as far as William the Conqueror's time. For hundreds, maybe thousands of years, many have sought to possess one." She stopped and looked up at him. "And many have died seeking the stone for the unusual powers it would grant them."

He blinked rapidly, his excitement growing and his heart grateful that for once in his life someone cared enough for him to make an ultimate sacrifice.

"Those with no knowledge of alchemy would not know how to use it or even understand the power of what they possessed. This stone," Ursula gestured to the broken remnants, "had been in Rosalyn's family for hundreds of years. It was one of a handful her great-grandfather was given when he was initiated as an alchemist. At the time, even the well-educated did not know how to harness its powers.

"It's been said, having the power of the Philosopher's Stone is like having the power to create miracles, to be God-like. Throughout history, those who've had this stone and the skill, have either saved a life, extended a life or," she paused dramatically, "granted eternal life."

Lachlan's eyes widened, but Ursula anticipated his thoughts before he formed them. "Nay, you will not be given eternal life, but this potion will cure you. I can promise you that," she said with conviction, then her focus returned to the mortar and she began her work again in earnest.

"When alchemists discovered this stone also had the power to alter metals," she glanced up from her work, "like turn iron into gold, they did their best to keep it a secret. But not all in their community followed the code of silence. For the power was coveted by the wealthy, who coerced those with a Philosopher's stone to sell it to the highest bidder," she said, shaking her head in disgust.

"Once the full powers of the stone were known, alchemists took a noble oath, promising to protect it from mankind," she explained, her attention going back to her work.

"As a secret society, they kept their skills and knowledge from anyone who was not a member, so they were able to protect the precious stones, as well as use them sparingly until the circumstances were dire enough."

Ursula stopped pounding the powder with her pestle. "Dire, like they are now," she said, scooting closer to where he lay.

She reached her arm behind his head to prop him up. "You will need to drink this. Here, let me help you."

Lachlan gathered all the strength he could muster. If he were to get out of this cell and save Rosalyn, he needed to hold his head up high. As if already partially cured, he even propped himself up on his elbows to Ursula's shocked expression.

He grinned. "The power of love and positive thinking," he mumbled softly, even surprising himself that his voice was returning when she put the bowl to his lips.

"Then think of this red liquid as your love potion. Bottom's up," she said as she tipped the bowl forward and the cool concoction trickled down the back of his throat, smooth, a little like a fine mead.

* * *

Rosalyn had to assume Ursula was successful escaping Ethan, for three serving maids had arrived before Rosalyn's eyes had even dried from her tears.

As she watched one of her favorite young handmaidens, Devin, a girl of no more than ten and four braid her hair, Rosalyn thought hard about what was at stake.

Gazing at her reflection in the mirror, she remembered her da's visit and his blessing for a union of English and Scot. Clearly, history was riddled with pairings of the two bitter rivals, and her choice of Lachlan was no more controversial than most, and even blessed by the King of Scots.

When her journey had begun weeks ago with her uncle and a few hired servants, she'd dreamed of ending back here at home—a home she'd been barred from since her da's death over four years ago. Then she was only ten and seven.

Now that she was of age, even if the King of Scots did not agree, she was ready to fulfill the promise she made to her da.

That purpose had been foremost in her thoughts when she arrived in Berwickshire. She'd been prepared to lie, cheat, and even die in her efforts to return the rights of Fyvie to the Macpherson family.

Perhaps that's why she'd never had she thought much beyond that. Of marriage, of having her own children, until she'd found Lachlan.

Blind ambition could be deadly, she'd learned, and if anything, she was no longer that naïve, hell-bent activist who thought nothing of charging headlong into questioning traditions and challenging the laws of the times.

Her biggest threat lay ahead, but if she had to choose between her home and her heart, she knew which way she would go.

But fate would be a part of what happened next. Were her mother and sister safe? Would Ursula save Lachlan? Could she figure out a way to outsmart Ethan at the hearing?

When a sharp knock on the chamber door made her jump

and Devin drop the hair comb, Rosalyn knew the time had come to get answers.

The chamber door opened abruptly and Ethan strode into the room as if it was the great hall, taking little courtesy to see if Rosalyn was ready or not. Clearly, he'd take her there in either state.

"It's time," he said like an executioner, then he turned on his heel, not even offering her a hand from her chair or an arm for escort.

She made a *harrumph* sound only Devin could hear, and they exchanged glances.

"You look lovely, my lady, and courageous." The girl served the compliment with a bow and a blush.

"Thank you, Devin. Now I must go to meet my fate," Rosalyn said more to herself than the girl, who nodded and adjusted Rosalyn's dress once she stood.

After entering the corridor, Rosalyn found Ethan waiting at the cross section of the halls ready to descend the stairs to the great hall.

"Come."

She was already walking toward him. His demeanor was commanding. Once she reached his side, he started down the stairs ahead of her without offering assistance.

What a brute, she thought. "Clearly, your mother never taught you manners," she said over his head while he continued to descend. "Oh, yes, I forgot, you killed her before she could teach you any," she snapped, not concerned about the consequences at this point.

Once Ethan reached the landing, he gave her a cold stare and then continued toward the great hall.

Without any ceremony, Rosalyn followed him into the room where many of the memorable moments of her life had taken place. Birthdays, anniversaries, visits with family and dignitaries, even King Henry III had supped with the family on a peace-treaty mission. Now, one of the most important moments of her life awaited her in this very room.

But she felt quite alone. Greta was gone, her da was gone, the rest of the family absent. She searched the faces in the room, realizing quickly that most of the eyes were on her.

Devin had helped her choose a dark-red gown in velvet brocade with an underlay pattern of silver, reminiscent of her family's favorite tartan colors. Rosalyn felt her face heat but she held her head high. Without hesitation, she made a direct line to the dais. The nobles and clansmen who'd gathered in small groups about the crowded hall parted to let her pass.

Rosalyn moved as if the decision had already been made in her favor and the proceedings a ceremonious matter.

Walking through the groups of families, she recognized them all. And instead of being greeted with innocuous stares, she was welcomed with warm smiles and occasional off-the-brow salutes.

As she took her place in front of the temporary court bench, Ethan filed in right behind her.

CHAPTER 41

$\mathcal{A}$s James made his way toward the great hall, he weighed the options of awarding Fyvie. Although he'd expected to have made the final decision by now, he was more conflicted than before.

Last night, while he lay awake alone in his chamber bed, missing his feisty new wife, he was reminded why the decision was so important.

Yes, he'd killed his father Nicholas, not out of spite, or anger, or for personal gain. He'd killed him to protect his mother, Victoria, and his wife, Elena. Both had been threatened by his deceitful and malicious father. A man who did not raise him. A man who defamed his mother and stole Fyvie from her. Both women had been pawns in Nicholas's plan to regain his earldom, the castles he'd lost when King Richard III had taken the throne.

But because his father's cousin, King Henry VII, had reinstated the Luttrell family's holdings before Nicholas's death, his half-brothers now coveted the Scottish castle that had been in his mother's family for generations.

It had all started when Victoria' father, Sir Brodie,

banished Nicholas to Fyvie castle when James was a child and he was told his real father was dead. It wasn't until King Henry's coronation and his mother's kidnapping, that James met Nicholas in a battle to the death.

Oddly, that wasn't when he'd killed him, though the joust was the impetus to unraveling his family's story—that Nicholas was his real father, and uncovering his mother's ties to Fyvie.

Now from what he'd been told by Lachlan, his mother, Victoria, was related to the woman named Rosalyn. No doubt if his mother had a say in the matter, she'd insist that Fyvie Castle be awarded to the Scottish lass.

Yet, the word from his half-brother Ethan claimed Scotland's King James III refused to award the castle's title to a woman and had forced Lachlan's marriage to the young Macpherson lass to solve the issue. Now, not only did she covet the award, but so did her brother-in-law, Ethan.

'Twas a story many might think fictitious, gathered from his twin half-brothers and the Italian bishop, but the issues were real for James.

A final turn in the corridor brought him to his destination and the final judgement could be delayed no longer.

Taking his place at the makeshift court bench in the great hall, James scanned the group before him.

"Welcome nobles, clansmen, Lord Lachlan, and Lady Rosalyn." He directed his attention to the Highland lass before him. "I see you are now well enough to join us."

A few snickers surfaced in the back of the hall.

"Aye, Lord Luttrell, I am honored to be here," she responded, ignoring her husband beside her. "You see it was not that I was sick at all. Instead, I was held against my will in the dungeon of this castle to prevent me from making a claim."

The sounds in the room went from the snickers to shocked *ahhs* of surprise and hushed voices.

Lachlan's expression turned from neutral to nervous. James responded by slamming the gavel to the table.

"Go on," he encouraged her.

"You see, Sir James, Fyvie is my home, where I was born, as was my father, his father, and his father before." She glanced behind her. "I was told my servants stood before you earlier today to support my stake. I see the men of families who've protected the Macphersons for hundreds of years gathered here."

She swept her hands in a broad arc and gazed about the room from one side to the other. "I am willing to lead Fyvie, because I am willing to die for Fyvie."

The men cheered as she clasped her hands in front of her heart. "Sir James, I would like to do something unconventional."

"My lady, you've already accomplished that so far. Please," he said, gesturing her to take his place and speak. He shifted to the side while she walked onto the dais and Lachlan stepped back into the crowd.

Rosalyn held her composure as she readied to address those before her. "When I left Aberdeen a few weeks ago, I tried to take over Fyvie dishonestly." She paused, after a few hushed words interrupted her, but she pushed on. "And I married for convenience, hoping that would bring me closer to my goal."

More mumblings of disbelief sounded, and she waited to finish.

"But to make matters worse," she started again, "I was lied to by someone close to me pretending to be another." She stopped then and appeared to search for that someone, perhaps Lachlan? But she seemed undeterred.

"But during my journey, I was reminded that God had

showed me a path that was true and if I traveled that path, I would be able to find my way home.

"Of course it was not easy, and I feared for my life and those I care about, but the road has brought me home to stand before my countrymen," she said, her arms sweeping outward.

"Because for me, home really isn't a place, it's people. So with your permission, Sir James, I request that the choice of lairdship of Aberdeen and control of Fyvie Castle be awarded instead of by decree, by vote, here and now."

James weighed her request for a few long moments. He was thinking about what he would report back to the King of Scots. Not only was her request at stake, but so was his reputation. He joined her and raised her hand with his.

"Good people of Aberdeen. Is this your new laird and leader? Will you follow her orders, wishes, and if called upon, fight to the death to protect her and all those within these walls?"

When James ended his plea, the room went silent. But then a wave of hands began to rise. Before long, every hand was in the air, including his.

Then room erupted in cheers and *huzzahs*. When the group finally quieted down, a voice called out from the back of the hall, "Aye, she will. I can testify to that."

The large crowd of only men began to part as a dark-haired man made his way forward. The widow's peak was unmistakable. His other twin brother.

Ethan?

"Hello, wife, you can do this all on your own, but I am here to support you," one of the twins said, gazing at her lovingly.

"Lachlan?" she said, dazed, as if she'd seen a ghost. Then Rosalyn spun around. "Where's Ethan?"

James took her elbow. "Don't you mean, Lachlan?" Now

he was confused. There was only one twin standing with them.

She turned around in a circle looking out over the heads of men who'd just chosen her as laird, searching, then beseeching, "Donnae let him get away."

"Lachlan or Ethan?" James needed clarification.

"We must hurry and save one and jail another," Rosalyn commanded as if she'd been their leader all along. Then she took the hand of the twin standing weak-kneed before him. "This is Lachlan," she said with a huff, as if it was easy to tell them apart. "*Ethan* is the one trying to escape."

James raised his hand, a signal to his Garter knights to join him. They were stationed around the perimeter of the hall.

"Ethan!" she shouted the name. Rosalyn's gaze swept the room, the others turned about in their places as his eight Garter knights joined him on the dais.

James pulled her aside by her elbow behind his men. "Clear your head. Speak directly. You'll need to provide specific directions and explain why," he instructed.

"Hear me!" Rosalyn shouted, accepting his advice and coming forward to the front of the dais.

"Aye, Laird Rosalyn," many shouted in return.

She squared her shoulders. "I know this may sound confusing, but the man who first stood with me before Sir James was not my husband, Lachlan. It was his twin, Ethan, who locked me in the dungeon and later coerced me into this farce, knowing he could not win Fyvie without me."

Then she stopped her confession and scanned the crowd until her gaze landed on her husband and she pointed to him. "There is the real Lachlan, poisoned by Ethan and left for dead in the dungeon. But because of prayers and the will of God and those who fight alongside him, my husband has escaped."

"We'll fight for you, Laird Rosalyn!" one man shouted.

"We'll bring Ethan to justice," another called out.

"Kill the bastard," said a third.

Rosalyn held up her hand. "As much as I'd like to kill the bastard, Ethan should be brought to justice first," she said with a level voice.

"Those who are willing, now is the time to search the grounds, every corner of the castle. Take a good look my husband. Remember, he's dressed in noble robes, not a kilt."

James laughed at that and added, "Should make him easier to find considering there are few on the grounds who aren't dressed as Highlanders, knights, servants or squires."

Rosalyn nodded. "The other Garter knights will be instructed by Sir James to secure the gates and entrances of Fyvie, then Lachlan and I will go take care of my mother and sister."

In an orderly manner, the Highlanders, knights and servants left the great hall to follow Rosalyn's orders.

The lass reminded James of another lady with passion for what's right; and courage, worthy of envy.

osalyn didn't know where her courage had come from. Perhaps she'd channeled the spirit of her dead father, but even though she was thrilled beyond measure she'd been awarded Fyvie and Lachlan had joined her, she wanted nothing more now than to find her mother and sister.

Bursting through entrance to the serving kitchen, she scared Ursula into shrieks.

"There you are," Rosalyn shouted, embracing the frightened healer.

Ursula was gasping. "What a scare you've given me."

"What relief you've given me," Rosalyn said releasing her friend. "Why did you not join Lachlan in the great hall?"

Ursula was quick to answer. "With Ethan claiming to have taken your mother and sister, I wanted to make sure they were still safe. I just left them in my chamber with two servants, and ordered them to stay put until I returned."

The healer's words eased her fears, but she was anxious to join them. James had offered a Garter escort and she was ready to make her way there without delay.

But before she could voice her concerns, Ursula asked, "Are you the new laird of Fyvie?"

"Yes." Both she and Lachlan agreed at the same time, then he pointed to her.

"Yes, my lady is the new laird," he clarified, tossing her one of his dashing grins.

"We must celebrate," urged her friend, taking her hands.

Rosalyn gave Ursula's hands a squeeze, but quickly released them when she grew serious. "Aye, we must celebrate, but Ethan is still a concern. The Garter knights and loyal Highlanders are searching the castle now. Blocking all exits, combing all corners of the castle. But we are all still at risk."

Lachlan placed a protective arm around her shoulder. "Do not worry, he's more apt to escape than cause harm when he's lost a wager. He's a poor loser. All he wants to do is brood and drink away his sorrows."

She wanted to believe him, but he'd killed Greta. "Nay, Lachlan, he's grown more desperate than you know."

But Rosalyn got her way and once they'd recruited two Garter knights, it wasn't long before their group was heading down the corridor toward the healer's chamber.

Ursula was the first to knock on the door and call out their arrival.

It cracked open slightly and a servant's head popped out.

"Greta!" Rosalyn shrieked. "I thought you were dead!" She paused, emotional over finding her nursemaid alive. "Ethan said he'd killed you."

"'Twould take more than one evil lord to deter me from helping you win Fyvie, my lady." Then she bowed slightly.

Lachlan gave Rosalyn's shoulders a gentle squeeze. "Your efforts have not gone unrewarded, Greta. This is the new Laird of Fyvie," her husband announced proudly.

"Come," the maid gestured. "Donna stand in the corridor.

Come, your mother and sister will want to share in the good news," Greta offered, stepping back and the four of them filed in to the welcoming shrieks of her family.

After hugs and tears of joy subsided, there were enough seats for all as Rosalyn told her mother and sister about had transpired.

Grateful for the reunion, but troubled by Ethan's escape from the great hall, Ursula's question thankfully turned the conversation to Bishop Passarelli. "Pray tell, then, has the holy man found the Golden Rose of Scotland?"

The Golden Rose. Yes, if he couldn't have Fyvie, the pope's gift of honor would be Ethan's next target. The Rose was valuable beyond measure and could command a king's ransom. But first Ethan would need to elude the most accomplished knights in all of England.

"Should be safe in its hiding place," Rosalyn finally answered when no one else had. She coughed nervously as all eyes were on her.

"You have the Rose, Rose?" her husband asked softly, making all the women twitter with laughter, but Greta remained serious.

"Lady Rose, the Golden Rose may not be safe," she warned, more guarded than before. "I must confess to ye now that Ethan did nae kill me because I gave him my skeleton key."

When Roslyn gasped, Greta shuddered. "Not only does he have the key, my lady, he forced me to reveal the Rose's hiding place," she confessed, hanging her head.

Rosalyn immediately went to her side, as did her mother and sister. She gently reached for the nursemaids hands, unfolding them from her lap.

"Dear Greta, you are alive and that's more important than any treasure. Donnae believe you've done any wrong." She squeezed her hands and gazed at her nursemaid lovingly.

"We must rescue the Rose before it's stolen away again," Lachlan declared, standing with his hand on his hilt.

Greta's eyes brightened, but Rosalyn patted her hands hoping to discourage the idea.

"Saving the Golden Rose of Scotland would be a most noble act, Husband, but none of us should risk leaving this chamber until we know Ethan is found first."

"Not all are at risk." Ursula stood when she spoke. "Ethan has no quarrel with me, nor does he consider me a threat. In fact, he may find think me an ally."

"Or a distraction," said Lachlan.

"And that's the point," the healer pressed. "Tell me where the Rose is hidden, for I am willing to save it for Scotland," Ursula stated proudly.

The silence in the chamber was more distracting than if she'd heard arguments for or against Ursula's brave offer. As the new laird, even her husband awaited her decision.

"Then I'll be going with her," her nursemaid volunteered, walking over to join Ursula.

Judging by their determination and willingness to volunteer, Rosalyn could not be insensitive to their requests. As much as she wanted to honor their offer, she could not. For it was her responsibility to protect the Golden Rose. And although she questioned his decree, the bishop had insisted Rosalyn was the chosen one.

With an appreciation for all her da had accomplished leading the clan afore her, Rosalyn strode stoically forward to stand before the two volunteers.

"I wish I could grant your request, but I cannot put the two of you in danger," she announced, glancing to her husband. "From the very start, the Rose is what brought Lachlan and I together. We must finish it."

Ursula's eyes narrowed, but she nodded. Greta bowed. It

was settled. Leadership wasn't easy, and Rosalyn imaged it never would be.

* * *

THE CASTLE WAS EERILY silent as Rosalyn led Lachlan through a vacant servant's work area and down a dark corridor. She stopped finally before the foreboding, iron-latticed door that guarded Fyvie's supply of surplus and ancient weapons.

They'd traveled with no torch through the castle and as she entered, with Lachlan at her heels, the vast war room appeared even darker than she'd expected. The moonlight shining in through the rooftop loophole windows provided little illumination.

Rosalyn held her finger to her lips as she waved Lachlan to follow her into the massive room, where her favorite treasure chest stood. Where she hoped the Golden Rose still rested safely inside.

Using one of her hands as a guide along the wall, she held Lachlan's with her other, inching her way toward the far corner doused in darkness.

Forced to leave the security of the wall after they'd gone as far as they could, Rosalyn reached out her free hand to wave away the darkness as if she could push it to each side and clear a path for them to pass.

When her knee slammed into something hard, she bit her tongue to keep her from crying out. At the same time, Lachlan ran into her backside, knocking her forward.

With little time to react, but with both arms free, she braced herself for a fall. What she didn't expect was to land softly on the other side of her tumble. More so, she'd landed in someone's lap.

A low rumble of laughter followed, but it wasn't Lachlan's.

Rosalyn froze, fearful any movement might cause her harm, even with Lachlan standing silent somewhere close by.

"Fitting isn't it, that we meet again?" Ethan asked, breaking the silence. "Comfy, my dear?"

When she stayed mum, he ambled on. "I'm surprised, though, I thought winning the castle and the lairdship would be enough for you. Won't you give me something for my trouble? Perhaps the missing Rose?"

Stalling, she contemplated her options. Surely, Lachlan was doing the same. She hoped Ethan assumed she was alone.

"But wait. You and I have some unsettled business. We should take care of that first," he said, placing his hands on her breasts and squeezing them so hard tears welled. Biting her tongue to keep from swearing, a rush of air passed Rosalyn's ear.

Whack!

When Ethan's head snapped back, he finally released her.

"Brother, let's hope my fist reminded you of your lack of manners." His voice was cold and laced with anger, but her heart warmed at his defense.

"This lady is my wife, no longer the missing Rose," Lachlan continued, lifting her out of his twin's lap. "And you, Ethan, are no longer welcome in our home."

Relieved to be rescued by her husband from Ethan's hold and for the moment safe, she was also mindful of his madness. Perhaps Lachlan had grown accustomed to his brutality, for she'd learned when he was brooding, he was dangerous.

"Come, Brother. You've won again," Ethan whined like a young child, "the earldom in Somerset, the fiefdom of Fyvie, the lovely lady Rosalyn. Let me have an award for my trouble. Give me the Golden Rose."

"Why did have you not made away with it already?"

Lachlan asked what she'd wondered. "You've had ample time."

"The skeleton key let me in, but the box would not open," he griped. "And it's too awkward and heavy to carry, or I would have been halfway to England by now," Ethan admitted.

The keys are not identical! Rosalyn now realized. She looked up to heaven and whispered, "Thank you, Da."

CHAPTER 43

*E*ven though he deserved to die, Lachlan had resisted killing his twin. When Ethan molested his wife, he'd come unhinged. Given the opportunity again, without Rosalyn as witness, he would have pummeled his brother to death with one of the castle's ancient weapons. There had been plenty to choose from and he'd had the provocation.

Now that he thought back on yesterday, he was still angry. Ethan had laughed off the whole affair after he'd begged Rosalyn for the Rose, saying he'd never been serious about any of it.

After the Garter knights found the three of them in the war room, Ethan had surrendered. He'd been escorted to the dungeon where he belonged, to protect others from a madness Lachlan could never understand.

But fortunately for Ethan, his half-brother James had been the voice of reason when they'd met this morn to sort out their family affairs.

It was decided each would have a hand in maintaining the family castles. Nunnery and Cadbury belonged to James's mother, Victoria, and the Garter knight was satisfied with that. Ethan would reside at Dunster, but Lachlan would retain the title of earl, for Rosalyn would have Fyvie. Even James promised Rosalyn his mother, Victoria, would visit.

But Lachlan swore to himself he'd never forgive Ethan for all the pain he'd caused. The death of their mother, stealing Rosalyn from his wedding bed, poisoning him. And it was a relief when he and James finally escorted Ethan out of the gates of Fyvie.

Word circulated rapidly among the servants that Ethan was gone and a celebration was promised to be ready in a few short hours.

Lachlan recruited Greta in helping him plan a feast that would honor his wife and see Bishop Passarelli off to Edinburgh with the Garter knights.

When the time arrived and Lachlan walked into the great hall with his beautiful wife, a loud applause welcomed them and well-wishers rushed forward.

Lachlan navigated the crowd, grinning politely until he was able to seat her at the head table next to Sir James.

All the important people were there: her mother, sister, Ursula, Bishop Passarelli, Greta and even her Uncle Angus. Once all were settled, Bishop Passarelli stood and motioned Lachlan and Ursula to join him.

When the holy man came forward, he carried a large object covered in a purple silk cloth. "Good people," he said with a modest bow. "*Scumasi*, although I am an Italian guest, I am also a man of God, your brother first."

When the room erupted in applause, he raised his hand. "Hold your adulation and respect for the man next to me, Lachlan Macpherson. He is one who has earned it."

The bishop turned to Ursula and with one dramatic gesture, she lifted off the purple cloth to reveal the stunning Golden Rose of Scotland.

The bishop put one of his arms around Lachlan's shoulders, even though he had to stand on his toes to reach him.

"In this great hall of Scotland, let the record show that it is not Lachlan Macpherson who was guilty of stealing the Golden Rose, holding Rosalyn hostage in her own dungeon, or trying to trick the Highland nation of Aberdeen into awarding him lairdship, it was his twin brother, Ethan."

He turned to Rosalyn sitting at the dias. "And you, my dear, have won a king's ransom."

She smiled shyly. "Bishop, I've already won what my heart desires," she said, gazing at Lachlan.

After the ceremony was complete and the guests had eaten all the food that had been prepared, Lachlan took his wife by the hand and led her back to his chamber. She'd chatted with him about the meal, how she'd miss the bishop, but more importantly, how she was ready for what lay ahead.

And it wasn't long before Lachlan had her unencumbered on his bed. It had been more than a week since he'd gone looking for a feather to seduce her a second time on their wedding day.

"We have some unfished business to attend to, my sweet Rose," he said, realizing only after he said those words, he'd forgotten his promise not to call her by that name.

It must have been the look of dread on his face as he gazed down on her perfect naked form that made her laugh.

"Oh, Husband, you may call me Rose." She batted her lashes. "But only when we are alone," she added with a wicked grin.

He reached for her taut nipple and rolled the delicate nub between his fingers, making it harder than before. "Wife, I cannae think of a better way to celebrate the day."

When his gaze met hers again, she was looking at him curiously. "Did you hear yourself?" she asked with a surprised grin.

"What?"

"You said *cannae?*"

"I donna," he said, goading her.

"Are you making fun of the way I talk?"

"Nay, woman, everyone talks that like here at Fyvie." He shrugged. "Donna be keeping me from my purpose." He paused and blew out the tapered candle by the bedside. Now only the embers from the fire showed him where his hands should go. No, he didn't need light to follow the path his body wanted to travel.

Although he'd had the experience of pleasing Rose once, he was as nervous as a first-timer when he pressed his lips to hers, wanting nothing more than to show her she was the most important thing to him other than land.

Damn the property. She was more precious than land, surname, or title.

When did it happen? He could not recount. Perhaps it was when he found out she hadn't run away, but that his brother had stolen her. And fortunately, not forever.

Rosalyn had assured him that Ethan hadn't hurt her or taken her virginity. He trusted her of course, but he was about to find out.

"Remember, love, a little pain and then pleasure," he promised.

"Let me start the pleasure," she suggested, shoving him down to the featherbed. He closed his eyes and the sensation of her hard nipples rubbing against his skin started at his thighs and traveled up toward his groin, her long, luscious hair trailing behind like soft silk.

He almost jumped up from where he lay when her soft stomach pressed over his shaft. After her lips locked with his, it was she who started the tongue repartee. Darting in and around his own. Then she pressed her warm and moist channel to his hardened cock, the sensation had him clawing at the covers.

When she released his lips for a moment, he seized the opportunity to move her higher up on his stomach.

"Pleasure, is mine, m'dear," he said. "You are a quick study but let me show you the way."

He moved her about his chest until he had her right where he wanted her. "Now, my love, you are good at riding horses, yes?" he asked softly.

"Aye, husband, you've watched me," she said, taking in a huge breath as if to go on, so he put a finger to her lips.

"Yes, I have and now I want to watch you, ride me."

He heard her suck in another deep breath, but it was different this time.

"Reach behind your arse and place my shaft where it was before," he instructed.

After a little awkwardness, like grabbing on to a horse's rein, she took hold of him and followed his lead.

Once she was in the right spot, his insides felt like they were churning with a fire that couldn't be extinguished. When she let out a moan, he knew she'd found her sweet spot.

"Now, I'll grab your waist and help you ride. Just hang on."

And ride she did. Rosalyn tossed her head back and her hair flew behind her as if caught by the wind. Lachlan held on to her narrow waist and brought her up and down as if she was cantering on a saddle.

The sweat formed between her breasts and glistened as it dripped down her body.

He was working to control his passion. He hadn't pushed forward through the final gate, but his wife appeared ready to jump across.

"Hold on, here we go," he warned, and with one last thrust, he passed the final barrier.

When she let out a tiny shout, he slowed his movements, waiting.

"Donna stop now," she demanded. "You cannae be finished," she said in a reprimanding voice.

He chuckled against her neck. "No, my darling, the ride has just begun."

So it was that night, after years of loneliness, loathing, and loss, that Lachlan had finally found the love of his life.

The trappings of land, a noble title, and purse, were no longer of purpose.

As their pleasure began to escalate, he waited until she had her release, then he gave her his. After a pleasure-filled gasp, she collapsed against his chest.

With a gentle embrace first and a deep sigh, he moved her to his side. "My lovely Rose, how rude of me not to thank you," he said, turning to face her. Gently brushing the falling bangs from her brow, he smiled at her.

"Well, Husband, I didnae think it rude to thank me before taking my virginity, but if you are now, then you are most welcome."

She answered him with such sincerity, he burst out laughing at her misunderstanding and began to speak through his amusement. "No, Wife, although I do thank you for the mating ritual, I had forgotten to thank you for saving my life, for your sacrifice of the stone."

She blinked hard a few times.

"I love you, Lachlan. Once I realized it, I couldnae let you die. Even if Bishop Passarelli says I will go to hell playing God, it will be worth it," she promised.

He gathered her into his arms and kissed the top of her head. "If that's where you go, I'll go, too."

They both laughed. "But you are the chosen one, Rose,

and I believe you've only used your healing for good. If you'd taken it yourself, well then you might have to answer to God for your actions."

She moved toward him and gave him a seductive kiss. "You could have left me in the dungeon at Berwick-upon-Tweed."

"And you could have left me in the dungeon, here at Fyvie."

She snuggled up in the space between his chest and arm, fitting perfectly. "If it is time for confessions and if we donna live to see the dawn—"

"Do not jest, Rose," he cut her off, rising up and giving her a serious look, then his expression softened. He did have questions that needed answers.

"I'll go first," he volunteered. "Confession. You were beautiful and in distress. I was cocky, but not heartless. I couldn't tell the judge my name in an English court and considered I would have better chances in Scotland." His words made her smile. "You go."

"Why did you nae use the king's seal against me in the court at Edinburgh?"

"You are supposed to confess, not ask a question."

"My rules."

"Confession. I didn't trust myself not to use it, so I left it at Berwick Castle."

When her eyes scrutinized him, he shrugged and asked the question he'd been stewing over since they'd met, "Was it a forgery?"

"Nay, it was stolen." She laughed at his smirk.

"You would have kept your pretty head after all."

She ignored him. "Was yours a forgery?"

"It was," he admitted, "but it was nae of the kings seal."

"*Nae?*"

"Not." He gave her a peck on the lips.

"Why did you continue to insist than I needed a guardian, even to the judge?"

"Confession. I believed I could charm you into my bed and win the land."

She laughed loudly at that. "You charm me in bed?"

He ignored her. "Now 'tis my go."

She nodded reluctantly.

"Even though your first attempt failed, because Ethan was pretending to be me, why did you want to poison me?"

The brightness in her eyes faded. "I would like to say it was all Ursula's idea, but it wasnae. I didnae have enough poison to kill you, just to keep you from following us."

"How could you have ever been fooled into thinking Ethan was me?"

She frowned. "Your brother James asked me if I really knew my husband, not long before Ethan locked me in the dungeon. I should have asked him for an explanation instead of being blinded by my anger."

Lachlan wasn't surprised by her comment. "When the bishop and I first met James, he knew we were related."

"How?"

"His mother Victoria warned James about us and she expected one or both of us to claim Fyvie."

"Do you fear James?" Rosalyn asked, appearing overly concerned, but he understood, considering the family's murderous history.

"Nay, he's a good man and he put me at ease right away. We are more alike than I expected. We equally despise the Luttrell name."

Rosalyn snuggled even closer, making him want to love her all over again, but he needed one more confession first. "Did you believe I'd stolen the Golden Rose?"

She giggled and the light returned to her gaze. "At first,

yes. I thought you might use it as a bargaining piece to take Fyvie from me."

Lachlan mimicked an arrow going into his heart. "Me take Fyvie from you?"

She narrowed her gaze on him.

"Do you love me as you've professed?"

She held his gaze and her pupils almost danced with mischief. "Let me prove it to you," she said in the softest whisper.

Then he groaned, happy he'd asked the question.

Also from **Crown & Castle Publishing** and **Marisa Dillon**:

THE LADY OF THE GARTER (The Ladies of Lore Book 1)

When Henry VII takes the throne, not all are loyal to the new king. Garter knight, Sir James, is charged with bringing dissenters to justice. Determined to fulfill his vows, he's unprepared for Lady Elena, a girl from his past.

Lady Elena defies her family and disguises herself as a squire to reunite with the man she's always loved. Determined to thwart the norms of the day, she risks all to learn the secrets of the Garter knights. Although she wields a sword like a man, she must fight with her feminine heart.

Thrust into a world of danger and family rivalry, James and Elena must each choose between personal sacrifice and great consequence as they navigate a second chance at love.

Will Elena find the courage to fight to save James from a dark knight set out for revenge, but loose her chance at knighthood?

Can James avenge his father's death and find passion, or

will his Garter oaths hold him to a life of service without love?

The Lady waits to tell her tale.

Available on Amazon: **THE LADY OF THE GARTER**

THE SECRET OF SKYE ISLE (The Ladies of Lore Book 3)

A lifesaving antidote grows as a rare rose on an isle full of faerie lore. Healer Ursula Fraser won't risk delivering her best friend's twins without it, but first she'll need a guide and a miracle.

Both come in the form of battle-scarred laird Alasdair MacLeod, a Highlander who seeks to avenge his father's death and claim the title, Lord of the Isles. He requires an heir, not a wife. But when he offers her his guidance, he also offers her his bed and a bargain.

Insulted, but fearless, Ursula expects she'll convince the laird to do her bidding without sacrificing her morals. Her ability to conjure herbal potions gives her great power until she discovers the Scottish laird is the only one who can save her from the murderous MacDonalds.

Will this Highlander who harbors a family secret keep her from returning to Fyvie Castle in time for the twins' delivery? Or will a faerie prophecy filled with magic and a roll of the dice settle all the scores?

The answers lie in *The Secret of Skye Isle*.

Available on Amazon: **THE SECRET OF SKYE ISLE**

THE DUCHESS HEIST (The Art of Love 1)

What is the cost of a nude painting from the Royal Academy of Art?

That depends on who you ask.

Possible ruination . . . for Lady Lillias St. Clair, the daughter of a gambling-addicted duke, when she discovers a partially completed portrait of herself reveals her identity and much more. But before she concocts a scheme to steal it from the prestigious academy, the artwork goes missing.

Perhaps salvation . . . for Lord William Cavendish, who hides his dark past behind a cavalier air and his good deeds. Yet, to earn true redemption and raise funds in time for a grand gesture, he must enter an international art contest with a scandalous pose of an unknown figure model, who turns out to be the daughter of the duke who stands between William and his dreams.

Worth dueling over? Both families have fought a generations-long feud between them. So when a fake engagement presents a chance to recover the missing nude portrait, Lillias and William agree the ruse may prevent a scandal.

When reputations are at stake, and a nude painting hangs in the balance, the cost could be too high for either of them until they find what Shakespeare once wrote to be true: 'love's not time's fool.'

Available on Amazon: **THE DUCHESS HEIST**

CONNECT WITH THE AUTHOR

With a bachelor's degree in journalism, Marisa has spent many years writing for the television industry. As an award-winning producer/director/marketer, she has worked on commercial production, show creation, product branding and social media.

Marisa has always enjoyed reading romance novels and now fulfills a dream by writing romantic adventures not for the faint of heart.

Visit Marisa at: www.marisadillon.com.

Goodreads:https://www.goodreads.com/author/show/10792736.Marisa_Dillon

BookBub:https://www.bookbub.com/profile/marisa-dillon